DRAY PRESCOT

To those unfamiliar with the Saga of Dray Prescot all that it is necessary to know is that he has been summoned to Kregen, an exotic world orbiting the double star Antares, to carry out the mysterious purposes of the Star Lords. To survive the perils that confront him on that beautiful and terrible world he must be resourceful and courageous, strong and devious. There is no denying he presents an enigmatic figure. There are more profound depths to his character than are called for by mere savage survival.

Educated in the harsh environment of Nelson's navy and by the Savanti nal Aphrasöe of Kregen, he is a man above middle height, with brown hair and eyes, the quiet movements of a hunting big cat and a physique of exceptional power.

Taking on the job of Emperor of Vallia, with the Empress Delia by his side, Prescot is determined to press on with his schemes to unite in friendship all the peoples of their half of Kregen in the union of Paz. Vallia and her allies, Djanduin, Hyrklana and some of the realms of the Dawn Lands, have defeated the puissant Empire of Hamal; but Hamal is not laid in ruins. From over the curve of the world dark and more terrible dangers sail down to destroy the bright civilization of Paz. Together with Delia, his family and his comrades, Prescot sees this as a time to make a fresh start. This is the opportunity to forge new alliances against all perils under the Suns of Scorpio.

"The wild men were there, flying high against the sky."

ALLIES
OF
ANTARES

by
Dray Prescot

As told to ALAN BURT AKERS

Illustrated by *Clyde Caldwell*

DAW BOOKS, INC.
DONALD A. WOLLHEIM, PUBLISHER

1633 Broadway, New York, N.Y. 10019

FIRST PRINTING, DECEMBER 1981

1 2 3 4 5 6 7 8 9

DAW TRADEMARK REGISTERED
U.S. PAT. OFF. MARCA
REGISTRADA. HECHO EN U.S.A.

PRINTED IN U.S.A.

TABLE OF CONTENTS

LIST OF ILLUSTRATIONS

Chapter One

Ructions in the
Peace Conference

During the second week of the Peace Conference only forty-nine duels were fought so the delegates realized they were making real progress.

The main sessions took place in a long-disused assembly chamber of the palace of Ruathytu and here day by day the benches filled with vociferous people all determined to have their say about the horrible fate to be meted out to defeated Hamal. The people divided by nation and race and each faction felt convinced its own solution was not only the perfect one, but the one to be adopted by everyone else.

This led to differences of opinion.

"A gold deldy per person," shouted a king from the Dawn Lands. In the overheated atmosphere with the drapes drawn away from the long windows and still the air stifling, his face looked a bronze mask of sweat. He shook his fist. "Nothing less—"

"Less?" A king from a neighboring realm of the Dawn Lands sneered, white lace kerchief to face, not bothering to rise to speak. "Less? Make it two gold deldys."

"Aye!" called a high-ranking noble, gold-bedecked. "Hamal has the gold. Hamal can pay!" Then, no doubt feeling that although no king he must maintain his dignity, he bellowed: "And make it three gold deldys!"

Stylors wrote busily at long tables positioned near the center of the open space between the ranked seating. They covered reams of paper with what was said, proposals and counter-proposals. They recorded very few agreements.

Other delegates joined in the raising of the indemnity and shouts of "four!" and "five" and "seven" brought the blood flushing to forehead and cheeks, brought a sparkle to eyes, brought feathers ruffling dangerously and fur sparking with static. The punishment rose until there was scarcely gold in all of Paz, let alone merely the empire of Hamal, to pay what would be demanded. Then someone raised the question of saddle flyers being taken in compensation, demanding their fair share of zhyans in preference to lesser birds. This caused fresh outbreaks of acrimony. Another delegate banged his sword on the floor and demanded full restitution plus damages for all the airboats his country had lost.

"Take all the fliers that Hamal has!" he cried. "And—"

"You would fly your own airboats home and claim they were lost!" challenged a puffy-faced king with hair noticeable by its absence, for it had been torn off by a wild animal seasons ago. "The Peace Conference demands a full accounting from you—"

"Aye! And from you, King Nodgen the Bald! We have sure proof you flew undamaged vollers back to your black-hearted kingdom and—"

The ensuing sword-flourishing and blade-whickering was dealt with by the marshals. On this day that task fell by rotation to four-armed Djangs, who had no trouble separating the combatants and escorting them back to their seats. Djangs, aside from being among the most superb fighting men of Kregen, are less in awe of kings and nobles not of Djanduin.

"You are not allowed to fight in the Peace Conference." The Djang Hikdar in command of the marshal detail carried off his duties with that Djang blend of competent military expertise and wild warrior fanaticism. He made sure the rival kings were both sitting in their seats before he marched his men off. No blood was spilled on that occasion over that particular quarrel in the chamber; blood flowed in the duel that followed. Outside.

All in all, the Peace Conference to decide what to do with Hamal presented a sorry spectacle.

From Vallia, Drak, the Prince Majister, and Kov Seg Segutorio made eloquent appeals for progress. King Jaidur of Hyrklana expressed his contempt for the delegates. His queen, Lildra, hushed him in her queenly way; but the feeling was abroad that the Peace Conference was doomed.

Young King Rogpe of Mandua announced that he did not feel secure enough on his throne to waste time in Hamal. He had only turned up after the battles, his armies being commanded by Kov Konec and Vad Dav Olmes, because his succession to his father had been challenged and the law had, tardily, upheld his claim. If everyone began to go home, Hamal was likely to be plundered without check in revenge for her own sins of the past.

The Kingdom of Djanduin was represented by O. Fellin Coper. As an Obdjang—equipped by nature with a cheerful pert gerbil-like face and only two arms and a keenly incisive brain—he was no fighting man. At his side sat K. Kholin Dorn. As a Dwadjang—equipped by nature with a ferocious assemblage of fighting equipment and a brain completely at sea in the arcana of Higher Command—he was a warrior who upheld O. Fellin Coper's decisions. The aerial assault delivered on the Hamalian capital city of Ruathytu had decided the issue and won the battle. That assault had been a Djanduin affair. The forces commanded by Seg Segutorio had joined in the final assault.

Now that mere mortal kings and princes and kovs sought to put together a Peace Treaty, the actual course of the fighting was conveniently pushed aside. Everyone demanded an equal say. That proved perfectly acceptable, provided common sense prevailed. As the Prince Majister of Vallia said: "Common sense seems to have fled! By Vox! Are we all a pack of ninnies unable to agree on anything?"

Some of the delegates from the Dawn Lands left off arguing and quarreling among themselves long enough to shout answers. Then, they went back to slanging one another.

Seg said, "I suggest we take into consideration the views of those members of the conference—"

Jaidur interrupted. "We take no notice, Uncle Seg! We tell these idiots from the Dawn Lands what we decide!"

Drak, serious, intense, dedicated, leaned forward, frowning. "The Dawn Lands contributed greatly to the success. And to ignore them because we are united and thus stronger is illegal."

Seg sat back, saying nothing. His blue eyes revealed nothing of his thoughts, and his reckless face was composed.

"Illegal!" Jaidur laughed. He was still a right tearaway despite having come to the throne of Hyrklana, a rich island off the east coast of Havilfar, and with the realm its queen, Lildra. His mother, Delia of Vallia, had great hopes that he would

reform and become a dutiful king. Now he roared his enjoyment
of the jest. "Illegal, brother! What we decide will settle the
fate of Hamal for many seasons to come. We must decide in
our favor. If these fools from the Dawn Lands—"

"Gently, Jaidur, gently," said Seg.

King Jaidur sat back in his chair. He put a hand to his lips
and Lildra put her hand down on his shoulder. Jaidur leaned
back, closing his eyes, and he touched Lildra's hand. He drew
reassurance and strength from the contact. Just so had his father
gained reassurance and strength from Jaidur's mother.

"The problem is the Dawn Lands will not choose a spokes-
man. They are individuals, and are contrary for the sake of
contrariness and drive everyone else into frenzy by their quar-
rels."

"True, prince," said Seg.

"We have complete agreement," said Ortyg Fellin Coper,
brushing his whiskers, being brisk. "Between Djanduin, Vallia
and Hyrklana. That combination is, indeed, very powerful."

"Powerful!" shouted across that king from the Dawn Lands
who had begun the escalation of the gold indemnity. "But we
in the Dawn Lands can put more troops into the field, more
vollers, more saddle flyers. Woe to anyone who forgets that."

Jaidur burst out: "More! Of course! And woe to you for
forgetting it as Hamal destroyed you piecemeal!"

Seg moved with the speed of a Bowman of Loh. He stopped
in front of Jaidur, half-bending as though talking, and he mo-
tioned to Lildra. It was nicely done. The fatuous king was left
talking to Kov Seg's backside, Lildra was smiling at him, and
Jaidur was being masked—and, no doubt, having a severe and
nostalgic telling-off from his Uncle Seg. Had a duel been
fought Jaidur would certainly have won, being a Krozair of
Zy; but the deplorable publicity would have done Hyrklana
and Vallia no good. Kytun Kholin Dorn, clever enough in
matters of this nature, rolled over to the Dawn Lands king and,
taking him in comradely fashion by the elbow, lifted him away,
saying something like: "And I can show you a Jholaix we dug
out of the wine cellars you've never dreamed existed."

The Peace Conference survived these bruises; but no one
was prepared to say how long such damage could go on.

In all these arguments and statements of opinion and position, no one bothered to think what the Hamalese might say.
They had been beaten. Ergo, they must pay up and do as they

were told and thank all their gods they were still alive. Yet to claim that no one bothered to think of the Hamalese is to avoid the real issue. Everyone shied away from the central point, the overriding question, the problem that put all the others—including the details of compensation and punishment—into the shade.

All the delegates to the Peace Conference were only too acutely aware that they must think of the Hamalese. And they kept fobbing off that dominant issue.

Who was to rule Hamal now that the old Empress, Empress Thyllis, was dead and buried?

"Dismember the damned place," was a commonly voiced solution.

"Split it up into kovnates and vadvarates and stromnates and do not allow a single kingdom. Divide and rule." This was a solution favored of many. The rulers from the Dawn Lands would feel far more comfortable if north of the River Os lay instead of a single huge nation a whole series of little ones in reflection of themselves.

It was left to Drak to point out: "And have continual warfare between the little countries—as you do all the time?"

By Vox! You win a battle and take a city and have a peace conference—and you start to find out where the problems really are!

Seg said, "Little is beautiful, and big is beautiful. Big is unwieldy and little is plain suicidal. We have to find a median way."

Because the invasion from Vallia had sidestepped the island of Pandahem and gone straight into Hamal, the future held problems there, also. As Drak said, "Now the nations of Pandahem have the dread of the devilish Wizard of Loh, Phu-Si-Yantong, removed, they will rapidly throw out the Hamalese occupation forces. I am sure they will want a say in what is decided for Hamal."

One of the Dawn Lands rulers—King Nafun of Hambascett, who had begun the auction in increasing gold deldys—snorted his disgust. He reared up in his seat, glaring about, the sweat now appearing to be melting from a wax death mask. "Pandahem? Pandahem? Have they sent troops? Have they aided us? No! They have no right to sit at the table that decides the fate of Hamal. We who fought, we—"

His neighbor-king, wily King Harmburr of Ezionn, bellowed out at that. "Fought? Fought? I saw no troops of Hambascett the Treacherous when I fought the Hamalese mercenaries—"

"And I saw not a swod of Decadent Ezionn when I routed the Hamalese heavy cavalry—"

"By the Veiled Froyvil!" said Seg. He let rip a sigh that was more like a stentor blowing to gain passage for a swifter than a lovesick swain languishing for his lady. "Cannot you two either leave each other alone, fight it out, or just shut up?"

Now a kov does not ordinarily talk to two kings in quite those terms.

Drak sat forward anxiously, and Jaidur looked with swift concern over at Seg. Both Drak and Jaidur—with their brother Zeg—had known and loved Seg Segutorio from the moment they had been aware of his existence.

King Harmburr of Ezionn and King Nafun of Hambascett turned to look at Seg. He continued to sit. He had prevented a confrontation with Jaidur, only to precipitate a worse one on his own head.

Drak said, "We have done enough for the day. Let us depart and reconvene on the morrow when—"

"Softly, Prince of Vallia!" quoth Nafun. He wiped his face with a sodden kerchief. "I have been insulted—"

"You!" snapped King Harmburr. He was a waspish little fellow. "You! The lout insulted me—"

Seg stood up. He moved lazily. He smiled. "I shall not fight either of you, or your hired champions. You two are stupid cretins and what is more, you know it. Aye!" He drowned out their protestations. "I can see ahead. I can see perhaps things that would not please you. You both know we must deal with Hamal fairly, or there will never be peace. So think. Act like kings. Even if it is difficult to act like men."

"The kov speaks with the words of the gods," said Drak. He knew when to bring religion into it. Cunning, resourceful, ruthless, Drak, Prince Majister of Vallia, and yet upright, honest, loyal, a man of the highest principles. Sometimes those high principles made life for lesser mortals damned uncomfortable. Jaidur, his brother, was of altogether more volatile a nature. As for Zeg, the middle brother, who was now King Zeg of Zandikar miles and miles away in the inner sea, the Eye of the World, I'd not heard from him for just not long enough to make me worried. Pretty soon, when this Hamal nonsense was cleared up, I was due a trip to the Eye of the World. . . .

The two kings were in nowise chastened. But other delegates were growing tired of this incessant wrangling. Even rulers of countries of the Dawn Lands traditionally opposed to one another cooled in face of the problems ahead. Various candidates for various sections of Hamal were touted. We all agreed that those nations of the Dawn Lands with frontiers on the River Os, the southern boundary of Hamal, had a prior right in the decisions affecting the parcels of land across their borders. This seemed fair to the delegates.

Even that caused disagreement. A number of the nations right in the north of the Dawn Lands immediately to the south of the River Os, He of the Commendable Countenance, had been in subjection to Hamal for so long they had not contributed anything to the armies of the alliance. In fact, some of them had actually had their own men in the ranks of the Hamalian army. These difficulties had to be discussed and agreements reached.

What at first glance seemed fair on closer inspection turned ugly with imponderables.

Many of the delegates supported rival claimants. No one was aware of any legitimate issue of the Empress Thyllis and her nonentity of a husband. He had disappeared long ago. A number of relations existed: distant cousins aplenty, and a group of men and women claiming the emperor as their uncle. After Thyllis had been shot to death by a crossbow bolt, loosed by Rosil, the Kataki Strom, Phu-Si-Yantong had proclaimed himself as Emperor of Hamal. Now what seemed to many of the delegates a ludicrous legal situation arose. Did this brief occupation of the throne acquire legality, and, if so, how did it affect the claims of Thyllis's husband's cousins and nephews?

Intriguing.

Nothing would stop the lawyers from inflicting day-long speeches upon the subject with all the happy hunting ground of the inflexible Laws of Hamal in which to play—short of nipping the problem in the bud. Drak, Prince Majister of Vallia, did just that.

"No legitimacy accrues to the Wizard of Loh, Phu-Si-Yantong, now dead—thanks be to Opaz!—or any of his assigns or heirs through this illegal usurpation of the throne." Drak looked around the chamber meaningfully. There was so much gold and silver displayed, so many gems, that the delegates could blind with radiance the unwary eye. "We have enough problems sorting out who is to take over in Hamal without saddling ourselves with more."

"Agreed!" The shouts were unanimous. On one subject, then, the famous Conquerors of Hamal could agree...

In the tiny hush of reaction to the outburst, young King Rogpe of Mandua stood up. He drew his sumptuous robes about him in the instinctive gathering of resources gesture of one about to plunge into unpleasant argument; almost immediately he loosened the fur-trimmed velvet, for Hamal was warmer than Mandua. "There is a matter I must have settled before I return." He held up a hand as some delegates started to protest.

Young and uncertain, Rogpe might be; in what he had to say he was in deadly earnest and therefore articulate and convincing.

"Here me! I speak of the case of those countries who actively allied themselves with Hamal! Most notably that of Shanodrin!"

"Slay 'em all!" and, "Burn their towns around their ears!" The suggestions on what should be done with collaborators bubbled up merrily and uglily.

"Prince Mefto A'Shanofero, known as Mefto the Kazzur! He stands indicted before this assembly! He and his accomplices must be brought to trial."

No one there in that glittering chamber was unaware that Mefto the Kazzur had sought through his alliance with the Hamalese to dominate much of the Dawn Lands. The Kingdom of Mandua had suffered. Now Rogpe put a hand to his quiff of fair hair. He smiled, a nervous smile yet one which revealed his feelings of triumph at delayed revenge accomplished.

Puffy faced, impatient, King Nodgen the Bald leaped to his feet. He shook a fist at Rogpe.

"Yes, yes, my young fighting king, yes! We will deal with the traitor Mefto the Kazzur. But we have more zhantils to saddle here. There is no doubt that if Hamal is to be kept under proper control the empire must be given a Hamalese to rule. That man is King Telmont—"

Nodgen the Bald's words were lost in a chorus of catcalls and fiercely amused expostulations and accusations.

"King Telmont is not related in any way to Thyllis—"

"He cowers in his kingdom in the far Black Hills—"

"He is spineless!"

The knowledge of family relationships and intricate blood ties and links and alliances through marriage were meat and drink to the rulers in the Dawn Lands. Such knowledge was of vital consequence. By understanding why one king did this and one queen did the opposite through the promptings of family loyalties enabled a tricky course of diplomacy to be set. The delegates had to keep themselves informed of the intrigues that fomented all the time. It was a matter of survival, along with always remembering names, for by forgetting a name one might lose a kingdom.

The rival king who had accused Nodgen the Bald of flying his airboats back home and then claiming compensation for their loss rose to shout with great scorn: "We know why you champion this King Telmont, Nodgen the Bald! How much gold has he paid you? What promises has he made?"

The marshal Djangs eased forward, wary.

"I spit on your robe, King Nalgre the Defaced! I deny your accusations, I hurl them back into your teeth—"

Fresh fuel was heaped on the fire of enmity; the duel that would follow later might enlarge catastrophically to include two entire countries, at each other's throats—as usual. These local wars had been contained in the mutual onslaught on Hamal. Now, with the sad inevitability of human nature, they would burst out again, raw and red and bloody.

The damping down of that squabble—a damping down only, for to extinguish it would take longer and demand harsher means—was left to Drak. By the grimness of his demeanor he left no one in any doubt of his anger and contempt. He tried to bring the Peace Conference back to considerations of what lay immediately to hand. "We each have a rapier to sharpen, and so accommodations must be made. If the delegates from the Dawn Lands insist on fighting among themselves, we deplore that but accept it as a burden of history. The future of Hamal must be assured. Let no one forget that all of us face a greater menace from the Shanks who raid us from over the oceans."

"Aye," said Jaidur. This was a matter touching him and his new kingdom nearly. "And I suspect the damned Shanks will soon stop raiding and attempt permanent settlements—"

Fresh uproar at this statement could not conceal the wave

of dread that swept over the chamber. All men of this grouping of continents and islands called Paz who lived near a coastline were dreadfully aware of the menace of the Shanks. Fish heads, they called them, Leem Lovers, any scurrilous name a man could put his tongue to, all revealing the horror their name conjured up.

As though the mere mention of the Shanks put a pause to the precedent proceedings, a fresh session opened with a concerted attack on the delegates from Vallia, Hyrklana and Djanduin.

Nodgen the Bald, irked at the dismissal of his claims for King Telmont, pointed a forefinger at Drak. He swept that indicting digit around to encompass Seg, Jaidur, Kytun and O. Fellin Coper. The unmistakable result of the gesture was to isolate these men and to range the other delegates against them.

"You sit there fulminating against us. You sit there pompously pontificating. Yet who are you? You are not of Havilfar North and Central—"

Kytun bellowed: "We are of Havilfar South West!"

Jaidur said, "We are of Hyrklana off Havilfar East!"

Drak and Seg remained silent, very sensibly.

"Look at you!" Nodgen waggled that forefinger. "All of you, lackeys. Aye, lackeys!"

Kytun's four arms windmilled and Ortyg, with a squeak of alarm, tugged at his comrade's military cape. "Let him chatter, Kytun!"

"Lackeys!" roared K. Kholin Dorn, fearsome, ferocious, a warrior four-armed Dwadjang. "Explain yourself—king!"

"That is not difficult!" shouted another delegate.

"No! Lackeys—all of you—lackeys of one man!"

"Let me blatter 'em!" pleaded Kytun, his face a black sunburst.

"Hold still, Kytun, do!" Ortyg's gerbil-face expressed concern for Kytun, nothing for the shouted accusations.

Nodgen the Bald bellowed: "One man commands you, the father of the King of Hyrklana; the King of Djanduin; the Emperor of Vallia. One man—and where is he? Why is he not here to talk to us—does he think himself so far above us—?"

The picture wavered.

As though heated air rose before the scene in the assembly

chamber the whole glittering assemblage shivered and undu-
lated.

"Your pardon," said Deb-Lu-Quienyin. "I must admit I
allowed my concentration to lapse."

The Wizard of Loh's eyes encompassed the world. I stared
into those eyes and looked through the sorcerous power of
Deb-Lu into the Peace Conference. People in there were shouting and waving fists although, I was thankful to observe, no
one was foolish enough to draw a sword.

"It is all right, Deb-Lu," I said. "I must be tiring you. And
what they say is right, in one way. I do not wish to go down
and sit among them for these dreary proceedings."

"Very practical."

"And if that is being high and mighty—so be it."

"Shall I go on?"

"It is hardly worth it. They will decide nothing. But Drak
tries hard. No, I need a wet and—"

The picture I saw through the Wizard of Loh's eyes came
into focus. We sat comfortably in a small aerie high in the
Mirvol Keep of the palace of Ruathytu, the Hammabi el
Lamma. Whoever had lived here before, probably a Chuktar
of saddle birds, had done himself well. There was ample provision of wine and fine fare. The picture steadied and the
resplendent assembly came back into focus. Deb-Lu-Quienyin
had arranged a signomant, a device which eased his powers
of observation at a distance, and its placing discreetly in the
chamber allowed us excellent vision all around, if in a little
foreshortened a fashion.

The wet I promised myself had to wait for the double doors
at the far end of the assembly chamber crashed open. The
Djangs on duty there recovered swiftly and their stuxes thrust
steel heads at the man who burst in. They halted their instinctive
reaction at once, for the man was clearly a merker, a messenger
who had flown hard. His leathers were glazed with dust.

He held up a hand and shouted so that all could hear.

"Lahal, notors! King Telmont has gathered a great army
and marches on us. He vows vengeance. He has sworn to
retake the city of Ruathytu and to place the crown of empire
upon his head. And his chief promise is this: he will seize by
the heels and utterly destory the man called Dray Prescot."

Deb-Lu let out a cry and the picture I saw through his eyes
vanished instantly. I blinked.

"Jak!" said Deb-Lu. "This is serious—"

"What?" I said. "Not you, too? You did not think, like those delegates down there, that by one battle and the taking of their capital the whole puissant Empire of Hamal would be conquered?"

Chapter Two

We Fly For the Mountains
of the West

"But we must find him! From what you say of him he is the only one. It is certain this King Telmont is a buffoon."

"Drak is right," said Jaidur. "We must find him—and damn quickly."

The Peace Conference had closed the session for the day and those delegates who had been so scathingly denounced by King Nodgen the Bald gathered with Deb-Lu and me in one of the apartments given over to our use in the Hammabi el Lamma.

"I can vouch for him," said Deb-Lu. He still wore his turban, and it was still lopsided; but for all that he looked what he was—a Wizard of Loh and among the most feared and respected of sorcerers of all Kregen. "Yes. Prince Nedfar is all your father has said."

"And," said Jaezila with a force that for all its passion did scarce justice to the tumult within her, as I could see and, seeing feel for her, "if we do not quickly tell Tyfar the truth, I, for one, will not answer for the consequences."

"That settles it," I said. We were all supposed to be relaxing after a hard day, and we were all tensed up and unhappy and aware of the pressures. The idiot King Telmont had scraped an army together and was marching on Ruathytu. The delegates from the Dawn Lands squabbled among themselves. And everyone wanted the business finished quickly so they might go home to the problems that awaited them there. "We must find Nedfar. He is the man who will be emperor. Just how we convince the others is another problem."

"We will convince them, Dray," said Kytun, using all four arms to express his feelings and to feed himself.

19

"Not by edge of sword."

"Of course not!" said Ortyg. His shrewd face expressed pained surprise at my suggestion. "We will discuss this—"

"I'll discuss it," promised Kytun.

"And Tyfar?" Jaezila was really worried. She and Tyfar were at one and the same time madly in love and forever at loggerheads, a most intriguing situation.

"I'll fly out, Jaezila," I said.

Drak looked cross. "I do wish, Father, you wouldn't call Lela Jaezila all the time. She is my sister, and your daughter, and she calls you Jak and you call her Jaezila. Most unsettling."

"We were blade comrades, Drak. I know Jaezila as Jaezila more than I do as Lela. Anyway, Tyfar must be told."

Jaidur swallowed his drink and said, "And where was this Prince Nedfar during the Taking of Ruathytu?"

I said, "I do not know. But I give thanks to Opaz and to Djan that he was not here. I do not like to contemplate what would have happened had we met in battle."

Kytun's fierce Djang face contained an amazingly placid look as he said, "I am glad we did not meet in the fight."

There was no mistaking his meaning. My Djangs would allow no harm to come to their king. I did not make the mistake of assuming I could overrule their loyalty by my desire to promote a new emperor in Hamal, for all my admiration of the emperor-elect and my affection for his son.

"Well, then, Jak," Jaezila stood up, tall and graceful and superb in her hunting leathers and in no mood to stand any nonsense from her father. "If you're flying out with me let's get started."

"Lela!" exclaimed Drak, outraged.

"We can't shilly-shally around. Tyfar is stuck out there by the Mountains of the West and being attacked by those confounded wild men, I expect, and getting all kinds of garbled messages about what's happened to Ruathytu. What do you think he's imagining, feeling? By Vox! Have you no heart!"

Not one of those fighting men who swore allegiance to me even thought of saying that, well, Prince Tyfar was a Hamalese, after all. They had fought the Hamalese; now they understood my dreams and desires for the future.

I stood up. I put the wine glass down.

"Wenda!"*

So, when we'd sorted out who was going and who staying to attend the tiresome Peace Conference, we all went up to the most convenient landing platform where a selection of captured Hamalian airboats rested.

Drak could not be released from his lynch-pin position in the conference. Lildra was reluctant to let Jaidur go as they were comparatively recent newlyweds, and this appeared to be just. Ortyg was not too keen on Kytun going, preferring him rather to stay to keep an eye on the unruly elements here.

Seg said, "I'm going, my old dom, and joy in it."

I admit I felt a leap of my spirits as Seg spoke. What it was to go off adventuring with a blade comrade, a true friend, the greatest bowman in all Loh!

Drak looked stern. He could have stood for a portrait of an elder judging a tribe, a statesman adjudicating on empires—well, he was all those things, of course; but he so looked the part. "I do not like the idea of you going haring off all over the place, Father. It is—it is undignified."

"I've never save in one instance bothered about dignity."

"But you are the Emperor of Vallia! Emperors do not go off flying—"

"This one does. Oh, and don't forget to mention when Kytun and Ortyg are here the King of Djanduin. Anyway, Drak, you will have to shoulder the burden of being Emperor of Vallia soon."

This, as you will readily perceive, was one of my very good reasons for leaving Drak. He had to be made to understand I meant it when I said he was to take over. He was perfectly capable. It was only his damned rectitude and sense of what was fitting that made him declare he would never become emperor while his mother, Delia, and I lived.

"You know my thoughts on that—" he began.

"Enough! Let us take off—"

Drak went doggedly on. "And we are supposed to be concerning ourselves about this Prince Nedfar you have selected to be the Emperor of Hamal. Where is he? He is who—"

"Listen, Drak! It is my guess Nedfar has flown to the Mountains of the West. He's visiting his son, Tyfar. That's what I think. If we hang about he will be rushing back here and no doubt become embroiled with some stupid idiot from the Dawn Lands, or this King Telmont, or anything untoward—" I finished speaking somewhat more lamely than I'd begun. I could hear myself talking, and that is always fatal to ordered thought.

Over our heads a few clouds scattered pink and golden light from their edges, radiant whorls of darkness, as they obscured the face of the Maiden with the Many Smiles. The stars clustered thickly, fat and bright and twinkling merrily, and a tiny night breeze blew the scents of moon blooms festooning the walls of the landing platform. I breathed in deeply. The air of Kregen is sweet, sweet....

Everything had been prepared. Now that the decision had been made I was anxious to be off, for I well knew what would happen if word of this got around to my people. There would be an instant outcry. To tell the truth, I found it uncanny how well my decision to fly off was being taken. If my lads of the Emperor's Sword Watch, or the Emperor's Yellow Jackets, got wind of an adventure in the offing—well! And Delia's warriors of the Empress's Devoted Life Guard—they'd want to come, too. And, I saw, if we didn't get off sharpish, nothing was going to stop Kytun from leaping aboard the flier and joining us.

Drak looked up at us three lining along the rail of the airboat. He gave us a smile. Suddenly, I wondered if he was pleased to see me go, to get me out of his hair. Well, if that was the case—and I doubted it—then it would be mutual only in the sense that what I was going to do where we were going was all a part and parcel of what had to be done for Hamal and Vallia.

Deft-Fingered Minch stared up at us, his bearded face as crusty and concerned as ever, for he was a kampeon I counted as a comrade, and I have no doubt at all that he was running over in his mind the preparations he had made for us. We had given him little time; but Minch was not called Deft-Fingered for nothing. I had no doubts that the airboat had been stocked, and fully stocked, with all that we would need.

Seg suddenly leaned even farther over the rail and shouted down to a fiery-haired fellow with wide shoulders clad in sober russet who looked up in just such a way as Minch.

"Lije!" shouted Seg. "Did you put in that knobbly stave I have in pickle?"

"Aye, I did that. And you shouldn't be flying off alone without me—"

"By Vox!" said Drak, as though struck by a shaft from Erthyr the Bow himself. "That is right! What am I doing allowing you and Lela to fly off—"

"By the Veiled Froyvil!" sang out Seg. "Your mother and father, and Thelda and me walked all through the hostile territories of Turismond together—"

"And Jak and Tyfar and I have gone adventuring, Drak," called Jaezila who was Lela to her brother. "So stop worrying."

I shot a hard look at Seg. He had the grace to brace his shoulders back and tilt his head, but he knew he had roused a storm that might delay us. "Get her up, Seg!"

"Aye, my old dom. Let's get away from all these nannies."

As the remberees were shouted and our voller lifted up into the night sky I looked closely at Drak. Already he was swinging away, cape flaring, to bellow at his people standing further back on the landing platform.

"Make it fast," I said to Seg at the controls. "Drak will send half the army after us."

"More likely your Sword Watch," said Jaezila.

"If that rapscallion bunch get half a chance to go off aroving you won't see their tails for dust. And," I said, feeling the injustice of it all, remembering Delia's father and his complaints about the way his pallans and guards cramped his fun, "and they'll stop us enjoying ourselves."

The flier sped swiftly into the moonshot darkness, speeding above Ruathytu, heading due west.

ESW and EYJ had been formed to protect the emperor. They did this with such devotion that a wall of bodies stood between me and danger. Only by an impassioned call for their loyalty to Drak, who was doing the fighting, and to Seg, who led the major portion of Vallia's forces, had I managed to keep my guards off my neck. Delia had given Nath Karidge permission to take three quarters of the Empress's Devoted Life Guard off to the war against Hamal. Nath wouldn't hang about if he could follow me, well knowing he'd see action. Into the equation I must add the crew of *Mathdi,* the voller used to such good effect in the days leading up to the Taking of Ruathytu.

So we slammed the speed lever over to the stop and we hurtled beneath the Moons of Kregen, for now there were four shining between the clouds, the Maiden with the Many Smiles, the Twins, and She of the Veils.

In an attempt to shake off these forebodings—which were selfish and ungrateful, to be sure—and lighten our mood, I said to Seg, "Why bring a bowstave you have in pickle, Seg? Surely it is better to keep it in a vat?"

"So some bowyers claim. You know I've been used to pickling 'em on the move." Here Seg glanced sideways at Jaezila, her face flushed in the rose and golden light of the moons. "And this is a very special stave. I want to keep an eye on it."

"Oh?"

"It is not yerthyr wood. I've learned a very great deal since I left Erthyrdrin, believe me. For one thing, the rose-colored feathers from the zim korf of Valka are as good as the blue feathers of the king korf of my own mountains."

"As good as?"

Seg laughed. "Well, my old dom, you can't really expect me to admit they are better!"

"And the other thing?"

"Why, that the wood of the lisehn tree of Vallia is as good as erthyr wood—"

"As good as?"

And Jaezila laughed.

Seg composed himself, for we all knew we'd tease him over these arcane points of archery and bow-building. "This brave young prince of yours, Lela—you say he is a bowman?"

"Yes, Seg, but—"

"For a Hamalese," I said, and ducked away in mock reaction as Jaezila struck out in mock buffet. "He is an axeman, Seg, superb. Not like Inch, though. But Jaezila can best him with a bow."

"She can best just about anyone," said Seg. "I know. I trained her."

"Then, Seg," I said, speaking comfortably. "Tyfar owes you his life, for Jaezila—Lela—feathered a thing all fangs and jaws in a swamp. It would have chomped Tyfar's head for dinner; but Jaezila's shot was precisely through one red-slitted eye."

Jaezila looked at me over a shoulder, all round and firm under her russets. "Aye, Jak! And in the next heartbeat you sworded the monster's mate that would have had me for its dinner."

"I remember. You asked me if Tyfar was my son—"

"I did. And you were my father all the time! Opaz plays strange tricks on us, to be sure."

Seg laughed, turning back to the controls. "And if all I hear and see is true then this Prince Tyfar will be your son Dray, after all."

"If he has any sense," I said in more of a growl than I intended.

The airboat bore on marvelously, for to Seg flying a voller without constant fear that she'd break down at any minute was liberating. We rummaged in the wicker hampers provided by Minch and Lije and munched and talked and ate and talked and drank and talked. Seg expressed himself as of the opinion, by the Veiled Froyvil, that it would be capital if Inch was with us.

"But I knew he had a stern task up in those Black Mountains of his. He has done very well to clear out the mercenaries and slavers. With Korf Aighos to the south clearing out the Blue Mountains, and Turko to the east managing to make something of Falinur—" Here Seg paused, and Jaezila started to say something and, behind Seg's back, I cautioned her to silence.

Presently, Seg went on speaking. "Turko will make those Falinurese understand what is required of them. But, had I to do it all over again—"

"You did the right thing, Seg. Turko will be harder than I could wish for; but we must work with what we have. In Hamal, for instance, do you think we can stamp out slavery even when Prince Nedfar is emperor?"

This was a stumper of a question, and we ate in silence for a time. Slavery at the moment was an intractable problem. One day, in the light of Opaz, one day, we'd be free of the blight.

Jaezila said, "And as well as our friends what of our foes?"

Well, there was enough of them about, by Krun!

We flew this leg of our course a few degrees south of west and, to the south of us and about halfway to the River Os, rose the Black Hills. From this range of heights flowed the River Mak, to empty into the Havilthytus at Ruathytu. King Telmont, then, must be marching along from the kingdom, a part of the Empire of Hamal, which gave him his name. Jaezila mentioned our foes; there was a man down there, a vad from Middle

Nalem to the west of the Black Hills, who would as lief put
me in an oubliette as kill me out of hand. This fellow, Garnath
ham Hestan, Vad of Middle Nalem, had been associated with
two other scoundrels, the Kataki Strom and Phu-Si-Yantong.
Well, Yantong was dead, blown away by the Quern of Gramarye. Now, I suspected, Vad Garnath had transferred his evil
allegiance to King Telmont.

Jaezila lowered her goblet and the wine shone on her lips.

"Jak—would you think it weak of me if I said I wished
Shara was here?"

"Not in the least," I said at once. "I always feel more at
ease when Melow the Supple goes with your mother, and Kardo
with Drak."

Melow the Supple and her twins were safely out of Faol.
They were Manhounds, horrific beings genetically structured
to run on all fours and to rip and rend and destroy, more
fearsome than hunting cats. Yet they were as essentially apim
as I was. Chance had given Melow the opportunity to win free
of her malign masters, and now she, and Kardo and Shara,
were our friends. And the truth was that with a Manhound at
your side you could wish for very few better comrades in a
fight.

The voller proved a swift craft and we took turns to sleep
and before dawn threw ruby and jade sparks onto the lesser
heights we closed with the Mountains of the West.

Not as lofty or awe-inspiring a range as the Stratemsk, the
Western Mountains of Hamal present a solemn and splendid
spectacle. Probably not every hidden valley has been trodden
by the foot of man. There are secrets in those interleaved folds
of crag and scarp still. We aimed our flight for Hammansax
where Tyfar had said he could be reached.

Color throbbed in the early morning. The air held a tang.
Seg knuckled his eyes and stared all around and stretched,
elbows back, spine arched, chest expanded, all the physique
of a master bowman eloquent of his strength and skill. I clapped
him on the back.

"Hai! Seg! A day for deeds!"

"Since our dip in that magical pool I feel like a youngster.
May Opaz witness that it is good to be alive!"

Jaezila called from the side, turning to face us, still half
leaning over. "There is a stream down there. I'm for a swim."

So, down we went in that dawnlight and stripped off and

plunged in, our daggers belted around our waists. Had there been any of the wonderful gallery of nasty creatures of Kregen swimming around hungry for breakfast he, she or it would have had short shrift from us three.

Dripping wet, we shouted and laughed and threw handfuls of water about and generally acted in a way that might have made Drak dub us undignified. I had a shrewd idea he'd join in . . .

By the time we'd dried off and cooked up some breakfast and stuffed ourselves to repletion with vosk rashers and loloo's eggs and masses of tea and palines, we felt in remarkable spirits.

Hammansax lay over the next ridge, far enough from the main mass of the mountain chain to afford it warning when the wild men attacked. As I told Seg, "It's not a question of if the wild men attack. It's always when."

Seg looked up, squinting against the morning light.

"Like now?"

We whirled.

They were there, flying in long skeins, sharp and dark against the brightness. The wings of their saddlebirds beating up and down, up and down, and the wink and glitter of weapons and armor, the flare of feathered decorations driving home with force their power and contempt for opposition. Not one of the civilized races, these moorkrim, these wild men.

"They haven't seen us." Jaezila threw her cape onto our little fire and the few last wisps of smoke died. "That was a nice cape. I particularly liked the zhantil-motif edging."

Still staring into the sky at those distant malefic figures, I said, "You can pick out the edging and stitch it back onto a new cape."

"They're flying away," said Seg.

"Aye."

"They've been up to mischief, then, if they're like any reivers I've known."

"Aye."

Jaezila bent for the cape and bashed it on the ground. Seg and I turned our heads to watch her, and I felt the quick spurt of love for her as she banged the cape on the dusty ground. The wild men up there, so like flutsmen and yet not civilized to any degree that would enable easy parleys to be held, undulating on beating wings, flew away, far away to the west.

"So we'd better go and see."

"If—" said Jaezila and she held the burned rag between her fists. "If Tyfar is—"

"Let us go and see."

Like any sensible Kregan in unfamiliar territory with a voller to consider, we'd concealed the airboat in the trees. The wildmen had not spotted her. We scuffed the fire out and Jaezila marched off to the voller. She let the cape fall to the ground. It was of a russet color, with a high velvet collar and those golden zhantils entwined and leaping as edging. Seg started after Jaezila.

I picked up the burned cape. I rolled it up. I shoved it under my arm. I started for the airboat. Jaezila was damned upset and I didn't like that.

She took the controls and sent the little craft up in a violent surge. We swung over the trees and pelted for the ridge. The gray rock and the trees whipped away below and we looked over the ridge into the valley folded between the mountain arms.

Fire, smoke, destruction. . . .

Hammansax burned.

"Tyfar—"

"He'll be all right, Jaezila. You know how resourceful he is."

"That's the trouble. He's likely to go rushing out and get himself killed."

We did not speak much as the voller shot down toward burning Hammansax.

The town had been a small prosperous frontier post—the sax in the name indicated that—and the raiders had failed to destroy the character of the place. Walls still stood, a few roofs remained unfallen. But smoke choked everywhere and people ran and yelled among the flames. They had come out of hiding after the wildmen flew off and now strove to save their town from further destruction.

In a flierdrome to one side, the wreck of a green-painted Courier voller lay twisted grotesquely, the flames little blue devils amid the smoke along her frame. Beyond her the flierdrome was empty.

"No one here when the wildmen struck," said Seg.

"Perhaps Tyfar wasn't here." Jaezila hurled the airboat down into the principal square. Only two sides burned, the other two containing stalls remained intact. People looked up and shouted as we landed on the beaten earth of the square.

We soon discovered the story. Prince Tyfar had not been in Hammansax for a time. The stink of raw ashes, hot and shiny, got up our nostrils. Whirls of black cinders swept into the air from the burning houses. The people were dazed. This was a disaster which, although always a possibility in their imaginations, had really arrived and with it—horror. No matter these folk lived on the frontier and expected trouble; when that trouble came it was always fresh and terrible and so much greater than the anticipation could prepare. Yet we could not stop and help.

"We have sent off messengers," one of the chief men of the town told us. "The army will follow the moorkrim and try to get our people back; but the wildmen will fly far, far." He wiped black soot around his eyes, which were red and inflamed. "May Havil rot their wings."

Despite all the ridiculous toughness I am supposed to have, be and represent, despite all the aloof power and authority vested in me, despite all this flummery, I felt the keen dagger of guilt. This was my fault. By invading Hamal we had drawn off vitally needed men to guard these frontier posts against the wildmen. Oh, yes, the burdens hanging on the shoulders of men and women foolish enough to rule empires crush their victims unless resisted with other weapons than simple brute force.

If you cannot make an omelette without breaking eggs, then one innocent person will save a city of guilty people.

We did what we could to help the people, but that was little enough, Zair help us.

They were aware that their empire had been defeated in a battle in the capital city. But that was a long way away. Cultivation and husbandry and constant vigilance against the wildmen from over the mountains was the reality, was the here and now.

They'd go on living this way, living their lives, and whoever ruled in Ruathytu would demand taxes and would send not enough forces to help in defense. We had done little for Hammansax. Prince Tyfar, we were told by the landlord of what had been The Jolly Vodrin—now a pile of rubble and burned timbers—had taken what the Empress Thyllis had left him of

his army to a high pass in the mountains called the Jaws of
Laca.

"How do you know that for certain?" demanded Jaezila.

She looked splendid, fierce and radiant and burning with
anger and anxiety.

The landlord, half of whose hair had burned away, wiped
blistered hands gently on an ointment rag. He was Hamdal the
Measure.

Seg said, very gently, "He will know, Lela."

What Seg did not say, what I did not say, was that Jaezila
would also know why a landlord of an inn popular with the
soldiers would be aware of their orders. This is a fact of military
life in certain quarters. Cautious generals must legislate against
it by counter-cunning.

"Where is the Lacachun?" asked Jaezila.

Hamdal the Measure held up one blistered hand, pointing
to the southwest. "Between the two tallest peaks within view
from that peak, the Ivory Cone. You can't miss it."

I said, "How many men did Prince Tyfar take?"

Hamdal made a face, and winced. "Two regiments? I do
not know. Perhaps more. A lord came asking these questions
just before the wildmen attacked—"

"Another lord?"

"Aye, notor. Another great lord. He sought Prince Tyfar
with great urgency—just as you do."

Seg looked across at me, questioning.

"Thank you, Hamdal the Measure," I said. "We must leave
you. But help will reach you soon—"

"Aye," said the landlord. "Aye—too late, as usual."

We went back to our flier.

"Another lord—" said Seg.

"Prince Nedfar," said Jaezila. "It must have been."

"Yes." The coaming of the voller struck warm under my
hands. "Probably." The twin suns burned down. "Possibly.
Let us hope that it was Prince Nedfar."

Chapter Three

Concerning Shooting Wagers

From the Ivory Cone the two distant peaks looked very much like the jaws of a dinosaur, head upturned, gaping at the sky. That was why they were called the Lacachun.

"If they've crunched down on Ty—" Jaezila gripped the rail and her voice was unsteady. I did not touch her.

"You know Tyfar."

"As I said—I do!"

The Ivory Cone passed away to the side, sleek and pointed and shining white, with long gray falls between the snow slopes. We all wore thick flying furs. Our faces glowed, nipped by the chill. On we drove and we looked keenly ahead, ready to sight whatever of peril lay before us.

This airboat—she had no name, only in the Hamalian way a number—carried us over the snow sheets and down past the saddle. We corkscrewed between sheer rock faces. A fear that we were entering a massif took hold of us and had to be resisted. We sped along over gulfs and soared up over slopes of scree and so whirled out again into space. We three were old campaigners. Not one of us even considered rising into the higher levels and simply flying over the top.

We wished to arrive unseen and unheralded.

The wildmen who had trapped the voller below were not so careful. These were their mountains and here they ruled.

The situation was laid out for us as we hovered in the rock of a striated rock cliff. A ledge protruded from the crumbled rock face, perhaps halfway up from the stream below, a mere silver thread. The lip high above threw shadows over us. The wildmen circled and shot at the stranded airboat on the ledge. Others had alighted and crept up between boulders tumbled on the ledge. They approached from each end, yet they hesitated, and we saw shafts lifting from the airboat and the stones about her.

"It is just a matter of time," said Seg. He reached for the longbow that was never absent for long from his side.

Jaezila had the controls.

"Can you—?" Seg started to say, and then stopped. Jaezila deftly brought the voller in among the shadows close to the cliff. She eased her along. Like a ghost we slithered with our starboard flank against the rock striations. Ahead and below, the ledge and the voller there and the swirling forms of the wildmen stood out in suns shine.

I picked up a longbow. Seg nodded. "A good choice, Dray. That stave I built when I was Kov in Falinur."

"You never stop making bows, Seg; how you keep track of 'em all is the mystery."

But, of course, that was no mystery. . . .

"Each bow is different," said Seg, selecting the first arrow from the quiver strapped to the voller's rail. "Each one has character. You know that."

"Yes. And there are no bows in all Kregen to match the ones built by Seg Segutorio."

"That," said Jaezila, bringing the airboat to a halt in midair and relinquishing the controls, "is true."

"How many d'you make 'em, Dray?"

There were eight moorkrim flying like the crazy savages they were in the air space before the ledge, rising and falling, swinging in to loose and diving or zooming away.

"The young braves of the tribe," I said. "You know the kind of pecking order they're likely to have and the necessity of gaining credit among their peer group. The more mature warriors will be on the ledge, under cover."

"Yes. I make seven saddle flyers this side—"

"And ten on the other end," said Jaezila. She took up her longbow. Like the others, this was a Lohvian longbow built by Seg. If you have to have a hobby on Kregen it is useful if it is connected with survival.

"Twenty-five," said Seg. "We've shafted more than that before breakfast."

"Maybe so, Seg. And each time we do it it could be the last. So, my old dom, watch it!"

He laughed, throwing back his head. His black hair waved wildly and his fey blue eyes looked now with the steady regard of the bowman—wild and impulsive and shrewd and practical are the folk of Erthyrdrin, and Seg showed all that blend now as he fitted nock to string.

"Father!" Jaezila looked at me, the arrow in her fingers as long and lethal as those held by Seg and me. I felt surprise that she thus called me.

"Lela?"

"You told me, I seem to remember, when I was little, that you and Uncle Seg used to wager when you shot."

Again Seg laughed, lifting the bow. His russet tunic hid what was going on among the muscles of his back and arms, but they would have made a sculptor weep for joy.

"So we did, Lela, my love, so we did! What is it to be, then, a gold talen a hit?"

Macabre, gruesome, unfeeling? Wagering on killing other people? Of course. Once we began to shoot, the wildmen would not bother about anything as decadently sophisticated as gambling on how they slew us. They would simply whoop in with the one blood-red desire to chew us up and hurl the refuse into the gulf. That is the way of wildmen.

Perhaps, if you thought about it, that was more savagely honest? All I knew was that I was on Kregen, my comrade and my daughter were about to face deadly peril, and a man I admired was about to die unless we stopped his killers.

We shot.

Three of the eight pirouetting in midair before the ledge were shafted, and then three more. The remaining two swung away, the wings of their tyryvols beating madly and Seg and Jaezila saw to them as I switched my aim.

The targets among the boulders proved more tricky, and I know two of my shafts missed. Return shots started to come up; but we were a small and protected target in the voller among the clustered shadows.

We three worked together sweetly in the shooting.

When the wildmen at the far end of the ledge broke from their boulders and, leaping astride their saddle flyers, shot up into the air and headed for us, Seg and Jaezila went methodically to work on them while I remained winkling out the fellows in the rocks this end.

A crossbow bolt punched clean up through the skin of the voller.

Seg said, "That looks nasty."

"They capture crossbows from time to time. They can't make 'em, can't even do repairs. When they break they throw them away. They tart them up with feathers and skins and hair. But they can shoot well with them."

Seg loosed and flipped a fresh arrow into place and loosed again, all in a smooth twinkling motion, before he spoke.

"That's one crossbow fellow won't shoot again."

And Jaezila laughed. "Two shafts, Uncle Seg, for one cross-bow man?"

"I'll pay you the gold talen, Lela, don't fret."

The ten flyers were whittled down to four before they reached the voller. Seg shot and took out a moorkrim with his hair black and greasy braided into a fantastic halo. Jaezila's shot merely transfixed the wildman's arm; that wouldn't stop the savage from advancing.

"Swords!"

As the three wildmen flung their tyryvols at the airboat in a welter of thrashing wings, we drew our blades. That churning of the air, a favorite trick of men who fight astride saddle flyers, prevented accurate shooting. The three hit the deck and came for us. Their stink preceded them.

When fighting on foot wildmen employ shields, usually of wicker and skins, and spears or swords if they can come by them, for they find the metallurgy of swords a little above their capacities. These three screeched war cries. They snatched their shields up and into place. One had a sword, a Hamalian army thraxter, and he pressed on boldly. The one Jaezila had wounded didn't seem to know he had been hit. The arrow transfixed his arm and with a petty gesture he broke it off, fore and aft, and then slapped his shield back across again.

You had to admire the fortitude of the wildmen, if nothing else.

Not caring to waste them, for the fellows below kept up their pressure on the stranded voller, I whipped out the Krozair longsword and cocked it between spread fists.

"Let me have 'em," I shouted at Seg and Jaezila. "You see off those fellows in the rocks."

Giving my comrade and my daughter no time to argue I pushed past to the front, faced the small deck space where the wildmen ran on as only warriors at home in the air can run, and met the first onslaught.

A Krozair longsword does not take a deal of notice of a wicker shield.

The first man sank to the deck with a cleft skull.

The next two, rushing up together on bandy legs bent like springs, leaped for me. The Krozair brand switched left and as I rolled my wrists flailed back right. Two swift and unmerciful blows, and the two moorkrim toppled aside. Both fell, slipped and, shrieking, pitched over into space. I put my foot against the first one, whose blood and brains oozed out, and pushed him over the side.

The smell of the wildmen, which comes as much from themselves as from the muck they smear on their greased and braided hair, hung about the voller. It would persist.

Seg bellowed, "They are rushing the airboat!"

"Down!" Jaezila sprang for the controls. She slammed the levers hard over and our flier pitched down as though the bottom of the world had fallen out.

She brought us in with superb piloting. We flashed over the boulders. Seg leaned over, very thoughtfully, and sent two flashing shafts into billets as we passed. It is my unalterable opinion that there is no greater bowman in all Kregen than Seg Segutorio.

We landed slap bang in the middle of the rest of them as they rushed the flier. The ensuing dust up was interesting, for Seg and Jaezila can handle blade as well as bow.

The tyryvols fluttered their wings but could not rise as the wildmen had tethered them with rocks for the final foot charge. Our blades glittered and fouled with blood. We fought fiercely for a space and then there were no more moorkrim to fight.

Seg had a small nick along his right wrist, a nothing, and Jaezila a score along her side. I frowned.

"Damned careless of you, my girl. Let me look."

"It's nothing, Jak!"

It was nothing, really, but we dug out the first aid which consisted of a gel in a bandage, and slapped it on. Seg looked up from the crashed flier. He shouted.

"You won't believe what's here!"

We went across the rocks. The aftermath of a fight is often a strange time, when noises ring in your ears, and the air seems irradiated with color, and the world moves under your feet.

Seg was right.

There were dead men sprawled here and there, curled up

in nooks and crannies, huddled behind the rocks that had punched through the voller's skin in the crash. She was done for. One of the silver boxes had broken and—it being the paol box—the cayferm it contained had wafted away to be lost in the air. A shivering man crouched behind a box which had saved him, for its stout wooden side was feathered with arrows like a pincushion. He held the windlass of a crossbow.

"Look," said Seg.

Prince Nedfar lay half on his side, his hands outstretched gripping the crossbow. It was clear what had been going on. The man behind the box was a Relt, a gentle specimen of a race of diffs who are not warriors, and he had been spanning the crossbow for Nedfar. Nedfar's face showed greasy and strained, dirty with grimed sweat. His eyes were sunken.

Among the dead men a few living men rose to greet us.

They were retainers, the Relt stylor, the cooks and valets, a groom, and I felt the pang at what must have happened. I bent to Nedfar. His sunken eyes looked like plums, bruised against bruised flesh.

"Prince!"

He opened his eyes.

In his right shoulder the butt end of a quarrel stood up. It looked obscene. Judging by the amount of wooden flight showing, its steel head was buried deeply into Nedfar's shoulder. He saw me. He recognized me. He spoke one word.

"Traitor!"

Chapter Four

Of a Walk in the Mist

"Now, now, prince. That's all over." I tried to take the crossbow from his hands. "You're safe now. We have to make you comfortable—"

"Jak the Shot—traitor! You betrayed Hamal!"

"He's off his head," said Seg. "And I can see he is a fine-looking man, just as you said. A real prince."

"Yes. We've got to take care of him."

What had happened was clear enough. The fighting men with Nedfar had fought. They had been killed. They must have held off the wildmen for a goodly long time. The end was in sight when we turned up. I judged that the twenty-five we had dealt with had been left to finish the thing from a larger warband.

"Hamal—" Nedfar looked in a bad way. His face was of that color of the lead in old sewers. "You betrayed our plans to our enemies, Jak—"

Jaezila brought water and moistened his lips. He saw her.

"Jaezila—what—the man Jak the Shot—do not, do not—"

"Prince!" Jaezila spoke in a voice like diamond. "Where is Tyfar?"

"Tyfar? My son Tyfar?"

"Yes, yes! Is he still in the Pass of Lacachun?"

"Oh, yes. He is still there—"

Nedfar's mind was not wandering; but he was very tired and his wound gave him a distancing from reality. No doubt past and present clashed in his brain. He sounded very weak.

"We must take Nedfar to a doctor." I tried to sound matter of fact. "We could take the bolt out of his shoulder; but the

37

pain might do for him, brave though he is. A needleman is absolutely vital."

"You're right. And we'll have to go in our airboat."

Again Jaezila bent to Nedfar.

"Tyfar." She spoke with compressed urgency. "Your son Tyfar. Is all well with him?"

The prince's voice rasped weakly. His head rolled.

"All is—is not well—with Tyfar."

We bent closer, intent, concentrating on the halting words.

"They trapped him—the message was—was a trick. A trap. I flew for help—help—Tyfar! They will slay him and all his men—"

Nedfar tried to lift himself, fighting back the pain. He glared up at Jaezila; she bent over him, her soft brown hair a glory about her face. On that face an expression of loving care was replaced by horror and then by a savage determination. The whole story was there, on Jaezila's face, to be read.

"He will be killed." She jumped up, swinging about and the suns light caught in her hair and across her russets and she looked glorious, glorious. "No time, no time—"

She was out of the wreck of the voller in the rocks, leaping to the nearest tethered flyer. The tyryvol's black and ochre scales glistened in the light. She gave him a clip alongside those ugly jaws and freed the tether. All in a fluid line of motion she leaped for the saddle, clamping those long slender legs in hard, giving the flying beast a licking flick with a loose rein, sending him bolting up, legs trailing, tail splattering dust and rock chips, flung him high and hard into the blaze of suns light.

"Jaezila!"

She did not bother to answer but strapped up the clerketer and stretched out to reduce headwinds. The tyryvol opened his wings and beat and beat again and soared up and up.

"Jaezila!"

Seg said, "We'll have to go after her, my old dom."

"Aye," I said. "I will. But you will have to take Nedfar back to the needleman—"

"Me!"

We looked at the prince, who slumped back, looking dreadful. His eyes closed.

"Yes, you, Seg. Don't you see?"

"No, Dray, I do not! You're the one who wants to make this Nedfar fellow the Emperor of Hamal."

"I do. But I can't let Jaezila fly off—"

"No more can I! By the Veiled Froyvil! You know you're the one to handle those idiots at the Peace Conference—"

"Drak can do that! So can you, come to that. There's no time to waste—"

"There's no time, agreed! You—"

"Nedfar is to be the Emperor of Hamal, that's all arranged—"

"I don't give a rast's hind parts for the Emperor of Hamal! But I give a very great deal for Lela! Don't you understand! She's the Princess Majistrix of Vallia, flying off alone into these confounded mountains with packs of wildmen out ahunting! I'm not going the other way—"

"This is—"

"Listen to me, Dray Prescot! You're the Emperor of Vallia and my old dom and your place is with the Peace Conference sorting out these idiot Hamalese and setting up this Nedfar fellow as their new emperor! By Vox! Why can't I ever knock any sense into that vosk skull of a head of yours!"

"Just because Jaezila is my daughter!"

There was no question of my giving orders to Seg. We did not operate on that level. He was right. I knew he was right. But Nedfar had to be taken to a doctor and I had to go after my daughter. The decision was made, irrational and selfish, maybe, but made.

I bellowed back as I vaulted out of the wreckage, "I'll be back soon! Get Nedfar to a doctor!"

As I laid hands on the nearest tyryvol, Seg yelled something I will not repeat. But I knew he would care for Nedfar. I'd trust Seg Segutorio to the ends of both Earth and Kregen.

There existed no doubt in our minds that one of us had to go with Nedfar. Unable to care for himself and a prince of Hamal, he would be at the mercy of any of the many folk who might see profit in his hide. His retainers left alive were not fighting men, and they had been unnerved—shattered—by the viciousness of the wildmen's onslaught and the carnage and blood all about them. Not everyone on Kregen is a bold brave roistering warrior, or a hunting-leather-clad girl ready with whip and rapier.

The tyryvol smashed his wings down under my intemperate

handling and we rocketed into the air. Grabbing at the leather straps of the clerketer, I glanced down. Seg stood there, hands on hips, head upflung, glaring up. As he dwindled away I could visualize the expression on that face of his and although I did not laugh I felt the affection bubbling up.

Good old Seg Segutorio!

That forkful of dungy straw he'd bunged in my face when first we met away there in the Eye of the World had paid dividends in the best comrade a man could ever hope for.

As we lifted away the tyryvol showed his disinclination to rise too high past the ledge. Ahead the world was blotted out in a swirl of mist, dank and gray, writhing down from the higher peaks and spreading out in the cleft between the precipices. I let the flying beast hurtle on at the level he chose, only making sure he was aimed in the right direction and going as fast as he could.

They are splendid flyers, tyryvols, adapted to the tricky cross-currents hereabouts. Of all the wonderful array of saddle flyers of Havilfar, the flutduin of Djanduin stands supreme, in my estimation. I think the snow-white zhyans are truly regal among flyers, but overpriced and tricky as to temper. We flew on and followed the windings of the cleft in the mountains. The silence, apart from the rush of air and the beat of wings, fell strangely after the bedlam of only moments ago.

If Nedfar died, then my plans for Hamal would be thrown out of joint. This buffoon King Telmont was quite unsuitable to be emperor. And if, as I darkly suspected, Vad Garnath had thrown in his lot with Telmont, that was another and even more sinister mark against the king from the Black Hills.

I suppose we could have ignored Nedfar's pain and pushed the crossbow bolt through his shoulder. Drawing it out would have been tricky; but we could have done it. We had a few simple medicaments. But the chance of the prince's death would have been too great; in our own reckless argumentative way, Seg and I had done what had to be done, albeit with suppressed feelings. We'd taken a shaft from old Larghos the So, cutting it off level with his skin and then putting a rod against it and giving it one hell of a thwack with the flat of a sword. Larghos had yelled blue bloody murder. But Nedfar?—Larghos had survived. I wondered if Nedfar would have weathered that kind of treatment. As the tyryvol carried me on strongly I found I was working out just how many seasons ago it was that Seg and I had fought at old Larghos the So's side.

Too many. . . .

He was probably dead now. When a mercenary earns the coveted title of paktun and wears the silver pakmort at his throat he stands a better chance of survival than an ordinary mercenary. He stands an even better chance when he becomes a hyr-paktun and wears the golden pakzhan.

The mist lowered down and tendrils swept away in long cobwebby strands. The tyryvol's wings lathered the mist. He was a fine strong beast, and his scales were polished up. The saddle was relatively crude, being made of wicker and leather and very little padding. It was practical, and from it the ukra, the long polearm of the flyer, could be wielded to deadly effect. The peaks around us seemed to stab like ukras, like the toonons of the flyers of Turismond; seemed to thrust jagged barbs to stop our onward passage. The mist forced us lower and lower.

I'd often pondered a scheme to bring some of the impressive coal black impiters over from the Stratemsk in Turismond. They were hardly flyers and would do well in any new environment of Vallia or Havilfar. And you don't need barbs in an aerial polearm. . . .

I cursed. I realized what I was doing. My thoughts were maundering on like this because I could not face the truth.

My daughter Jaezila had gone flying off to find Tyfar, alone, hurtling into danger. And I was flailing along after her and this pestiferous mist shut down and prevented me from finding the way.

By Zair! If the mist clamped in. . . . That I might be dashed to death on the rocks seemed to me then a mere trifle, a passing side effect of the greater tragedy. I had to get to the Pass of Lacachun!

Tyfar was trapped. Nedfar had mumbled something about a message being a trick. So Tyfar had gone to the rendezvous with a couple of regiments or so and had been trapped. If Jaezila flew into that scene. . . . I used the loose strap on the tyryvol and he responded, beating strongly and churning the air. It was cold and dank and miserable; I scarcely noticed. The furs lay back in our voller. I barely missed them. All the chill deadliness of the Ice Floes of Sicce would not have worried me then. I flew after my daughter, and I refused to think

of the time in the Eye of the World when I had flown after
Velia, my daughter. . . .

Zair would not allow that to happen again. He could not. . . .

To left and right the craggy mountainsides lifted up to vanish
into the clouds. Ahead the mist hung like congealed cobwebs.
Below lay a boulder-choked stream, a mere ligament of silver
wire. As we flew on and the jaws of the mountains closed the
river spouted closer and closer. Ahead of us now the pass lifted
with the stream tumbling down in fronds of spouting silver and
the mist crushing down from above. Most birds and flying
animals will balk at flying through clouds, although some—
the flutduin par excellence—can manage that tricky evolution.
The wise men say the flutduins have an extra sense in their
souls. Whatever the truth of that, the tyryvol flew lower and
lower above the stream spouting amid boulders in the pass and
would not fly higher into the mist.

Eventually the mist and cloud touched the ground ahead.

The way was barred.

No use hitting the flying animal. He craned his neck around,
hissing. Each scale carried a drop of moisture. The leather was
dark with water. I jumped off and, gripping the reins in a fist
like a knobbly tree bole, I started walking, leading the flying
beast along. He strutted, lashing his tail, most unhappy.

Boulders sprang away under my feet. Sharp edges of rock
snapped at my ankles. I almost fell and dragged on the leading
rein to support my weight.

The animal balked, rearing, flailing his wings.

"Come on, tyry! You can do it!"

A ferocious haul on the lead pulled him on. He saw there
was nothing else for it. Wings folded, tail tucked, head outstretched, he followed me into the mist.

Dampness clung everywhere. The chill bit to the quick. At
least, the stink of the wildmen eased from the saddle and
accoutrements. It was necessary to keep on hauling on the
lead, pulling the beast along. His clawed feet clicked and
clacked among the stones. He maintained a nasty hissing
sound, which indicated not vicious anger but rather a sort of
misery. No time to feel sorry for him. Somewhere ahead in
the Pass of the Jaws of Laca Jaezila might be facing dangers
that would appall a paktun. . . .

The whole world of Kregen consisted merely of a silvery
gray whirl. Nothing existed except the stones under my feet

and the leather leading rein in my fist. Sounds thinned. The clatter of the tyryvol at my back sounded as if it came from the other end of Kregen. The mist got into my body. I felt as though I floated. Yet upward lay the way. Upward over rounded boulders which rolled treacherously, and sharp-fanged slabs of rock that gashed at ankles and legs.

My state may be imagined when I say it took me a long time to realize what this mixture of rock and boulders meant. . . .

A rushing sibilant sound gradually intruded on my dulled senses. In these dolorous conditions I half expected the Star Lords to appear with their blue radiance and their Giant Scorpion and snatch me up and away. But the roaring welter of sound growing louder as I stumbled on came from the stream. Here it must be leaping off some higher crag to the side and splashing onto the rocks. In a few moments drops of solid water flew out of the mist, stinging like hail.

I stopped, turning my head. The tyryvol, a mere shapeless blot of shadow at my back, hunkered down. The waterfall was wearing away the cliff, and every now and again a cascade of sharp rocks would fall. Hauling on the rein I started off, edging a little to my left, away from the fall.

The mist looked to be in agitated movement over to the right; the boulders slicked with wet. I stumbled and half fell, gripping the rein. The tyryvol let out a tremendous squawk and dived over me, wings out and flapping, and giving me a welt with his tail. I sprawled forward under the flying beast. He went on, and I could still see him, and he dragged me after him, bursting out of the mist and soaring out over nothingness.

Spinning like a spider at the end of a thread, I dangled beneath the flyer; all below me, thousands of feet down, spread out a vast rock-enclosed valley. Helplessly, I swung along under the flyer, who thrashed his wings in an ecstasy of flight after the prison of the mist.

The leather rein cut into my hand.

Gyrating like a bobbin, I saw the mountains circling me, spinning around and around. The stream spouted off the cliff and hissed down to hit at the side of the path where the tyryvol had dived into space. Mist pressed down above, shading everything into tones of gray and slate and purple. Across the valley the opposite cleft shot into view and out again as I spun. Up there lay the Pass of the Jaws of Laca.

My weight at the end of the rein dragged the animal's head down. He kept trying to lift himself and wagged his head from side to side. I swung. Freed from the goading manthing who rode his back, the tyryvol wanted to free himself from the weight dragging his head down.

He began to claw and bite at the rein, twisting his head to seize the leather between his fangs, grasping it with his talons to steady it and wrench at it. The leather was good and strong and would last; but not for very long. Below me lay a drop into the Ice Floes of Sicce, for sure.

Hand over hand, I started to climb up the leading rein.

It was a race and the dratted flying beast knew it.

Sweat poured off my face. My muscles knotted. I hauled up disdaining to use my feet, for there was no time. It was a case of heave up, grab, heave up. The wind whistled about my ears. The tyryvol's wings beat remorselessly, up and down, and his tail flicked about nastily.

The opposite side of the valley swam nearer.

His teeth were yellow and wicked. He tore at the rein. His head was dragged down with each upward lunge I managed. I jerked the leather, and then gasped; that might snap the stuff clean through. Up I went, and click click went his teeth. Oh, yes, a fine old to-do, sweaty and alarming and windy.

It was a damned long way down, by Krun!

He nearly had my hand off when I reached up for the last purchase. Snatching my hand away, I glared up at the beast. His eye glared back, malefic and wrought up. Clearly, he was saying, "If you can't fly me properly then drop off!"

Gripping the leather with both hands I swung back. On the return swing, face uppermost, I forced the swing on. Like a phantom bursting from the pits of horror and disappearing, a flyer whipped past. The impression was all of flailing wings and rippling feathers, of a sharp beak and bright eye, and of a wildman skirling and screeching and prodding with his pole-arm.

The leather cut into my hand as I spun. The newcomer volplaned up, turning, revealing himself to be a small fluttlann, all white and pale blue. His rider shook his pole-mounted blade at me. His teeth showed. He was laughing at my predicament! He kicked in and the fluttlann pirouetted and dived on extended wings. Not fast, fluttlanns, not one of the more prized saddle birds of Havilfar; but they are pressed into service when nothing better can be had. It was perfectly clear this wildman saw himself gaining a powerful tyryvol. All he had to do was fly in and slash the leather leading rein away, the idiot who had fallen off his saddle would drop into the gulf, and the tyryvol would change ownership.

My tyryvol lifted his head. I swung about underneath. The fluttlann straightened, turned into a horizontal bar with a double blob at the center. The sharp steel blade of the ukra did not glitter in that mist-shrouded light, but it looked highly lethal and unpleasant.

No time now to go through the contortions of fighting a way past the tyryvol's fangs up onto the saddle. By the time all that had been done the wildman would have finished it with a single blow.

Gripping onto the rein with my feet, catching a loop and drawing that over and down one foot to stand on it with the other, gave me a crazy kind of anchorage. My left hand held the leading rein. My right hauled out the Krozair brand. I nearly went head over heels into nothingness; but the blade whipped free. The fluttlann swerved at the last moment and the ukra slashed, wide and horizontal and deadly.

The Krozair brand met that sweep. Steel chingled against steel. The shock made the tyryvol's head bob up and down like a water duck. Gyrating like an insect caught in a spider's web, I got a breath, took a fresh grip on the handle of the sword, glared about the sky for the wildman.

He spun up, circled, turned and then hurtled down again.

This time, set, I angled the blow. The Krozair steel simply sliced clean through the stout wooden shaft of his ukra. The steel head spun away below.

He screeched—wild, incoherent mouthings. I shook the sword at him.

"If you want to finish it, come in! Otherwise—clear off."

He circled. No doubt he was waiting for me to put the sword away so as to climb up. It occurred to me to consider the way Seg would handle this situation.

Seg could have done it easily, I know.

It was more difficult for me.

The wildman circled, around and around. The little fluttlann was willing. The tyryvol ploughed on, heading for the opposite side of the valley. That was my direction, also. There lay the Pass of Lacachun.

The wildman wouldn't be going away. He'd wait. He had me. If I didn't tire and fall off, he could sweep in any time he liked. His patience would be rewarded.

Savage and barbaric tribesmen are noted for impetuous anger and headlong attacks; also they do not take kindly to fools. Often they are less noted for patience, although patience is one of the basic necessities of survival in barbaric communities. Yet this very readiness to wait blinded the wildman to a simple answer to the problem. It was simple only if he trusted his own skill, and I judged him a young man, an unfledged would-be warrior who sought to gain a great coup by the capture of this tyryvol. So as I put the longsword away and reached around on my back, the wildman drew his leather-wrapped bowcase.

His gorytus was decorated in only the most rudimentary fashion: a line of beads and a handful of feathers. As he gained in stature the gorytus would become smothered in applied marks of his prowess. But if I got my shot in first his gorytus would remain undecorated forever.

Now here was where Seg would have come into his own.

I held the leather leading rein in my left hand and into that hand, parallel with the rein, I transferred the bow. An arrow drew from the quiver with that initial little resistance to show it was firmly affixed and would not fall out when I stood on my head—an occurrence of routine nature, I assure you, in aerial combat.

The wildman had drawn his bow from his gorytus by this time. He eyed me, quite aware what I was up to. I saw his teeth again. We fitted shafts within the space of the same heartbeat. He nudged his fluttlann and I felt the choke of bile in my throat as he flew a little way to the side. I was dangling uselessly and swinging in the opposite direction.

I contorted my body like a chiff-shush dancer out of Balintol, all liquid wrigglings and writhings. The tyryvol poked his head down and I sagged in the air. I looked up.

"Hold still, tyry, you ungrateful beast! That wildman will beat you, for sure."

The leather coiled the other way. . . .

The wildman shot a tiniest fraction of time before I did.

His arrow buzzed off somewhere. My shaft took him in the thigh. That was not my point of aim. Seg would not have missed.

The moorkrim let out a shriek of rage and reached for

another shaft. He had not faced a Lohvian longbow before. His own flat bow, while a fine weapon for aerial combat, did not draw with the same long power as a Lohvian longbow. He had no idea that the steel-headed arrow, piercing through his thigh, pierced on into the body of his fluttlann.

The saddlebird faltered in the air.

His pale blue and white wings flurried, beat with a panicky stroke, another, slowed the rhythm, drew out to a wide-planing glide angle. The wildman shook his bow at me. His mouth was an oblong blot of shrieked anger.

I felt for the fluttlann. Like the freymul which is called the poor man's zorca because it lacks much of the superbness of the zorca, the fluttlann is regarded as a second-class saddle flyer. The strange and, if you care to delve, pathetic item to note about the freymul on land and the fluttlann in the sky is that, both being regarded a little slightingly, both are better than reports say, and both are willing and courageous and will serve to the utmost of their strength. This fluttlann tried to keep up; but his wound was sore and deep. Slowly, he gave up the unequal struggle and planed away, spiraling, looking for a good place to alight. With him he carried one moorkrim who was wilder than most wildmen in those dying moments of conflict.

My tyryvol tried to bite off my left hand.

I stuck the bowstave up, in a reflexive gesture, and knocked his head away.

My problems were not over yet, by Krun!

A quick grab saved me from falling. The bow went back over my shoulder. The tyryvol turned his head sideways and surveyed me with an eye that was not so much beady as downright voraciously calculating.

I started to swing, holding on with both hands, freeing my legs, swinging myself up and down like a pendulum. It was bend, pull, stretch, bend, pull, stretch. The animal's head went with me like an upside down yo-yo. Like a pendulum I swung horizontally, along the line of his body, and I got my feet into the base of his neck where it joined his scaly body. I'd have liked to have landed him one in the guts; but I couldn't reach that far.

He gave a choked up kind of squawk.

"That'll show you you won't shake me off, tyry!"

Down I swung and up and then down and around again,

swinging like a monkey after a coconut. In the wind rush and bluster the sound of a ripping, tearing, death-bringing parting of the leather rein told me this was my last chance.

On that swing, just as the rein finally parted, I got my leg hooked around the tyryvol's neck. I hung from one crooked knee. His scales cut into me. His head drove down and tucked in and his fangs, all yellow and serrated and sharp, slashed at my dangling head. His talons raked up from the rear to scrape me off and hurl me away.

I swung.

Sideways on my bent knee I hauled myself up. A flailing hand scraped on his scales, caught and gripped. With a frenzied cracking of muscles I heaved up. His talons gored my side and I swore at him.

His clashing fangs missed me by a whisker. His head shot up and he twisted around to get at me on the other side. I straddled the thick part of his neck. I held on. I held on!

I took three huge draughts of air.

The valley below swam dizzily.

By the disgusting diseased liver and lights of Makki Grodno! This was no time to test out Sir Isaac's theories...

I sat up, clipped the tyryvol alongside his head, told him that his fun and games were over. He would come under control all right. Mind you, he'd be frisky for some time. He'd quite enjoyed it all.

The sweat lay on me thickly, clammy, chill and damned unpleasant.

After that it was headlong for the Pass of Lacachun.

By Zair! I don't relish going through that kind of nightmare too often, believe you me.

Chapter Five

Trapped in the Pass of Lacachun

The landlord of The Jolly Vodrin, Hamdal the Measure, had told us Prince Tyfar had taken two regiments. The reason for the statement now seemed clear as I circled briefly between the peaks, glaring down onto the Pass of Lacachun. The men down there were of two kinds: crossbowmen and spearmen. Hamdal had seen that and reported. Just how many there had been to start with I did not know; I did know and with dreadful certainty that there were not many left now.

These soldiers were trapped. They huddled in what cover they could find on a projecting floor of rock standing proud of the south side of the pass. To either side the sheer faces of the lower cliffs lifted to the peaks above. Yes, rather like jaws, those peaks. And the tidbit in their gullet was being gobbled up by the clouds of skirling wildmen.

Against the north face I flew in shadow. The sounds of the yelling down there drifted up attenuated. The floor of rock jutting out into the pass, smothered with fallen boulders, provided the best—the only—place for defense.

The wovenwork shields of the wildmen were no proof against the crossbow bolts of the defenders. Salix plants of various varieties grew in the upland soils, and, stripped, provided light strong canes for weaving. Many moorkrim carried hide-and-skin shields, some fastened around wickerwork foundations. The Hamalian shields of the spearmen down there would keep out an arrow cast from a flat bow if the angle was not perfectly at right angles. All the same, the wildmen had bottled up this little force and were going about their business of exterminating it completely.

Nothing was going to stop me from bursting through them and landing among the survivors. Down there Jaezila stood in

49

the cover of a rock and, even as I watched, she shot in her longbow and took out a wildman who attempted to get his shot in first. He went over sideways, flailing, with the long rose-fletched arrow through him.

At Jaezila's side, Tyfar stood, his head bandaged, giving orders to his men.

A nasty situation....

Down I went, hurtling with the tyryvol now thoroughly of the opinion that this manthing on his back was no longer to be trifled with. Most of the wildmen had landed and taken cover the better to shoot up at the ledge of rock; but enough remained flying to make me punch through them with a rush and a whoop.

Even then, with me hollering like a dervish and crashing through in a thrashing of wings, a couple of the swods below loosed their crossbows. Both bolts hissed past. I yelled.

"I'm on your side, you pack of famblys!"

And then the wildmen took it on themselves to show their nastiness, and they shot my tyryvol under me.

I felt his body bunch and jerk with the bite of the arrows. He uttered a shrill squawk and then a dolorous descending moan. His wings trembled. He fell. We pitched down for the last ten or fifteen feet and I was only saved from a broken neck by his collapsing body. I leaped off, feeling immense sadness for him. After his little escapade over the valley with me dangling like a bobbin, we had come to an understanding. His bright eyes glazed over. His slim head on its slender neck shuddered and drooped laxly, and he was dead.

For a moment—a stupid, defenseless moment—I stood looking down on him.

"Jak! Get your fool head down!"

"All right, Tyfar, all right."

I stomped across to his rock. Two arrows broke against the face as I dodged into cover.

"Jak!" said Jaezila. "Prince Nedfar—?"

"He'll be all right. Seg went back with him to find a needle-man."

"And you two came after me." Tyfar put his hands on his hips and glared at us. Trim, defiant, eager, a true comrade, he shook his head. He looked as though he could go ten rounds with a dinosaur, bandaged head and all.

He winced when he shook his head.

"Jaezila raised her long bow and aimed."

"We came after you, Ty, because we didn't think you could be trusted out alone." Jaezila spoke sweetly.

He looked at her. "You mean you couldn't keep away from my funeral."

"Now, Ty—"

He gestured with a blood-splashed hand. "Well, look! We're boxed in here. I told Jaezila she was a ninny to fly in alone. Now you do the same."

He was right, of course. And we were not about to go into maudlin scenes of swearing eternal comradeship as we were chopped. For a start, neither Jaezila nor I intended to be chopped, and Tyfar wouldn't, either, once we jollied him out of his mood.

"What happened?"

"He fouled it up," said Jaezila, with her haughtiness of manner most pronounced.

"Well?"

Tyfar looked chastened. "I had a message to come here to catch a damned bandi—"

"We heard something of that. The message was a trap."

"Yes. I've been hitting the moorkrim hard lately and this is their way of getting rid of me."

"And all you brought was two regiments?"

He looked furious. "We're thin on the ground and just about nonexistent in the air. I'm supposed to command the Twentieth Army, and they stripped most of my troops. Tell me, Jak, for the sweet sake of Havil, what really happened in Ruathytu? We heard garbled reports of a battle—"

"First of all, what was your father doing here?"

"He wanted to see me. What about I've no idea. He heard where I'd gone and followed. He descried the situation and tried to go for help. It seems that wildmen brought him down. And then you—"

"Seg will bring up help. There is no doubt whatsoever of that."

"I don't know who Seg is—"

"A friend. A good friend."

"Now tell me about the battle—"

I frowned. How to tell a young keen general commanding troops that his country had been defeated not only in a battle but in the war? That his foemen lorded it in his capital city? I swallowed. I tried.

His face lengthened. He half turned away. He put a hand on the rock behind which we sheltered.

"You mean to say we lost?"

"Yes."

For only a heartbeat I doubted him; then he proved once again that he was Prince Tyfar.

"Well, we lost this one. But we won't lose the next—"

"I knew you would say that, Tyfar. I have to try to make you see that the Vallians and Hyrklese, particularly, desire friendship with Hamal."

"A fine way they have of showing it." He was suffering now as the enormity of what had befallen his country sank in. "You mean they just took Ruathytu? Just like that?"

"It was not easy. It was a bonny fight. But the Djangs settled the issue."

He listened as the story of the Taking of Ruathytu unfolded. He stood very still. I watched his hands. Slowly they constricted into fists, knobby and hard, the fists of a fighting man as, spread on a page, they were the shapely hands of a scholar. A man of parts, Prince Tyfar.

"We three have been through some rousing adventures," he said, stirring himself. "The Empress Thyllis made a pact with the Hyr Notor, who was a Wizard of Loh. I remember our times, Jak, with Deb-Lu-Quienyin. I could have wished he had been there, at the Battle of Ruathytu, to help us."

I could not look at him, at my comrade. Deb-Lu had been there. Without his sorcerous powers we might well have lost. In the end it had been Deb-Lu, aided by Khe-Hi-Bjanching, who had defeated Phu-Si-Yantong, the Wizard of Loh whom Tyfar knew as the Hyr Notor. Tyfar would have to know one day. How would he react when he recalled our conversation?

That was merely a smaller component of the greater puzzle. And now Tyfar, all unknowing, heaped fresh fuel on the blaze that would explode when the time came.

"So the Djangs took a hand? I know little of them but, Jak, you once said you were from Djanduin, that you had estates there."

"I did and I have."

He cocked an eye at me.

"The Hamalese were beaten by a combination of people who had grown tired of Thyllis's mad dreams of empire, and they were aided by the Djangs—"

"That is easy enough to understand." Tyfar sounded bitter.
"If Vallia entered the fight against us, then that arch devil,
Dray Prescot, is Emperor of Vallia and King of Djanduin. His
evil influence brought about our ruin."

"Ty—" said Jaezila.

She looked most unhappy. She stretched out a hand toward
this young Prince of Hamal, and a shower of insects burst from
a pot flung over the rocks. The pot smashed to bits on the
stone and the buzzing, winging, stinging insects swarmed out.
Instantly we were hard at work swatting and dancing and bang-
ing. Arrows flew in.

"Keep your eyes front!" bellowed Tyfar at the swods as he
flailed away at the clouds of maddening stingers. "We'll take
the insects off you! Look to your front!"

The Deldars took up his orders and the swods stuck grimly
to their posts, clutching crossbow and spear, and when the
attack came screeching in it was met by disciplined men under
orders. We stepped up to fight, and we met and rebuffed the
onslaught. When the wildmen retreated, leaving their dead,
we slumped back, exhausted.

"They won't repeat that trick in a hurry. It must have taken
them a long time to collect the insects. How many pots did
they throw in?"

"Twenty, at least."

"They'll try something else soon."

A number of openings into the cliff where the ledge joined
led into a series of caves. A stream ran through to fall away
into a sink hole. Into this sanctuary the wounded were carried.
Tyfar had brought a doctor with this little force; but he had
been wounded. Now he lay on a cloak and told other less
wounded men what to do to alleviate suffering.

Tyfar explained that he'd brought four vollers, small craft,
and all four had been burned by the wildmen. The men had
fought their way through to this outcrop and made of it a
fortress. The moorkrim clearly considered the affray and its
successful outcome for them to be merely a matter of time.
"We started with two regiments, crossbows and spears, and
they were weak, anyway. Now we're down to what amounts
to little over one reasonably strong regiment, five hundred or
so men. We take the roll call; but it is depressing."

I learned what had happened to the rest of Tyfar's Twentieth
Army. The bulk was spread along his sector of the frontier,

with strong contingents removed and sent east. I pondered this. I did not think any elements of the Twentieth had been in action against us in Ruathytu. I pursed up my lips, and then, casually, I said, "D'you know anything about King Telmont, Tyfar? What sort of fellow he is?"

"Telmont?" Tyfar turned back at the entrance of the caves with a final encouraging word to a spearman with a shaft through his shoulder. "Not much. He was called Telmont the Hot and Cold until he hanged and burned enough people to stop the name being bandied about. But it is true. He can't make up his mind on anything, except hanging and burning."

"Any chance that, now that Empress Thyllis is dead, the people would shout for Telmont as emperor?"

Tyfar swiveled to stare at me. His eyes opened.

"It is a thought—one that had not occurred to me. But—well, he is a king of some means. He could buy support." Tyfar frowned and then laughed. "No, no, Jak. He'd never make up his mind to reach for the crown. He'd have to have someone to kick him up the backside."

Thinking of Vad Garnath, and the Kataki Strom, I said, "Perhaps he has. He is supposed to be marching on Ruathytu."

Then Tyfar said something that stopped me in my tracks.

"He is! To throw out this devilish alliance! Then I must hurry and join him and drive back the Vallians and their despicable allies!"

"Oh, Ty!" exclaimed Jaezila.

She looked fierce.

"Now what's the matter? I mean, of course, when we get out of this pickle we're in."

We went back to the rocks, and there was a jaunty bounce to Tyfar's step. Now he had an aim in life. I refused to despair. Tyfar now believed our friend Seg would bring relief. Then Tyfar would collect what men he could and rush off to join King Telmont. That made sense to a loyal Hamalese. Sweet sense.

"Listen, Tyfar. I heard no good spoken of Telmont—"

"Of course not! He's a fool. But if he is raising the standard of resistance to Vallia—"

"Your father has a greater claim to the crown and throne of Hamal. Think of that."

"You have spoken of this before—"

"Aye! Even when Thyllis sat on the throne. Now that she

is dead I speak openly. I want to see you father, Nedfar, Emperor of Hamal."

Tyfar put a hand to his bandage. "Yes, but—" He walked on. "We have no real support. Thyllis saw to that. She maneuvered father away from the center of power. He was included in the high command only because he is an astute soldier. No, Jak. No one would stand with father—"

I took a breath. I said, "Suppose the alliance stood for him? Suppose Djanduin and Hyrklana and Vallia all said Prince Nedfar, Emperor of Hamal, Jikai! What then?"

He controlled his contemptuous anger. "You mean treat with our enemies? Supplicate them, be beholden to them? Fawn on them as slaves fawn on their master who brings the slopbowl of porridge?"

"One thing, Tyfar, you'd have to get straight." His honest anger nettled me. "If it is to work you'd have to get rid of slavery. I can tell you that is one thing the Vallians and Djangs won't tolerate."

His cheeks were pinched in and white. "I detest slavery, too, yet it is a necessity for ordered life—"

"We won't go into that now. I know your point of view. I respect you too much to think you a hypocrite. But leave that for now. Think about your father as emperor, with friends at his side—"

"Friends!"

"Aye, Ty, you ninny! Friends!" Jaezila was as wrought up as the man she loved and who loved her—although they fenced one with the other, afraid, it seemed, to acknowledge their own emotions.

"I don't understand this." Perplexity made Tyfar calm. "What authority do you have to make this suggestion?"

Not now. Not the right time. . . .

"It is a serious proposal I heard about. You and your father were not available, and so could not be approached. But you will be. The Vallians are in deadly earnest about this. They don't want continual war with Hamal. There are the damned Leem-loving Shanks—"

"I know, I know. But here come the wildmen and they are our first concern. . . ."

So we took up our weapons and went smashing into action again, slashing and thrusting and driving the moorkrim back over the lip of the ledge. They went flying over, their skins and furs and feathers a panoply of savage warriors, our steel in their hearts. We fought them. But we lost men and our numbers were thinned and we knew we would never last too many assaults of that ferocious nature.

Tyfar panted. "The devils! By Krun! If only we had a voller!"

The medicaments were holding out and we patched up our wounds. We drank thirstily from the stream. The water was ice cold. As for food, that was in good supply and we could eat heartily, in the grim understanding that we were likely to be killed before we starved to death.

Jaezila finished putting a gel-impregnated bandage on Barkindrar the Bullet's leg. He was a hairy Brokelsh, a faithful retainer to Tyfar, a comrade with whom we had gone through perils. Nath the Shaft, a bowman from Ruathytu, tut-tutted and said: "You stick your leg out when you sling, Barkindrar, and you expect to get a shaft in it."

"It's just a hole. Had it been a slingshot it'd have busted my leg—"

"All right, you two," said Jaezila. "Save your temper for the wildmen."

"Yes, my lady," they said together. They put great store by Jaezila, did these two, Barkindrar and Nath, Bullet and Shaft.

Intrigued by Tyfar's passionate yearning for a voller, I asked him what one voller would do, since he had lost four.

"Do? Jak! Why, man, get Jaezila to safety, of course!"

A pandemonium of yells and screams at our backs coincided with the next onslaught. Wildmen roared onto the platform and as we fought them others dropped like monkeys from the caves in the cliff, howled down upon our backs, trapped us in jaws of death.

Chapter Six

Seg and Kytun Are Not Repentant

Like big fat flies dropping off a carcass the wildmen plummeted out of the holes in the cliff. They howled down upon our astonished soldiers. The wildmen in front and now these suddenly appearing demons in the rear. . . .

"Steady!" Tyfar stood up, not so much fearless as indifferent to anything but holding his men. "Face front! You—face rear—" he bellowed in a voice that astonished me. He sorted the men out even as the two sides sought to close upon us and crush us in the jaws of death.

As for me—the Krozair brand leaped like a live spirit. The wildmen, hairy and shaggy and nasty, bore in with skirling bravery, scorning cuts and bruises, only dropping when some serious portion of their anatomy was chopped away, only dying when not enough remained of that anatomy to sustain life. Dust puffed under stamping feet. Sweat shone briefly, and the dust covered the sweat and caked men's faces and arms. That peculiar haze of dust and sweat hovered above the battle as brings back the memories to an old fighting man.

Jaezila swirled splendidly, her sword wreaking devastation upon the hairy skin-clad host. Diplomatically I left Tyfar and Jaezila to work out a modus vivendi between themselves. Contenting myself with keeping my own skin unpunctured I could watch out for them and knock the odd persistent fellow away and still let them fight on, back to back, defiant and splendid. And, by Vox! The fight was warm, exceedingly warm. We were overmatched in numbers. The very animal vitality of the moorkrim astonished by its ability to sustain damage and to leap from rock to crag to boulder, swinging sword or thrusting with polearm all along the way. It was like fighting a collection of Springheeled Jacks.

In the midst of the fight, Jaezila and Tyfar kept on at each other. Back to back for much of the time, they each made lurid guesses as to the activity of the other: "Have you untangled your feet yet, Ty?" and: "I should have worn a thicker backplate with you there, Zila," and so nonsensically forth. Tyfar's axe, dull and fouled with blood, cut mercilessly down with massive sweeps. No one was getting past him to sink a blade into Jaezila's undefended back.

For a moment or two it became vitally necessary for me to leap and skip about as a dozen or so scuttling horrors plopped down from a cliff-edge hole. They came for me as a target. These were the caving experts of the moorkrim, often called moorakrim, swarthy of skin, bent of back, grimed with the marks of soil. Their fingers were long, bony and taloned, and their hands formed scoops. Like all the wildmen, they were bandy. Without doubt once the Hamalese had been killed these two sorts of moorkrim would fight among themselves for the spoil.

They hurled javelins at me, they threw stones, and the stones were more dangerous than the javelins.

Great displeasure is taken by a Krozair of Zy if he is forced to beat away flung stones with his Krozair longsword. Beating away arrows and javelins is one thing; driving off a stone over mid-off is quite another. I felt the chunks of stone cracking against the steel.

"You mangy pack of powkies!" I yelled, and started off for them, howling all manner of abuse and swirling the sword, as much to scare them as to bash away their stones. They hesitated. One or two hopped about from one bandy leg to another.

"Schtump!" I bellowed and ran faster, and caught the two nearest fellows, the two bravest or more foolhardy, I dare say, and swept them into four. I shook the Krozair brand at the others and charged at them, thinking among all the scarlet flashes of annoyance how my Krozair brothers would frown at this wanton display of vanity.

But the wildmen scuttled back on their bandy legs and with swinging skins about their shoulders disappeared into a hole in the cliff. To let them go was no decision. I started back to Tyfar and Jaezila and saw one of the commanding officers of the regiments fall. The Jiktar simply fell straight down. His helmet was dented by a thrown rock—a very large rock.

Up on a ledge over our heads a group of the moorakrim worked busily at what was—what had to be—a catapult.

I stared up. The suns were slipping down the sky and the light lay full on the cliff face. The wildmen up there did have a catapult, a small affair with a squat beam and a narrow twisted sinew spring. But it could throw.

The arm came over and the clang distinctly preceded the arrival of the stone. That one missed.

Then a wildman tried to spit me and I parried and riposted and looked up at the ledge and that catapult.

"Cover me, Deldar!" I said to the neatly groomed officer— he had a spot of dirt on his cheek and his right shoulder arm-piece was cut through—who staggered back with half a dozen of his men. They recoiled from an advancing line of wildmen, moving now with purpose as they sought to clear the platform.

There was no time for question and answer. I stuck the longsword through my belt, not in the scabbard, and shoved it back out of the way. The Lohvian longbow came off my shoulder sweetly to hand. The arrow nocked as it seemed of its own accord. Brace, push, pull, bend—shooting in a long-bow demands skill and skill I had been taught by Seg. The first rose-fletched shaft skewered the wildman about to place the next stone. He fell back, the shaft through him, and before he hit the ledge his comrade started to fall beside him, feathered through the chest. His arm struck the release latch and the arm, missileless, slapped forward. The whole catapult jumped and a crack of an exceedingly rich and juicy sound floated down.

"Bad cess to you," I said, loosing again and taking a wild-man in the rump who was trying to take cover.

The very neat Deldar had formed his handful of men in a line among the boulders and we were separated by a short open space from Tyfar and Jaezila. I shot again. Tyfar and Jaezila fought on, and I switched my aim and was able to take out a couple of moorkrim and so assist my comrades. I reached for another arrow and—lo!—the quiver was empty. So much for hotheaded intemperate rushings after people; Seg would be scathing with me for so glaring a dereliction of the archer code.

Dealing with the wildmen who lined out after us was not as difficult as I'd expected, for the neat Deldar was neat in swordsmanship and neat in his handling of his men. When we straightened up after that small affray within the larger, we were down two men and the wildmen, those still alive, drew back.

I said to Deldar, "Your name, Deldar?"

"Fresk Thyfurnin, notor."

"If all the swods fought like your men, I'd be easier."

"I think, notor," said this Deldar Fresk Thyfurnin, "that this is our last fight."

"I'll not have that kind of talk—" I started to bluster. Thyfurnin simply pointed along the cleft of the Pass of Lacachun.

They flew up and they seemed to fill the air between the two rock faces. The cliffs echoed to the rustle of their wings. The mist drifted past, very high, shredded now for some time to allow the radiance of the twin suns to burn through. Below the mist they flew on, hundreds and hundreds, it seemed, drawn to the pickings to be found at Laca's Jaws.

"Well, now, Deldar Fresk. I still do not think you right. We will have to pull back to the caves and defend ourselves there."

"Of course, notor. And guard our backs against the moorkrim creeping along their holes in the cliffs. Our wounded were lucky to have escaped them. But we will fight."

Tyfar and Jaezila dispatched the last of their opponents and walked across the open ground toward our group. Everyone looked depressed. The darkness in the air shadowed from that enormous flying host was enough to make a laughing hyena weep. We gathered together before the entrances to the caves.

"We've won this fight." Tyfar sounded as though he would burst a blood vessel. "No one thought we could win; but we did. We beat 'em.—And now we have this whole new force to reckon with."

"How many men do we have?"

Deldar Fresk, it turned out, was the senior surviving officer. All the Hikdars, each commanding a pastang, and the two Jiktars had been slain. The roll was a lamentable affair.

The host in the sky flew nearer.

In defeating the flying wildmen and the cave wildmen we had lost over two hundred men. We had, counting lightly wounded, some two hundred and twenty remaining.

The noise of beating wings filled the air now, close and closer. The volume of sound caught and re-echoed from cliff to cliff bore down oppressively, making the nerves twitch. We took a fresh grip on our weapons and positioned ourselves among the boulders and the cavemouths. In that small breathing space I took the opportunity to fetch what arrows I could find embedded in moorkrim corpses. I managed to bring in ten.

So a moorkrim bow and a few full quivers had to be brought back. Each arrow was a life. The flying host began to descend and the leading elements planed in for the platform. They could see the dead people lying everywhere.

Deldar Fresk served in the crossbow regiment.

Tyfar called across, "As soon as they are in range."

"Quidang, prince," said Fresk, and set himself.

Now this Deldar Fresk was a fine fellow and the swods were of value. But there was no shadow of a doubt in my mind, no shadow of doubt whatsoever, that what I was going to do would be done, and would be the right thing to do. I anticipated no opposition from Tyfar. The moment I laid my hands on a tyryvol—or any other quality saddle-flyer—I'd have him or her and get Jaezila away. Tyfar would help. We'd get Jaezila out of this debacle alive if it was the last thing we did.

The leading tyryvols alighted on the platform and Fresk opened up on them, the crossbows clanging and hissing in rotation. Of the two hundred and twenty swods some ninety were crossbowmen. Shooting in the harshly disciplined Hamalian way, they carried out considerable execution. Return shafts came in, outranged by the crossbows but brought into range by the advance of the shooters between the rocks. Such was the weight of the enemy's dustrectium* and the numbers of his swordsmen that this snapshooting party would not last very long. The force on the ground built up and positioned itself nastily and neatly and started the advance.

We watched the vulpine forms of the wildmen slipping between the rocks, skulking forward, jumping across open spaces and affording no chance for a shot. They edged forward.

"I—" began Tyfar.

"Not so, Tyfar." I put a hand on his shoulder. We stood just within the overhang of the cave so that descending arrows could not strike us. Jaezila stood at the side, her face calm, brooding, perhaps. We all had a deal to brood over, by Zair! "In this the task falls to my hand."

*dustrectium: firepower

"You do not know what—" Then he stopped speaking. He closed his mouth, opened it deliberately, said: "I am an onker! All this time we have been comrades, and still I try to make stupid suggestions that you and I do not think alike. Of course. Except, Jak, except—the task falls to me."

"You are the general of the Twentieth Army, and this handful of men is your total command here and now. If you make a run for it and they see you—and, believe me, they'll see you!—what will they think of Kapt Tyfar, Prince of Hamal? Hey?"

"You are my blade comrade, Jak, and you have a damned sneaky underhand downright illegal way with you!"

"See that wildman just alighting?" I nodded toward a splendid-looking saddlebird and a splendid-looking rider. Among the others fluttering down to be hidden in the rocks, this man stood out.

Tyfar said, "Just grab the first one—"

"Oh, come now, Ty! While we have a choice, let us exercise it. That is the flyer we will have."

"The wildman is a leader, a Jedgar, and he'll have a canny bunch of his fellows with him."

Jedgar is simply a corruption of the word Jiktar, and generally denotes barbarian or irregular captain, and what Tyfar said about this moorkrim Jedgar was perfectly correct. In my frame of mind, with Jaezila in such dire danger, I rather fancied going as near to the top as I could contrive.

"His canny bunch will be no crazier than we are."

"That is true."

"So that is settled."

"You have the besting of me," Tyfar grumped, "in this argument. But I fancy I shall rank Deldars again, and soon, and then we shall see."

The moorkrims rose from their places of concealment. Screeching their battle cries they hurtled on. Difficult to kill, yes. Not as difficult as reptilian schrepims, with their phenomenal speed and insensate capacity to stay alive and battling when they should be dead, having been cut up into pieces. The eyes of schrepims contain the pigment rhodopsin which confers good night vision and which also glows in reflected light. As Kregans say: "To see the eyes of schrepims glowing at night is to look on the watchfires of hell." As the wildmen raced in I took a silly and, although stupid, real comfort from the

thought that I was glad they were not schrepims. This is par-
adox of a low-volume capacity, of course; but it serves to
illustrate the frame of mind I was in. Jaezila *had* to be flown
away to safety. Besides that—nothing else mattered.

Tyfar agreed with me. Honor meant nothing to either of us
if honor meant Jaezila would be killed.

We'd both cut and run, escorting her to safety, and leave
those brave swods to fight on to the end.

Contemptuous on our part? Yes. I do not deny it.

I remembered Velia.

It was what I would have done, without doubt.

There was no need.

Glorious!

Men shouted and pointed. Among the flying clouds of wildmen swirls became visible. As though a broom clashed along
sweeping up autumn leaves, so some force brisked along the
pass driving the tyryvols and their moorkrim riders before it.

The mist darkened as the twin suns struck more sharply
upon its upper surface, and the level rays of jade and ruby
pierced through below to shine along the pass. In that strange
almost undersea radiance, a hollow luminesence, powerful
winged shapes bustled through the whirling tyryvols. Black
beaks slashed left and right, and frightened flyers fluttered
away from wicked polished talons.

The massed feathering of yellow wings heralded the storm-
ing onslaught of ferocious four-armed fighters. Impetuous,
unstoppable, superb, my Djangs roared onto the platform and
chopped the wildmen up fine and served them up frittered. The
fight exploded in a frenetic movement of blades and was still.
Kytun rolled over toward me, shaking drops from his sword,
his dagger being wiped with an oily rag—already!—and his
remaining hand lifted in cheerful salute.

Up there over Kytun's head the roiling mass of wildmen
pressed back and we could see the aerial conflict clearly.

If you cared for aerial evolutions it was extraordinarily
clever. The maneuvering and pirouetting were of a high standard; but everyone watching saw instantly that the flutduins,
whether flown by Djangs or apims of Valka, had the mastery
of the wildmen no matter what saddle flyer they flew.

I frowned and, staring up, called to Kytun: "Is that all of
you?"

"All of us—"

I yelled then, loudly, at him and bounded out onto the platform, hurdling boulders, reaching him as he thought to indulge in our back-slapping, arm-gripping, gut-punching rhapsody of delight in meeting. Instead, I said in his ear: "Call me Jak or I'll three-arm you! No king! Is that clear, Kytun?"

"But, Dray—you are the—"

"Jak and no king!"

"Very well—"

"Is that all of you, up there and here?"

"That's all, Dra—Jak. And I am fortunate my party found you. We split up and split up, and in the end I imagined looking for you all on my own."

"Where's Seg?"

Kytun laughed in that huge Djang way and looked about. At that moment a moorkrim fell from the sky to splat on the rocks. My eye was caught by the movement and as Kytun said, "There he is," I saw the rose-fletched arrow, a clothyard shaft, through the wildman. Moments later Seg landed and leaped off his flutduin and hurried over. He said: "Jak!"

"All right, Seg," said Kytun. "I forgot."

Seg sighed. "Djangs," he said.

"And not many of you." Looking up and around, it seemed to me there were barely three or four hundred in this relief force, Djang and Valkan combined.

Tyfar and Jaezila came over. The introductions went well and when this pappattu was finished it was a general "Lahal!" and the remark from Jaezila: "It looks as though you've just brought in more fellows to be trapped with us."

Again that massive Djang laugh scorched up echoes from the cliffs. "Not likely, by Zodjuin of the Silver Stux! Look, up there. The wildmen have had a bellyful. They fly."

It was true. Not only did they fly, they fled.

"Remarkable." Tyfar had not cleaned or put down his axe; it cocked up in his fists, ready for action. He looked at Kytun, a magnificent, fearsome, four-armed fighting man, and he looked at Seg, lithe and limber, broad with an archer's build, and he saw the way they greeted me. His open face bore the shadow of a frown. I felt for Tyfar. My heart—to use one Kregan expression—turned over for him.

Jaezila felt more. She was pale, very pale. Her head was held up, erect, and her eyes were brilliant. She was a woman who had made her own way on a harsh and hostile world; she may have been my daughter, she was her own woman now.

Slowly, Tyfar said, "I am beholden to you, Kov Kytun, and you, Kov Seg, and your people, for my life and the lives of my people. But, if I mistake it not, you are no friends to Hamal."

"Of course they're friends, Ty!"

"They are your friends, Jaezila."

"Oh!"

But it was not a moment for lightness.

Tyfar went on: "Djangs overthrew my city of Ruathytu. Valkans are from Vallia, and they joined in the fight. And here we are, a Djang kov and a Valkan kov and—" He turned to look at me. "And you, Jak?"

I could say nothing.

Tyfar turned and looked at Jaezila.

"And you, friends with these enemies, Jaezila?"

Seg said, "The Empress Thyllis asked for trouble, bought trouble, stored up trouble ahead of time. Now she has paid. And, by the Veiled Froyvil, she's only paid a tithe of the mischief she caused." He lifted a hand, and he was not smiling. "No, Prince Tyfar, wait and hear me. You talk about Hamal as 'your country' and we respect you for that. But you must know the stench and offense Hamal has become because of mad Empress Thyllis."

"And that maniac Phu-Si-Yantong," chipped in Kytun.

One thing was sure, they weren't repentent about beating the Hamalese and taking their capital city, and they weren't about to become remorseful now because a defeated prince chose to feel sad.

"And you, Djang and Valkan, sack my capital—"

"No, prince. No sack."

"I would like to believe that. But soldiers tend to go berserk if they have to fight to take a city—"

"True. Damage was caused, mostly by the Wizard of Loh. The Djangs," said Kytun, "keep the peace and ensure order in Hamal these days."

"The truth is, Ty, Hamal is much better off without Thyllis. You know what you have to do to secure the throne for your father—"

"Zila! How can I—in honor? With enemy help?"

I put my teeth together and clamped my jaws. I refused to speak. You can drive, as they say, and never make.

Seg was in full command of all the details, all the plans, all the emotions of what we hoped for.

"Hamal used to be an enemy to the lands surrounding her and also other countries over the seas. That is no longer so. The alliance embraces Hamal. Safeguards—"

"Conditions and terms of servitude?"

Tyfar's contempt cut like a quality blade.

The suns' rays lay long and level through the pass. More Djangs and Valkans alighted and began to tend the wounded Hamalese. Fires were lit from the provision commissariate birds' loads together with what of brush and gorse grew sparsely in crevices. Water heated. Food was prepared. The group around Prince Tyfar was left alone, and the talk and wrangling went on. After all, Jaezila was in a privileged position here in Tyfar's eyes—as, I suppose, was I, had I cared to exercise that option—and Tyfar was a prince talking with two kovs. So it was easy for me to ease back and observe.

"Do you believe I want the best for you, Ty? The best personally, I mean?"

"How can you ask such a question?"

Jaezila bit her lip.

"I know, I know. We spar and fence. Something makes me treat you badly, and laugh." She looked away, and back at Tyfar. "But you respond, now. You never used to."

"Maybe I have learned—"

"Precisely! But you have not learned enough! We all want the best for you, for your father, and for Hamal. Yet you will not listen to us!"

"So you do ally yourself with—"

"Ally? Of course if you were going to say our enemies—"

"Our late enemies, it seems."

"Or do you want to see King Telmont on the throne?"

Tyfar put a hand to his bandaged head. Over by the lines the lads staked out for the flutduins a commotion arose, to be settled quickly. You cannot expect Djangs to be plaster saints. The suns slid away beyond the hills. A breeze got up and blew along the pass. After the exertions of the day it would be nice to eat a gargantuan meal, to drink some good wine and to sing some of the old songs of Kregen. Then a profound sleep and a few pleasant dreams. The morrow would dawn and bring fresh problems, but, by Vox, we'd be fit to tackle 'em!

One of the Jiktars from Valka walked up, Erdil Avnar, talking to one of his Hikdars. They were lithe and agile men who had joined the Valkan aerial cavalry early. They wore equipment and uniforms of the particular splendor Valka brings to this kind of martial show, bullion, flounders, lace, pelisses, frogging—a parade of the tailor's art no less than that of the military designer's. They saw me and Erdil Avnar bellowed out: "Lahal, strom, lahal!"

"Lahal, Erdil. Lahal, Edin," to the Hikdar. "How was it aloft?"

"These wildmen fight like cornered leem."

"Aye. But you bested them."

"Of course they bested them," said Jaezila from over my shoulder. "And now we are tyring to make that victory worth something even more than simple victory."

Erdil and Edin straightened up into a rigidity like unto the pine forests of the petrified mountains. Their chests swelled, creaking their equipment. As one, they slapped up full salutes, and bellowed: "Quidang, majestrix!"

Now quidang means an agreement and acquiescence in orders rather like the terrestrial navy style of "aye aye, sir!" Tyfar looked hard at the Jiktar and the Hikdar, and then with a puzzled expression at Jaezila. For majestrix is the way empresses and queens are addressed, and the eldest princesses, the princess majestrix of her country. Tyfar was not called majister, not even Nedfar his father, although it was sometimes known in a strictly irregular way. So Tyfar frowned.

And I thought to myself—as though ice had started to melt in my head, for thought and I had been damned distant relations of late—I thought that perhaps if Tyfar knew what there was to know, it would help to crystallize the problem and force him to make up his mind.

Rather naturally, I expected him to see the advantages of what was offered in time, although I was prepared for his final refusal, and to join with us in persuading his father.

"Erdil, Edin," said Jaezila. "You are very welcome. You must tell me more of the fight."

"Right willingly, majestrix," barked out Erdil, straight and rigid and straining his equipment.

"Majestrix?" said Tyfar.

"You misheard, prince," said Seg, stepping up and putting a shoulder between Tyfar and the two Valkan flyers. "The Valkans compared the wildmen to masichieri.* Your head—"

"I'm not an imbecile, Kov Seg. Think that at your peril."

My daughter Lela, called Jaezila, looked at me. I stared back at her, and I raised my eyebrows. That was a giant grimace, in those conditions, meaning much. Jaezila nodded, hard.

She put a hand on Seg's arm. He turned at once, head bent and face intent, completely attentive.

"It is time Prince Tyfar of Hamal learned, Uncle Seg. Would you do us the honor of making the pappattu?"

"Pappattu?" said Tyfar. "Between us? We were introduced, as I recall, after our first meeting in that hayloft when you held an arrow nocked on us." He pointed off to the side of the cave where in firelight Barkindrar the Bullet and Nath the Shaft stood up to watch, sensing some crisis by the way we held ourselves. "When you cared for Barkindrar in the hayloft in Blue Vosk Street."

I said, "When the beastie tried to chomp you in the swamp, you both reacted, and we were using names. I recall it perfectly. No pappattu has been made between you."

Both Jaezila and Tyfar looked surprised. They began to cast back in their minds to see if I was right, and, more or less, so I was.

"Then this flummery cloaks a deeper design—"

"Of course, Ty. Now, Seg, you know who Prince Tyfar of Hamal is. Go on."

Seg cleared his throat. Kytun moved up a trifle closer and he casually freed one of his swords. Seg spoke: "Prince Tyfar of Hamal, you have the honor of being in the presence of and of being introduced to Lela, Princess Majestrix of Vallia."

*masichieri: low-class mercenaries

Chapter Seven

Of the Wounds of Prince Tyfar of Hamal

Well, and wasn't it right and proper, perfectly fitting, that Seg Segutorio should make the introduction? Should close one episode and open up a whole bushelful of new?

Seg stepped back, and he was smiling as only he can, the kind of smile that reaches right down into a fellow and curls his toes.

Tyfar closed his mouth. It had been open only just long enough to have trapped half a dozen flies, had any been foolish enough to enter.

"Lela. Princess Majestrix of Vallia."

Tyfar did not lose the color from his face. He stood up straight, watchful, like a deer pausing on the edge of a water hole. His head was lifted, and slightly inclined. He remained perfectly still.

"Ty?"

Apprehension—that showed in Jaezila.

We stood there among the mountains, on a dusty ledge blood-soaked and cumbered with corpses, and the sounds of men moaning and the crackle of the fires mingled with the snorting of the saddle flyers and the rustle of their wings. How to overemphasize the shock of this revelation to Tyfar? Warily, he looked at Jaezila, and warily I looked at him. In one way I could expect any wild reaction, and in another I guessed what his reaction would be. I could still be wrong....

"I loved you, Jaezila, and you worked against me, betrayed me—"

"Not you, prince," said Seg sharply. "Against that maniac Thyllis."

70

Tyfar barely heard Seg. His gaze fastened on Jaezila. She stared back, and after that first tremor, she did not flinch.

"I've called you a ninny, Ty, and it isn't true. How do you think I felt? Do you imagine I liked acting this part with a man—with the man—?"

"Why didn't you tell me?"

Kytun slapped that everready sword back into the scabbard with the hand that happened to be grasping it at the time, and gestured irritably with two others. "Act your age, prince!"

"A spy—" Tyfar drew a breath. "Sucking our secrets—"

Seg broke in, as annoyed as Kytun.

"We've offered to support your father's just claim to the throne. We've all heard excellent reports of you. We want to be your friends. You've got to accept the realities, prince, you have to accept the needle."

If this was the right way or the wrong way, I did not know. Seg and Kytun were in no doubt. Jaezila was in agony, and so was Tyfar, and all because a silly woman who was Empress of Hamal had been obsessed with ambitions and conquest.

I said, "That Jaezila is the Princess Majestrix of Vallia has no bearing on our friendship. We have said we are blade comrades. Well, then, let us prove it."

"You are right, of course." Tyfar spoke in a musing way that would, for anyone who did not know him, cause intense astonishment that he was not roaring and swearing away and dragging out his sword and threatening all kinds of dire retributions and hurling recriminations about like hailstones. "It was a shock. My opinion of Vallia has not been high."

I could feel keenly for Tyfar. A shock, he said. By Zair! What he must be feeling now! And yet his face remained calm and composed, a trifle too pale, and that bandage beginning to leak an ugly red stain.

Jaezila cried out. "Ty! Your head!" She swung on Jiktar Erdil Avnar, who had proved the catalyst in the revelation. "Erdil, run for the needleman—the prince bleeds!"

"Quidang, majestrix—"

"It's only a scratch, Zila," protested Ty.

I let out a breath. A big, a mighty big, hurdle had been leaped in those few words.

The dam broke on that, and a babble of words flowed out, everyone talking at once, and then stopping, and starting up again. Tyfar sat down on the ground, thump, suddenly. Jaezila bent above him, her face drawn with concern. The doctor with Kytun was a Djang, and he swung his four arms into action at once, putting a fresh bandage around Tyfar's head and sticking a few acupuncture needles artfully into him to take away the pain. Tyfar fretted under this fussing.

"I'm all right. And you—Zila—you're a damned Vallian, and a spy, and a princess—no. No. *The* Princess Majestrix—"

"I couldn't have told you before, Ty. Could I? You see that?"

"Of course." He looked up at me. "And you, Jak?"

"I did not know until very recently. It was a shock to me, too."

"And you didn't—"

"There was just one chance of telling you, Tyfar, and it passed away because I considered that this matter lay between you and Jaezila."

"I suppose we should call you Lela now, Zila."

"No. I like Jaezila."

I heard what I had just spoken. The words rang in my head. I had as good as said this was no concern of mine. Well, Zair knows, I've dropped myself into plenty of scrapes on Kregen in affairs that were no concern of mine. But, in this. . . .

I stood back a little. I looked down on Tyfar who had been made comfortable on the ground with a cloak, and on Jaezila who sat at his side, holding his hand. No doubt assailed me that they would reach their own understanding. Tyfar was probably more hurt and weaker than he realized. But my own words thundered at me, and the implications drew blackness into my face. This business really was between these two. Their lives were involved, not mine, their futures together were at stake, not mine. But it was my business, too.

Tyfar saw my face. At the sudden frown Jaezila twisted to look up at me.

I said, "Prince Tyfar, we must set the record straight, seeing we have been through much together, and have an empire to heal and a deadly foe across the seas to fight."

"Jak?" He was puzzled. "Now what—?"

I stared down at him, aware of the firelight against the rocks, of the evening breeze, of the silence now that the needlemen had tended the wounded and eased their pains.

"Prince Tyfar, Jaezila is my daughter."

He laughed.

Tyfar laughed. His head fell back against the bunched folds of the cloak. The bandage stood out in a streak of yellow against the blue.

"Your daughter? Does that devil Prescot, the Emperor of Vallia know? Is that why you two venture off—?"

He sat up. He sat up as though bitten clean through.

He glared at me, and the blood rushed and collided in his face, and his eyes caught the firelight and glared in red madness.

I nodded.

"Yes, Tyfar. That is the way of it. Jaezila is my daughter in all honor. So that makes me—"

He shook his head and did not wince.

"You needn't say it." He sounded drugged.

"So that I can and will have your father, Prince Nedfar, crowned Emperor of Hamal."

"Is that all you can think of, Father?"

"No. But it is a good thought to hold onto now."

"Dray Prescot." Tyfar savored the words, the name, rolling it around his mouth like a gob of rotten fruit. He spat it out. "The great devil, Dray Prescot. By Krun! You've had a good laugh at my—"

"Tyfar! Do not think that! By Vox, lad, never think that!"

"Oh, no Ty! Surely you can see Father would never laugh at you like that! For the sweet sake of Opaz! We are blade comrades!"

Tyfar fell back on the cloak. His face remained flushed and his eyes looked feverish. Sweat shone on his forehead under the bandage. Jaezila sponged the sweat away gently.

Seg rolled over. He put his hands on his hips, looking down on Tyfar. He said, "Prince, I can tell you this. Dray Prescot may be a cunning old leem hunter but he is a man who knows friends and what friendship means. If you are fortunate enough to count yourself a comrade of Dray Prescot, then you are fortunate above most men. And I know."

I repeat this, you will readily perceive, to illustrate the arguments various folk used to ease the torment Tyfar was experiencing. I think chiefly he felt used, diminished in his own eyes. But I believed in him. Jaezila was no fool. She knew Tyfar better than did I, and she was not deceived in him, I felt sure.

This scene had been painful for us all. Now it had to finish. In the ensuing hours, on and off, Tyfar would talk of the times we'd had together, and see them in a new light. "All the time I was working for Hamal, you were working for Vallia."

"For Vallia." Jaezila's face, caught in reflected fire glow, looked impassioned. "That is the point, Ty! Had you seen some of the terrible things the mercenaries and slavers did in Vallia, at the command of that horrible woman—and who weeps now that she is dead?—had you seen that..."

"War—"

"Not the kind of war the new Vallia fights. No. If those dreadful things had happened to your Hamal, wouldn't you fight?"

He looked weak, his face wan, the yellow bandage unhealthy against his skin. "I did fight—"

"The position is," said Seg. "Thyllis has been got rid of with the minimum of damage and trouble. Hamal is virtually unharmed. Your father can take over a running empire. Back in Vallia we still face the troubles your country has brought us."

At times desultory with exhaustion, at others impassioned, the talk went on through the night. No one slept very much. Too much lay at stake here. These hours witnessed events of the most momentous significance. We all felt that. The very night air seemed imbued with intimations of the future.

At one point Tyfar sat up, looking wild. "I feel so dirty!"

"That is a natural reaction, understandable. The name of spy is universally condemned. But if a spy acts in honor—"

"As we have done, Tyfar," I put in, speaking hard.

Jaezila nodded vehemently. "And you had better rest. I don't like that hole in your head."

And Tyfar said, "Which one?"

Barkindrar the Bullet and Nath the Shaft, who had been with us through many perils, looked numbed when they were told. They were flabbergasted. I watched them narrowly, believing they would take their lead from their prince; but ready in case they decided that their duty to their country called on them to attempt to slay the Emperor and Princess Majestrix of Vallia.

"Jak?" said Barkindrar in his uncouth Brokelsh way. "You're an emperor?"

"Of Vallia?" Nath the Shaft's brown fingers curled around

his bowstave. It was not a great Lohvian longbow; but he was a remarkable shot with the compound reflex weapon.

"When I am in Vallia. Here I am Jak the Shot, your comrade, and comrade to Prince Tyfar. You must help him grapple with this. After all, we went through the Moder together, and that underground horror was far worse."

Tyfar, whom I had thought asleep, rolled over and half sat up. "I wonder?"

That worried me.

"I must bathe myself," he said in a slurred voice. "I must take the Baths of the Nine."

Nath and Barkindrar looked concerned. "There are no facilities—"

"Here, prince?"

"Fetch the needleman!" cried Jaezila.

When the Djang doctor arrived and examined Tyfar he pursed up his lips.

"It is not promising, king, not promising at all. The prince will develop a fever and needs better attention than we can give him here."

"Like father like son," said Seg. "I left Nedfar with the best needleman in Hammansax. We'll have to get this fiery young zhantil to him as well."

"Yes."

"Except that I left the voller with him to take Nedfar on. Hammansax itself was in a bad way, as you know."

"We'll have to mount up, strap Tyfar on, and fly as fast as we can. If any bird can do it, a flutduin can."

"The flight—" The needleman spread his hands. All four of them. "I cannot answer for—"

"We understand, Khotan," said Jaezila.

Khotan the Needle nodded, not very happy at the prospects.

Barkindrar and Nath turned away, out of the firelight.

Some of the wounded were too badly hurt to move, and men and attention must be left with them until we could get a flier back. Jaezila looked across the fire at me, her cheeks shining and lined with shadow so that, for a moment, I shivered. I shook myself roughly. By Vox! Tyfar had had a shock; he'd get over it, get over the mental wounding as surely as he would the physical. All the same, one had to be prepared for him to break out as a high-tempered prince, strong on honor, had every right to do. This mess was nowhere near over yet.

If Tyfar took himself off into a voluntary exile to brood over
his betrayal, as he would see these unfortunate circumstances,
and then resolved to join King Telmont to strike against his
country's victors—who could blame him? In my view he
would be wrong; but I was prejudiced.

As the twin Suns of Scorpio rose between the mountain
peaks bringing with them a new day of puzzles and emotions,
I was thinking that, by Zair! what it would be to be just a semi-
brainless adventurer wandering the face of Kregen with a ready
sword, instead of a semi-brainless emperor attempting to guide
the destinies of a world. Shouts of mingled anger and mirth
lifted and I turned to see a group of swods manhandling somebody out of a cave entrance, somebody who struck me instantly
as strange, weird, eerie.

Chapter Eight

Pale Vampire Worms

Over by the flutduin lines Tyfar was being assisted into the saddle by his own people. The Djang owners of the saddlebirds stood back. Jaezila hovered, anxious, with Seg and Kytun beside her. We all sensed that at this moment Tyfar wished to have his own people about him. This mood would pass. I had to believe that.

The group of yelling men dragged their captive down toward us. My first reaction remained, reinforced the nearer he came. A shock of wild hair, brown and gray, sticking out like a porcupine's quills, a raggedy collection of skins and leaves, scrawny arms and legs, those bandy legs of the wildmen, and a face like a squashed rat's convinced me this fellow was bad news to anyone. He was gagged tightly with a strip of leather so that his face was drawn back into a stretched grin.

"A Havil-forsaken moorkrim sorcerer!"

"Cut off his head—*now!*"

"Burn him!"

The uproar continued as the swods roughhoused their prisoner across the rocks to their Deldar. Deldar Fresk Thyfurnin looked grave. Like us all he was exhausted from the aftereffects of the fighting and the lack of sleep. He said to me, "They were lucky to catch the Arditchoith. Nasty customers, as dangerous as a wounded leem."

One of the sub-officers, a matoc, reported in that the wildman sorcerer, the Arditchoith, had been snapped up by a party as he tumbled from a rocky ledge in the cave. Both sides had been surprised and shocked. But here was the sorcerer, wild as all hell, safely gagged and bound.

"Make sure the gag is tight, matoc."

"Quidang, by Kuerden the Merciless!"

77

The uproar attracted Seg and Kytun and they walked across from the flutduin lines. Presently we would have to take off with Tyfar and pray he survived his ordeal.

Seg was just saying, "They'll never get any information out of him if they rough him up like that," in a judicious way when the sorcerer—by some sleight of thaumaturgy, no doubt—broke momentarily free. Those few moments were enough. His bandy legs twinkling, he broke through the startled swods, leaped for a boulder, balanced, leaped for the far side, and tumbled clean into the all-embracing arms of a party of Djangs come to see what the excitement was all about. They held him, and he would not escape them.

"By Zodjuin of the Silver Stux!" rapped Kytun. "This fellow is a man! Let's find out more about him."

The Djangs grasped the wildman and he was run up to stand defiantly before Kytun. Now Kytun is a majestically impressive figure, broad, bulky, regal of mien, and his four arms are so evidently capable of dealing out punishment and destruction that he inspires universal respect. Also, as I know, those same four muscular arms and deadly hands can be infinitely tender in caring for those he loves, and in looking after the flowers that so delight him in his garden back home in his paradise island of Uttar Djombey. An imposing, dominating, intimidating figure, then, Kytun Kholin Dorn. The wildman sorcerer, the Arditchoith, stared furiously up through his shock of disarranged hair with a look of malignant hatred. His whole posture, the jumping of the muscles in his face above the gag, spoke eloquently of vivid resentment and animosity and nothing of fear or trembling.

"Spying on us, were you?" quoth Kytun. "Well, we'll soon find out if there are any more of you. Take off his gag. There are questions he must be asked."

Sinewy Djang fingers stripped away the leather gag.

A frenzied chorus of shrieks battered into the air.

"Don't take off the gag!"

"Stop! Stop!"

"Keep him tongueless!"

It was too late.

The horrified shouts of the Hamalese soldiers changed to shrieks of consternation and fear.

The wildman sorcerer spoke.

What he said he spat out in no language I knew, although

the language genetically coded pill I'd taken years ago enabled me to grasp at the essence of what he was saying.

Rather—at what he was calling up.

In a screeched invective-laden invocation he called upon the Pale Vampire Worms. His stutter of words seemed to swell and crackle among the rocks. The soldiers yelled and fought to climb aboard the nearest tyryvol or flutduin. A coldness dropped upon the platform in the canyon and clouds passed before the faces of the suns.

From a myriad cracks grazing the surface of the platform elongated white forms emerged. They writhed. Sinewy, puffed, bloated with pale slime shining, they oozed from the dank recesses of nightmare to swarm onto the ledge and descend upon the panic-stricken people.

A crack at my feet disgorged a plump white worm—I'd not noticed any crack there before—and as I stumbled back the thing lifted into the air. White, corrugated like a concertina, slime-running, the Pale Vampire Worm looked upon me with two round crimson eyes protruding prominently. Real power, then, he had, this wildman wizard.

The sword was in my fist and the blade went around in a horizontal slash before I knew what was happening.

The worm fell in two severed halves, and the tail end shriveled into a pale wormcast and the head spun about, the two bulging eyes red as freshly spilled blood, and began to grow a new tail.

The air filled with the horrors, and those of us left on the ledge slashed and leaped and flailed away—and many a man fell with a worm fastened to his throat, kicking and struggling as the Pale Vampire Worm turned the color of blood.

Kytun slashed with four djangirs and the frighteningly efficient short sword of Djanduin in his capable grip kept the horrors at bay. But they oozed from the clefts in the rock and swarmed upon us. Our blades ran with ichor and tails fell to shrivel; but the heads pirouetted and grew afresh and came on again.

Deldar Fresk tripped one of his men, running in blind panic. The man tumbled over and Fresk grabbed his crossbow. For a Deldar of Hamalian crossbowmen to span and load was a matter of training and drill and superb expertise. Even as I cut and hacked with sword and main gauche I saw Fresk aim the crossbow and loose.

"The pale vampire worm looked upon me..."

The bolt struck the wildman sorcerer in the head.

His head exploded.

Instantly, every Pale Vampire Worm vanished.

There was no craze of cracks fretting the surface of the platform.

Kytun used his lower left hand's forefinger to wipe away a scrap of brain from his cheek.

"Djan!"

"You!" said Seg. "Take his gag off. . . . Let's ask him some questions. . . ."

It became extraordinarily urgent for me to step up and speak in a bright voice which, with a sigh I confess, came out like a rough-edged file. But they listened.

"Forget the damned sorcerer and the Pale Vampire Worms. Where is Tyfar? And Jaezila?"

Seg and Kytun were my comrades and had recently been introduced to Tyfar, a fellow comrade. The simmer of the volcano heralding a verbal slanging match over the Pale Vampire Worms and the cause of their appearance was instantly forgotten. Down by the flutduin lines, as where the tyryvols had been tethered by their late owners, the confusion ebbed as men realized the worms no longer existed. Few birds were left. Men sprawled on the ground, drained of blood, and they remained and did not rise up returned to full health. Wherever the damned worms had gone they'd taken the blood with them.

There was no sign of Tyfar or his people, and Jaezila was missing also. I just hoped she was sticking like glue to Tyfar, caring for him and gaining protection from his people's sword-arms. I swung on Deldar Fresk.

"Well done, Deldar! We owe our lives to you."

"I have heard of these Havil-forsaken moorkrim wizards. I do not wish to meet another."

"Unless," said Seg with a look at Kytun, "unless he's well and truly gagged."

"I'll have the leather gag and thongs ready, I promise, by all the Warrior Gods of Djanduin!"

And—we all laughed.

Khotan the Needle had vanished and I sincerely trusted he was in attendance on Tyfar. I could guess that Barkindrar and Nath the Shaft, faithful to their creed and duty—not so rare a habit of mind on Kregen as it has become on Earth—had bundled their prince and Jaezila and the needleman aboard

saddlebirds and thwacked them into the air. I'd been skipping
and jumping and slashing at Pale Vampire Worms at the time.

Fresk said, "We shall be all right here, notor."

I looked at him.

He nodded to the flutduins remaining. "Clearly, you will
fly back to Ruathytu."

"Yes," I said. I roused myself. This burden of imposition
on men who were men like myself was a part of the punishment
I endured for the presumption of allowing myself to be made
an emperor. But I refused to become lost in self-pity. There
was another side to being an emperor. I had no authority in
the Hamalian army, but. . . .

"I shall see to it, Deldar Fresk, that you are made up to
Jiktar. I have noticed you."

He did not flush or stammer. He looked me in the eye and
I wondered if he wanted to spit in my eye.

Then he said, "Thank you, notor."

That was all.

Well, by Krun! And what else did I expect?

So, because we were lords and masters and of the high ones
of Kregen, we took the flutduins and the tyryvols and flew
away. We left Deldar Fresk and the men without mounts to
await subsequent rescue. I did not look back. By Zair! Only
overpoweringly important issues would cause me to fly off and
leave brave men in a plight like that.

And, the truth was, without question, that the problems I
faced were overpoweringly important. As we flew up into the
radiances of Zim and Genodras, it was the overpowering part
of that thought that was the most daunting.

Chapter Nine

I Mention the Emperor of Pandahem

The Freak Merchants and the magicians and the conjurers had returned to their usual haunts in Ruathytu. Under the strict laws of Hamal they found life harder than in most of the exotic cities of Kregen; but in the eternal strength of their kind they survived.

In the brawling sprawling smoking open-air souk the man next to the fellow whose trick was pouring boiling water over various parts of his anatomy without apparent effect caught up his ungainly reptiles and hung them about him, tails curling and fangs clashing. Copper obs rattled in the earthenware bowls. The noise and stink and confusion racketed to the bright sky where the twin suns shone down serenely. The uproar was truly prodigious.

Strings of laden calsanys trotted past. Slaves scurried about their business, for master or mistress, down-drooping of mien, sunk in the busy apathy of slavery. The riders who spurred through the throngs were cursed at and spat after; but they forced a way through. The dust lifted, thick and choking. The smells could have been sculpted by chisels.

"He's down here somewhere," said Seg, avoiding a brass bowl on the end of a chain at the end of a pole at the end of a procession of brass-bowl-bearing slaves.

"Somewhere."

"Well, by the sign of The Crushed Toad."

"That infamous place," said Hamdi the Yenakker, a very great rogue but tall and upright and carrying himself with a swagger, a Hamalese who had sworn eternal fidelity to Vallia as the new power, "that sink of iniquity is there." He pointed. The place was tumbledown and smothered in creeping vines; but a soldier would see the thickness of the walls and the placement of slit windows high in the angles. "But there is no sign of your man."

"Your man, Hamdi," said Seg, moving out of the way of a cowled woman with a bosom and a basket.

"I merely repeat what I was told. He can tell you what you wish to know about Spikatur Hunting Sword."

"And," I said, "I have the bag of gold he asks for and I'd sooner he took charge of it. I've had a dozen fingers clutching at it already."

We all wore nondescript clothes of the swathing kind concealing most of our weaponry. In here they'd take your favorite jeweled dagger off you at one end and sell it back to you at the other. The Souk of Opportunity, this place was called, and no one was in any doubt whose opportunity it was.

Opportunity was another name for Hamdi the Yenakker. There is little that needs to be said about him. There are Vicars of Bray on Kregen, but his wholehearted embracing of Vallia and all things Vallian after the taking of Ruathytu was most certainly not an unalloyed advantage. Oh, yes, Hamdi had his connections, and we were to find great use for him. But his attitude, which unkind men might dub fawning on Vallia, was like to offend others, others like Prince Nedfar and Prince Tyfar. Happily they were both recovered of their wounds and day by day as the Peace Conference broke up around our ears and King Telmont marched nearer, we worked on Nedfar to accept our proposals. It was not an easy time.

Nothing much to be said about Hamdi the Yenakker, and, yet, surely, there was this to be said for him—he was one embodiment of our desire for Hamal and Vallia to work together for the future of the whole of Paz against the Shanks. So, as shrewd Ortyg Fellin Coper pointed out: "The realization of honest plans does not always bring the expected result."

We pushed our way toward The Crushed Toad. This Souk of Opportunity had grown up over the seasons in a section of one of the two Wayfarer's Drinniks, and the wide dusty space was now more congested than usual. The reasons were simple. Hamal's commerce normally went by air but since the wars and our virtual destruction of Hamal's air arm, the various forms of land transport returned to favor of necessity. This Urn-Clef Wayfarer's Drinnik northwest of the city just outside the Walls of the Suns, with the sky-spanning arches of the aqueduct carrying water down to the Arena slanting across the

eastern section, sent off caravans to the northern parts of
Hamal. The River Havilthytus serviced the west. Lacking the
impressive canal system of Vallia, Hamal's land communi-
cations were superior, for ownership of an airboat remained
still a pricey business.

Inside The Crushed Toad Hamdi led us to a small upper
room which we entered with fists wrapped around sword hilts.
Only one man sat at table, his shirt open to the waist revealing
a forest of blackish hairs, his double chins partially obscured
by an ale jug. Liquid dribbled down the creases in his skin.
He slapped the jug down and bellowed.

"Lahal, Hamdi, you rogue! Where is the gold?"

Hamdi caught my eye and nodded, very stiff.

"This is Nath the Dwa.* His twin, Nath the Ob, did not
survive the Empress Thyllis's invitation to an outing in her
Arena."

"The bosks stuck him clear through the guts," said this Nath
the Dwa. "I own I was glad to learn that bitch Thyllis was
dead, although the manner of her death escapes me."

"She was blown away by sorcery," I said. The lesten-hide
bag of gold thumped down on the table. "Here is the gold.
Now tell us of Spika—"

"Hush, man! Hamdi—you were followed? Check the stairs."

Seg looked out of the door, went to the landing, came back.
"All clear. We were not followed."

Nath the Dwa took another draught. A heel of bread and
a chunk of cheese lay dying on a wooden platter. There was
no flick-click plant in the room; there were a dozen or so flies.

"I joined Spikatur, for I was angry and wanted my revenge.
By Sasco! I wanted to split the throats of as many nobles as
I could! But it went wrong—"

We did not sit down as Nath the Dwa talked on. He did not
explain why it went wrong or why he had been expelled. But
he told us details in return for gold, details that will become
apparent as my narrative continues. "And they're flooding into
Hamal, now. You must watch out for a fellow thin as a stick,
ferret-faced, with one eye, and the other covered with a patch
of emeralds and diamonds, crusted thick together."

"Gochert," I said.

Dwa: two. *Ob*: one.

He looked surprised. "You know him?"

"No. I have seen him."

"He is a master swordsman. He spitted Henorlo the Blade clean as a whistle. As a Bladesman he has few equals."

"Well," spluttered Hamdi, "I'm not going to cross swords with him!"

I said, "Are there really no leaders of the Spikatur Hunting Sword conspiracy?"

Nath the Dwa swilled ale and swallowed. "Not in the way you or I would understand leaders. But there are those who tell others their thoughts and desires, and these others do them with a gusto." No names had passed from us to Nath and we both wanted it that way, so there was no bandying about of polite forms of address. "Gochert is one such."

"The adherents of Spikatur believed in fighting Hamal and they assassinated Hamalese nobles. They gave their lives willingly. Why should they continue now that Hamal is defeated?"

Nath the Dwa wiped his lips. "And King Telmont?"

"His army will disappear—" began Seg.

"His army," pointed out Nath the Dwa, "is a fresh army containing many mercenaries. They are out for loot. They will fight you. Anyway—" he made a dismissive gesture "—the rasts from the Dawn Lands return home. Soon there will be only the detachments from Vallia, Hyrklana and Djanduin to stop Telmont. His strength will grow as yours shrinks. He will sweep you away."

"We're not here to discuss high strategy. Is there anything else you can tell us for the gold you have been paid?"

"Yes. A great lady has lately arrived in Ruathytu. She travels in secrecy. She is veiled—"

"From Loh?" said Seg.

"Who knows?" Nath the Dwa reached for a refill from the wooden ale bottle. "She keeps her own counsel on that." He poured with a gurgle. He did not offer us refreshment. "She is come, it is said, in Spikatur's name to wreak vengeance on her foes. She is seen by few."

"Her name?"

The jug paused on its way to his lips.

"Name? I have heard her called Helvia the Proud."

"But that is not her name?"

He drank and laughed. "Probably not."

"And where may we find this Helvia the Proud?"

The jug described a circle in the air.

"As to that, a man from the high council of Hamal who asked questions was fished out of the River Mak. At least, some of him was."

"We heard. So that is what befell him."

"He was not a very good spy."

A knock sounded on the door, a very timid knock. Nath the Dwa slapped down his jug and looked pleased. "That will be Filli with the so-lunch. And I am sharp set." He raised his voice. "Come in Filli."

A silver-gray-furred Fristle fifi entered, nervous, head bent, bearing a cloth-covered tray. She wore a blue bow tastefully adorning her tail, and her Hamalese clothes were of the short and skimpy kind. She placed the tray on the table and without looking at us went out. Nath the Dwa whisked the cloth away and delicious aromas lifted into the room. He wrinkled up his nose, closing his eyes.

"There is nothing more here," said Seg.

"No. You are right."

The tray contained thin slices of vosk and golden-yellow momolams, all in a rich gravy. At the side a green salad fairly sparkled with dewy freshness. For sweet an earthenware dish supported a pie, a glorious, crusty, honey-gold pie. A mixture of scents rose, fruits of many kinds blending into a heady mouth-watering delectation.

"Celene pie," said Nath. "How I dote on it. But first, the vosk and momolams. I shall spend your gold well, horters, very well, and grow myself a belly to astound the world."

Seg laughed and we went out, closing the door on Nath, who was already hard at work. "He sounds like Inch and his squish pie," said Seg. "Although celene pie is too rich for me." Celene, a common name for rainbow, describes in this case a pie or flan made from a mixture of fruits and honey. I led the way down the stairs and back into the Souk of Opportunity, mulling over what we had learned. One thing was sure, we had not heard the last of Spikatur Hunting Sword.

The noise and heat and dust smote us as we left The Crushed Toad. A train of Quoffas, enormous patient hearth-rug animals, shambled along drawing carts loaded with freight that would demand a dozen lesser animals to draw. A caravan was forming up, and the guards curvetted about astride a typical Kregan collection of riding animals, brandishing their weapons and screeching and kicking dust. The scene might be barbaric and intimidating to a sober citizen from a civilized terrestrial town, but these guards were only having fun and kicking up a shindig before departure to impress their employers. In times of trouble the bandits swarm up out of their rat holes, and caravans must be guarded.

Even in Hamal, strict as to laws. . . .

We walked across to where we had left our animals.

"The more I hear about this Spikatur thing," said Seg, "the more I am puzzled. I thought they sought to bring Hamal down to her knees. Well, haven't we done that?"

"Except for what mischief Telmont may get up to. I wish Nedfar would make up his mind. Once he decides to be emperor I'm sure people who want a peaceful life will rally to him."

"They'll have to fight before they get their peace."

"Aye."

"And if the Spikatur people turn against him?"

"That is something I wish we did not have to consider. But we do. They have already tried to kill him, and I can only hope that now that the situation is changed, their attitude will change as well." We passed an awning-shaded stall where brass pots glittered, spilling out into the suns light. One of those on a journey was useful. "I think that both Tyfar and Nedfar feel that in accepting our help they are in some way disgraced. It may be that the Spikatur conspiracy to destroy Hamalese nobles weighs on their minds."

"Not on Tyfar's! He is a right gallant young prince."

"Oh, he is. A good comrade. And that reminds me, Seg. The island of Pandahem. We have to settle that yet. How would you like to be a king in Pandahem?"

He gaped at me. Then he threw back his head and laughed.

"I was Kov of Falinur and look at the mess I made of that—"

"No! That I won't have. You did the right things—"

"And they failed. Turko will handle them more harshly, and that is probably what they want. As for me—a king? Anyway, the kingdoms in Pandahem are all spoken for."

"Precisely. We shall descend on the island and clear out all the slavers and mercenaries and the rulers will breathe easier again. It is in my mind that they could do with having an emperor to guide them, keep them from each other's throats.

Somebody who is above their feuding. How does Seg Segu-torio, Emperor of Pandahem, ring in your ears?"

He did not hesitate. "Like a passing bell on the way to the Ice Floes of Sicce." He stopped and stared at me. "Dray! What are you thinking of?"

"It's all right, Seg. I'm not crazy and I haven't allowed megalomania to overtake me. Just that I think it would be useful all around. Anyway, it would give you something to do."

"I'm busily rebuilding the Kroveres of Iztar."

"That is more important than being an emperor, I grant you. But think about it, for my sake."

We walked on through the crowds and found our riding animals and mounted up, giving a silver sinver to the slave who had held them for us. They were hirvels, for we did not wish to attract attention. The silver might have done that, all things considered. Then we trotted slowly off back to the pal-ace.

Chapter Ten

The scorpion and The Scorpion

In the following period as the Peace Conference fell apart and the delegations from the Dawn Lands returned home and King Telmont gathered his strength and advanced and reports came in of a buildup in the adherents of Spikatur Hunting Sword, Prince Nedfar deliberated.

"For the sweet sake of Opaz, prince! And for the equally sweet sake of the poorest family trying to scrape a living in the fish stews! Make up your mind!"

Nedfar looked steadily back at me. "You are the Emperor of Vallia, Jak, and I have not recovered from the shock of that yet. I called you traitor. No wonder you studied in the map room. But—"

"Look, Nedfar. We're talking about your country. So I fooled you. I have had to do many things in my life. . . . You have never—I do not guess but am certain—never been slave."

"Of course not."

"I have. It is not nice. If this is your sticking point, I well understand that manumission will not come overnight."

"Slaves like to be slaves."

We talked and walked about, gesturing irritably, in a splendid room of the palace, the Hammabi el Lamma, on its artificial island in the River Havilthytus. Strong bodies of Djangs and Vallians guarded the palace. Nedfar had to be brought to the point, he had to accept the needle, and, as I said, "It's not as though you have to come to the fluttrell's vane, either." Which is to say that this was not just making the best of a bad business. "Hamal needs you. By the disgusting diseased liver and lights of Makki Grodno! *I* need you!"

"Ah! It is for Vallia—"

"Spare me," I said, and stalked off to the side table where the flagons and bottles were ranked like a phalanx.

"The Emperor of Vallia," he said, and shook his head. "And you were slave down the moder."

"And other foul places. Look, Nedfar. You know how it is between your son Tyfar and my daughter Jaezila—"

"You mean, do you not, majister, Lela, the Princess Majestrix of Vallia?"

"I so do. But Jaezila has a sound to it that pleases us. And you do understand that Jaezila outweighs in my mind all this fancy talk of empires?"

He pursed up his lips. "I wonder—"

I did not roar out about whether he doubted my word and similar hot-tempered and rational retorts. I looked at him. Now he was a great Prince of Hamal, well used to power and unthinkingly accepting instant obedience. He lowered his eyelids and turned his head away, and a stain flooded into his cheeks.

"By Havil! You are the devil men say you are."

Often, to that remark, I had replied in the cheap way: "Believe it!" Now I took up a goblet, a thing of gold and rubies, and filled it with a fine Jholaix and carried it across.

"Drink, Nedfar. You will have to run Hamal with your own wits and resources, your own skills and statecraft. Do not misjudge the situation. We of Vallia will not be looking over your shoulder all the time, there will be no taint and no disgrace in this." I finished that up most bitterly. "We in Vallia have our hands full repairing the mischief you lot from Hamal have caused us."

He took that splendid goblet and held it, his fingers lapped around the gems. The red of the rubies glowed. He lifted his head and stared at me, a hard, calculating, shrewd assessment. Then: "I would not be beholden to an enemy for a throne."

"Agreed. Am I your enemy? Have I ever been—truly?"

It was a nice point.

We talked on, this way and that, and he did agree that I had never borne him any ill will—even when I'd been slave. Then he said, "I have heard the stories of how you became Emperor of Vallia. You did this entirely on your own, for all your friends and cronies, for some unexplained reason, deserted you."

"Wrong on two counts, prince. My friends did not desert

me. And no man or woman becomes emperor or empress
without help."

"But you were a lone man—a strange figure—the stories
are legion concerning Dray Prescot."

"And how many are true?"

"You know."

"I know that if Hamal and Vallia do not stand together and
show this example to the rest of Paz, the damned thieving,
raping, burning Shanks will ruin us all."

On that point, after hours of discussion, the decision pivoted. Nedfar was an honest man whose honor had got out of
hand when he was faced with the realities of the situation. I
convinced him at last that there was no dishonor in accepting
the throne, and the bargain was struck. As we shook hands the
bell hung by the door tinkled, and so I shouted and the doors
opened and they all crowded in.

Well! The hullabaloo was expected and soothing for what
it portended. Tyfar solemnly shook his father's hand. Jaezila
kissed him. Kytun boomed and Ortyg squeaked. All of us were
overjoyed—and I own my pleasure came from relief that the
thing was done and seen to be done. I was even cynical enough
to wonder if being an emperor would change Nedfar for the
worse. And then I relented and allowed the pleasure to creep
in. After all, emperors are not made every day—even on
Kregen.

With all the experience of his short time as King of Hyrklana
lighting up his face, Jaidur said, "Now we must get the whole
of Hamal to support you, Nedfar. I would say that a treaty of
friendship now exists between your country and mine."

"My hand on it!" exclaimed Nedfar.

Jaezila held Tyfar's arm. Kytun's hands were nowhere near
his sword hilts. Ortyg brushed his whiskers. As I say, we were
all very pleased with ourselves. . . .

Every one of our loyal friends wanted to come up and
congratulate Nedfar, and a sort of mini-reception was held. I
heard Tyfar say to Jaezila, "I look forward to meeting your
sister Dayra, Zila. You must miss her."

"I do." Jaezila put a hand to her hair. "Yes, to be honest,
I do. She was always a little minx. And she's done some things
that are too terrible even to think about, let alone tell a prince
of Hamal." Jaezila laughed, and turned and saw me looking
at her. The smile faltered through the laugh.

"I dearly wish to see Dayra again," I said. "I love her, as you know, and if you should happen to see her, Jaezila, be sure you tell her that. I do not think she understands." I looked over across the heads of the happily chattering throng. "Jaidur took long enough, Zair knows."

"I will tell Dayra, father," said Jaezila, and she was suddenly deadly serious. "She runs with bad company and there is a reckoning overdue for them. I will tell her."

The fear that clutched me then was that the overdue reckoning for the villains who had bedazzled Dayra would fall upon her also. She was a headlong, vivacious girl, known as Ros the Claw, and I found it well-nigh insupportable that her enmity for me so distressed her mother, Delia.

Nedfar still held the golden goblet studded with rubies. I believe he felt the same as did I, that this goblet formed a convenant between us, the act of drinking a sacrament to and for the future of our two countries.

The news spread and the gathering turned into a party and the party atmosphere permeated the palace and extended into the city so that Ruathytu exploded to the stars. Prince Nedfar was well-liked, and now that he was emperor people could look forward to getting back to normal after the war. Things would change, of course; but life could go on and folk could breathe a little easier. Hamalese nobles crowded in to swear their allegiance. I moved a little way apart—I confess I was looking for a piece of squish pie—and I saw a reddish brown scorpion peering at me over the lip of a chased silver bowl packed with palines.

I stood stock still.

His body-segments glistened. His stinger lifted, hard and black. He stared at me. I guessed no one else in the lofty chamber could see this scorpion but me.

His feelers and his stinger waved. They moved commandingly. Still gripping my goblet of best Jholaix, I walked slowly to the nearest door and went out into the corridor and turned along past two Valkan sentries, who managed to hide their smiles and who saluted with stiff and ridiculous punctilio. The scorpion appeared ahead, along the corridor, and with a quiet word to the sentries, I followed him. The carpet muffled my footsteps. The air was close and hot and spiced with scents. The scorpion led me into a small room where two slave girls, stark naked, lay asleep on a truckle bed locked in each other's arms. They were Sylvies. I took my gaze away from them, saw the domestic cleaning gear in the room, looked at the scorpion, wondering who had money to waste in buying seductive Sylvies to use as palace maids.

Blue radiance dropped about me.

The little reddish-brown scorpion vanished. In his place and glowing with the blue radiance of unimaginable distance, swelling and bloating over me, the immense form of The Scorpion told me I was summoned to the presence of the Star Lords. Huge, that phantom Scorpion, encompassing a crushing bulk far larger than could possibly be confined in this small room. The coldness swept over me.

The naked girls dwindled away. The room spun. I was falling and spinning, wrapped in the coldness of ice.

Winds tore at me, buffeting, roaring. Spinning end over end and still clutching the goblet, I whirled away into the vasty deeps of darkness.

Chapter Eleven

The Star Lords—Allies?

The cold lingered and clung chill, and then went away and I could breathe again.

Insubstantial tremors, gossamer strokings, thistledown brushings confused my senses; I stood on grass soft underfoot and strode granite floorings, and cavorted through blustery winds high in the air. Gasping with a shudder I made no attempt to suppress, I opened my eyes.

Silver-gray veils shot through with rainbow colors like butterflies' wings hung before me. Each hung alternately from right and left, curving gracefully to the center. Reaching out a hand I saw the insubstantial material lift away like a curtain before I touched it, rising to reveal a curtain beyond hanging from the opposite corner. As I advanced, each curtain lifted up and away to the side in turn, on and on. Do not ask why I did not look about me. The lifting veils ahead, innumerable veils, mesmerized me.

As though advancing along a corridor filled with veil after veil, I walked on, and beneath my feet the floor pulsed and banked like morning mist.

As if unraveling a tangled ball, I continued.

The beckoning veils drew away silently. The first chamber opened out ahead and on either side, walled in crimson light, floored with crimson tiles and roofed with crimson radiance. I walked on. Vague forms drifted at the edges of vision, to coalesce and glide apart again like phantom underwater fronds undulating in unfelt currents. The veils closed about like the wings of moths, soft and furred. So I went on.

The next chamber breathed a subdued greenness composed of spring grass and jungle fronds, damp and dewy, and the moss underfoot darkened with each footprint and faded as I passed along.

The third chamber after innumerable opening veils proved as I expected it to be.

All of yellow, golden amber yellows, bright brilliant yellows, light and sunshine and airiness, and that chamber passed and I went on following the opening way ahead.

In a myriad glittering lights like the eyes of dragonflies I stepped past the ultimate veil and put that curtain away and stood forth in massive silence into a chamber robed in ebon.

Here I stopped.

I looked about.

On the right hand wall of blackness three pictures were arranged in a horizontal row. They were oval in shape, thickly framed in silver, and each showed a painting of a world set against darkness, a world I recognized as Kregen, with the continents and islands of Paz clearly visible between bands and streaks of whiteness. I looked at the three pictures, and away to the other side of the chamber where the lights pirouetted. Perhaps a shape moved there; perhaps there was only a flicker of light upon shadow in my own eyes.

I opened my mouth.

"Everoinye! Star Lords!"

For three heartbeats the echo of my voice rang in the chamber.

Then—

"Dray Prescot, onker of onkers, prince of onkers."

"Yes," I shouted. "I am stupid, an onker, and I own it. And you—what are you?"

The rustling voice expanded within my head as well as around me in the warmed and scented air.

"We are the Everoinye."

I cocked my head to the side in a silly instinctive gesture. Was there the faintest ghost-echo of humor in the voice, a tiny trace of mirth, like the last bubble in a forgotten glass of champagne? The Star Lords?

"You, Dray Prescot, are much changed. You were the blowhard, the rough, tough warrior who swore and cursed and reviled us even when you faced what you imagined to be death or worse than death, even when you were slave. Now you are an emperor who makes emperors and kings, and you speak softly, owning to your state of onkerishness. Have you anything to say?"

The latter-day change in the character I ascribed to the Star Lords amazed me. They had treated me in the past not so much with contempt as with indifference. I carried out their missions for them or I was banished back to Earth. That, clearly, was a situation that had suffered change.

The black wall opposite the three pictures of Kregen was no wall as I looked broodingly in that direction, wondering what to say to the Everoinye that would convince them I was, indeed, the sober, sensible emperor and not the roaring tearaway I had been, still was, and no doubt would continue to be.... That wall was an emptiness, a void, a gulf. At least, I thought it was, for it seemed, as I looked, to extend beyond the confines of infinity, if such a thought be possible, and the flickering motes of light danced and danced like fireflies in the evening.

"Say, Star Lords? Only that I have work to do on Kregen and you interfere with that work, as you have—" I stopped.

"As we have always done?"

"If you say it."

The hollow voice sharpened and struck with a return of an ancient vigor. "Do not attempt to dissemble. We are privy to what you desire."

"Then you must know what lies before me."

"The continuation of our plans for Paz."

I sucked in a breath.

And then, in that fog of bewilderment, I suddenly realized I still held the goblet of wine. It lay in my grip, hard and polished and real. I lifted the goblet, and drank, and emptied it, and so looked about—most ostentatiously—for a table whereon to place the precious thing.

Like a speeded-up growth, a mushroom-shaped table sprouted from the ebon floor.

So close it was, so quick, it nearly caught me betwixt wind and water. I looked up.

"And, had it done so, Everoinye—would you have laughed?"

The voice ghosted in on a sigh I heard with an amazing clarity.

"We were once mortal men like you, Dray Prescot. We have not forgotten how to laugh, but there is no occasion for that these days. You say you have work to do. We must warn you—"

I opened my mouth; my fists were gripped on the goblet, I opened my black-fanged winespout and I almost bellowed in the old intemperate Dray Prescot way. And then I closed my mouth and clamped my teeth, and waited.

"—warn you that your work has just begun."

I waited.

"The Shanks."

"They have many unpleasant names and that seems a popular one. I do not care for the results of their operations. Their hobbies are not to my taste. My people fight them. And you?"

If I expected the transformation of the Star Lords to encompass their rising to that bait, I was mistaken.

"You will fight them, Dray Prescot, for that is what we wish."

A sudden, anguished, intolerable horror prostrated me. Was I to be hurled all naked and unarmed among the Shanks, the fish-heads, the Leem-Lovers? No, by Zair, that I couldn't bear. . . .

The all-pervading voice of the Everoinye encased me in words like spider-silk.

"We are old, Dray Prescot, old beyond anything even you with a thousand years of life could comprehend. There are objectives we must accomplish in due time. You have proved of value to us. We do not deny this. It is strange—as you would say, passing strange—that this should be so, for you are a harum-scarum miscreant, a rogue with delusions of grandeur, an emperor with charisma who can bring a whole world to do your bidding. And we understand the causes of your present meekness and level-headed tolerance. We approve and are not deceived."

If this was a trap I was not going to fall into it.

I said, "And what help can you give me?" I spoke with more harshness than I'd intended.

"We may not send you back to your planet of birth."

Again, was there that dying champagne bubble of mirth?

"And positive help?"

"That, Dray Prescot, you must wait to find out."

Then, understanding they would not elaborate on this point, I passed on to something I dearly wished to know.

"Tell me, Everoinye, why did you seed Kregen with so many wonderfully different races and animals?"

"You do not know that we did so, and, had we done so, it would not be for you to know the answer."

"So you're fobbing me off again? By Krun! I thought—"

The whispering voice was now—it had to be!—tinged with genuine mirth. "You are forgetful, emperor?"

I put the goblet on the table. It looked forlorn, perched there alone. I drew a breath. Before I could speak, the insufferable whisper said, "We had a hand in what was done on Kregen, as did Others of whom we will not speak."

"You will not give me reasons, if you will not own up to your meddling. I fancy the Savanti may have some answers—"

"They know nothing. They objected at the time because of what the Curshin did. But the Savanti understood only some of the results; they have no knowledge of the reasons or the causes."

"All the same—"

"Enough, Dray Prescot! We do not wish to send you back to your Earth."

That, as you know, by Zair! was enough to scare me witless.

The Savanti, superhuman but mortal men and women, in their Swinging City of Aphrasöe, had first brought me to Kregen in order to work for them as a savapim and help bring civilization to the world. I had failed their tests, now, I was beginning to understand, because of the inherent rebellious recklessness of my nature that abhorred unjust authority. The Star Lords in their inscrutable purposes had taken me up and employed me and thus served my own ends in returning me to Kregen where all that I really wanted in two worlds awaited me. Delia! My Delia of Delphond, my Delia of the Blue Mountains! All this flummery was for her, and only her, and I wondered if these disembodied ghost voices, these vast brains, really understood that.

"You know I will not willingly return to Earth. Your determination to have your own way does go against the grain, for you are not gods. . . ." I paused for only a moment, holding myself steady, wondering if they would blast me on the spot for what they would take as blasphemy. I went on: "You say you are old. You have plans for Kregen. Why me? Why—"

"You are not the first."

"I suspected that."

"Kregen is vastly different now from what it was. Our times run perilously short and there is much to do. You will do what you can against the Shanks. Perhaps that is all we can ask of you."

To say I was astounded upon amazement upon stupefaction is to phrase my feelings very slightly. I swallowed.

"Oh, we'll have a go at the Shanks. Nobody likes them."

"Precisely."

I ruminated. "What does that mean?"

"Precisely what it says. Now, Dray Prescot, lest you presume because we have told you a few small matters, be warned! The days ahead are filled with peril. Tread carefully. For all your intemperate hotheadedness, which you affect so cleverly, you may fall to the blade, to the arrow."

"And?"

Well, insult them how you might, you wouldn't startle a Star Lord easily this side of the Ice Floes of Sicce.

"And hew to your path."

"Is that all?"

"It is all and enough, for it contains all."

I rubbed the back of my neck and it was my turn to be startled. I looked down quickly. I still wore the comfortable lounging clothes I was wearing when talking to Nedfar. Odd. In encounters with the Star Lords material things like clothes and wine goblets tended to escape attention.

"Tell me," I said, squinting at the confusing dragonfly lights, "what of your rebellious young Star Lord who challenged you. What of Ahrinye?"

"He is on a task beyond your comprehension and it is no concern of yours."

"Et cetera," I said, and I own the rebellious ugliness sounded threatening in my voice.

The reaction was rapid.

"Enough, Dray Prescot, who is called Emperor of Emperors! Beware the wrath of the Everoinye! Begone!"

It was quick, damned quick, I'll say that for them, the invisible, black-humored pack of leems.

I was standing in the small room staring down at the entwined Sylvies, naked limbs glistening with unguents, hair glossy about flushed faces. They looked up at me, newly awoken, and before they could scream I'd slammed the door open and stalked out, clutching my robes about me, furious past anger so that I wanted to roar with laughter, and did not, because I hewed to a new path and would not be deflected.

My entrance following the scorpion into their room had awoken the Sylvies. When I returned to the party no one even remarked on my absence, everything was as it had been before, and the clepsydra could have dropped barely a score of splashes to mark the passage of time.

One fact I knew and kept in the forefront of my thick vosk skull of a head. The Star Lords possessed power, real power, terrible power. It was fortunate for us all that their wishes and mine coincided.

Chapter Twelve

What I Learned in The Leather Bottle

"You do intend to go to my father's coronation, then, Jak?" Tyfar spoke with such mirth, the young devil, I was minded to play dumb and plead prior engagements. "After all, you are by way of being an expert."

The main and overridingly important thing to notice here was that Tyfar and I could joke about a horrible experience through which I had gone when Hamal and Vallia had been enemies.

That she-leem Thyllis during the pomp and circumstance of her coronation had had me, naked and filthy and hairy, dragged around Ruathytu at the tail of a calsany.

That Tyfar could rest assured that he might make this nature of joke without offense heartened me. He now fully accepted that what we said we said in good faith. Only his own prickly sense of honor had stood in the way of immediate acceptance.

"Do you, Tyfar, have any particular calsany in mind?"

"I have my eye on a particularly fine animal. And we all know what calsanys do when they are upset or excited." Then a sudden seriousness brought his mockery to a close as he said, "Although, by Havil! I certainly would not, nor would my father, sink so low as to drag a defeated foeman around the streets like that. I saw it, and never knew who you were. It was something that, even then, revolted me."

Then we were joined by Hamalese nobles and Djang nobles and the conversation expanded. Now all our thoughts were set upon the coronation of Nedfar so that all the people of Hamal might have a lawful emperor, and the expected confrontation with the enormous raiding fleet of Shanks. This fleet was being watched and shadowed, and all men trembled lest it turn in their direction. The brutal fact was, the Shank fleet would turn in *someone*'s direction—without fail.

As for the rest of that evening, it remains a mystery to me. My mind filled with speculations on that remarkable encounter with the Star Lords. By Vox, but they'd changed in the time I'd known them!

On and off, thinking about the changed situation in the ensuing days, I fancied that the key words, the clue, lay in the words of the Everoinye: "We are growing old . . ." I had some thousand years of life stretching ahead of me thanks to the baptism in the sacred pool of the River Zelph in far Aphrasöe, and I had no idea of what length of time the Star Lords would count as making them old. Millions upon millions of years had been my feeling. Perhaps that was mere superstitious impressionism? Maybe the Everoinye grew old and dropped dead at far more frequent intervals.

The idea did not give me the same glow as it would have done a few seasons ago.

Here and now I had to assume the Everoinye would leave me to get on with the job. The ready acceptance of Prince Nedfar as Emperor of Hamal was no closeted palace coup, for the rejoicing extended in genuine feeling throughout the city and into the provinces as the news spread. Tyfar saw about making sure of the army, and many a fine fellow you have met in my narrative rolled up to swear allegiance, and many and many more I knew well and have not mentioned, also. The Air Service wanted to know when they could expect some vollers.

This exposed the whole vexed question of the position of the realms of the Dawn Lands. Most of those monarchs who had so bitterly quarreled had gone home, expecting dissension to rend Hamal for seasons to come. And there was always King Telmont. Our spies reported he had taken a wide swing around to the south. He and his army—which grew from disaffected mercenaries—were watched. So the few airboats left were handed over to the new Hamalian Air Service.

Many people have called me an uncouth fighting man, and that never worries me. It now occurred to me that it would be tactful if I left Ruathytu for a space, to give the new emperor room to swing his sceptre. We intended to begin as we meant to go along, and Ortyg fretted over the accounts due in Djanduin and Jaidur itched to return with Lildra to Hyrklana and

Kytun wanted to put into practice some new ideas for the army he'd picked up. So we agreed. We'd leave Hamal to the Hamalese for a space, and all return for the coronation. As for the detachments of our armies and their commanders—they would remain.

Tyfar said, "Only true comrades could do this, Jak."

"Aye."

"My father tells me he even feels shame for doubting you. I—"

"You are a young rip, who has a stern task before him. As for the emperor; he and I understand each other. Now I'm off to have a quiet look at King Telmont and his army. If Rosil is there, well, he will be a bonus, and Vad Garnath, the rast."

"Take care, Jak—"

"And you."

He continued to call me Jak at my express wish. Soon enough he'd be able to accept my name without a tremble. Everything is not sweetness and light in the blink of an eyelid.

Jaezila said she would stay with Tyfar. Saying the remberees to them I checked my impatient query: "When will you two knock some sense into each other's heads and get married, or whatever relationship you desire, instead of pussyfooting around each other like a manhound and a wersting?"

As we said the remberees, Jaezila kissed me. "And, Jak, Father, you might run into Mother. You never know."

As I fired up and demanded to know what she meant, she put a finger to her lips, laughing. "You know, Father, you mustn't know! It is Sisters of the Rose. Sufficient?"

"No. But no more than I expect." The Sisters of the Rose, that secret organization of women, was secret. No man was privy to its secrets, for that would have negated the art and craft of female autonomy. It was all sub-rosa, and with that feeble twin-world-language idiocy in my head, I took off.

There had been the usual to-do over getting away alone, but I'd managed it. Seg refused to be hurt. As he said, "I have the Kroveres of Iztar to see to. They will have a lot to do in Vallia now."

"And in Hamal and the rest of Paz, Seg."

"Of course."

So I flew south ready to act the spy again and see what this King Telmont and his associates were made of.

As I sped southwards in a fast two-place flier I wondered

if I would meet those two unhanged rogues, Rosil, the Kataki Strom, and Vad Garnath. I'd spoken to Nedfar about rewards. Deldar Fresk, who had not lost another man there in the Pass of Lacachun, was made up to Jiktar. I particularly wanted to make sure Rees and Chido were safe. They were very dear to me, bladesmen of my ruffling days in Ruathytu's Sacred Quarter and good companions. Chido, I was told, had returned to his estates of Eurys in the east, where he was the Vad. Rees, whose estates had blown away on the Golden Wind from which he took his name, had been badly treated by Thyllis. There were many people in the same position. It was not difficult to arrange with Nedfar to reinstate them, and reward them, and I'd put Rees's name prominently on the list. As to his whereabouts, no one seemed to know.

Rees had suffered most cruelly from the Kataki Strom and Van Garnath, his eldest son, Reesnik, being slain by their hired assassins. We'd spent some rousing times together, and I had brought his daughter, Saffi, the golden lion-maid, out of a hideous bondage. But Rees and Chido knew me as Hamun ham Farthytu, the Amak of Paline Valley. That was a name I owned to in honor and intended to keep inviolate. I'd have to do some fancy footwork when we all met up, by Krun!

The dwaburs sped past below. Hamal is a rich country and Nedfar would make of it a fine and wonderful place. All we had to do was deal with Telmont and his hired army, and then close our ranks against the Leem-Lovers from over the curve of the world.

Simple plans are very often but not always the best. All I intended to do was turn up at Telmont's current army camp as a simple paktun, a mercenary at the moment tazll and therefore willing to take employment. I'd have a good look around and nose into what did not concern me and then, having sized up things that spies could not tell from outside vantage points, return to work out ways of dealing with what I had discovered. It seemed a not unuseful idea to drop down into a town first and ask around before committing myself to the army. Anyway, I wanted to hide the voller first.

Take it all nice and easy. . . . No sweat. . . . Just fly down and stow the airboat and then wander into town. . . . All free and easy. . . . Ask around, casual like, all smiles. . . . Easy. . . .

Ha!

This was Kregan and I was Dray Prescot, and that combination is, I have to point out, volatile.

Stowing the voller was simple enough at the back of a stand
of timber. Walking around the curve of the hill along the dusty
yellow road into town was simple, too.

They grabbed me as I started off across the square toward
the nearest tavern. Now, my reputation holds different values
in different parts of Kregen, and had these folk known who
I was they would no doubt—without a damned doubt at all,
by Vox!—have used edged and pointed weapons. As it was
they tried to lay me out with cudgels.

Townsfolk, they looked, rosy of cheek, shocked of hair,
wearing simple country town clothes. But their bludgeons
whistled about my ears like billy-oh.

"Hold on!" I bellowed, weaving and dodging. "Hold on,
for the sweet sake of Kaerlan the Merciful! I mean you no
harm."

They meant *me* harm, though.

I dragged out my thraxter and used the straight cut and
thrust to parry blows, to thwunk a few tousled heads, to trip
up folk who insisted on trying to brain me. The townsfolk were
all hurrying up, screaming abuse, women hurling rotten gre-
garians and children flinging all kinds of unmentionables. The
mob bludgeoned and pelted and shrieked and I soon turned
into a dungy fruit-juicy lumpen scarecrow.

"By Krun!" I said. "I'm not standing for this!"

So, there and then, without more ado, I ran. I ran off. I ran
away from an indignant mob of townsfolk with their brooms
and cudgels and rotten fruit. Run! I ran, I can tell you!

They chucked refuse after me and a stinking bamber hit me
behind the ear, and squelched all glistery brown down my
neck, stinking to the heavens. I ran faster than they did, and
reached the voller and took off. They stood under the craft and
shrieked imprecations up at me, shaking their fists and their
clumsy rabble weapons. They were not shouting the remberees.
And, by Krun, I hadn't stopped to observe the fantamyrrh as
I boarded the voller.

Whirling away and up over the trees I turned to glance back.
They were still there, jumping up and down and waving their
weapons and no doubt bellowing fit to wake the dead. By the
disgusting leprous left nostril of Makki Grodno! Now what had
that all been about?

Moving this time with much greater circumspection at the next town along and mingling in unobtrusive clothes with folk entering the narrow streets in a religious procession, for the little towns in this section were unwalled, I discovered the answer to the riddle.

And, to an old campaigner, an old paktun, that answer was perfectly obvious and deucedly uncomfortable to a fighting man. I had laughed like a loon leaving that first town, for the ludicrous situation appealed to me; now I did not laugh.

The explanation, simple and ugly, was merely that the townsfolk had been plundered rotten by the mercenaries of King Telmont's army. Simple, direct, and, as I say, ugly.

My clothes, fighting man's gear, and my weapons, marked me for a paktun. These townsfolk, brave enough to remain in their little towns, would deal most unkindly with a lone soldier.

The religious procession wended along to an adobe temple erected to the greater glory of the goddess Dafnisha the Ample, a goddess much favored in these parts, having a deal to do with the births of healthy twins. The chanting and the shuffle of feet died. I hitched up the old blanket coat that, ragged and dingy, draped my left shoulder, leaving a not-too-clean blue shirt displaying a fringe of shaggy ruffles, and went over to the nearest tavern, The Leather Bottle. It is always the nearest tavern a fellow enters when he is thirsty—almost. I didn't want to share a place with the devotees of the plump and fertile goddess Dafnisha the Ample when they boiled out after their service with their tongues hanging out.

The Leather Bottle was like many another small tavern in this section of Hamal, quiet, dusty, provided with one good supply of ale and wine and the rest indifferent stuff. Three frugally produced copper obs started me off, enough to quench my thirst, and a few more brought an earthenware platter so that I stuffed chunks of bread and slivers of cheese into my mouth as I drank, chewing with distended cheeks, and thus conveyed the impression I wished to create. I had, also, given a little twist to my face, as Deb-Lu-Quienyin had taught, so that I seemed your typical laboring fellow on the lookout.

Soon I was in conversation. The suns warmed the room and a flick-flick plant stirred to life now and again.

"King Telmont?" The speaker, a fellow with a wooden leg and a cast in his left eye, spat. He was a good shot. "We hid what we thought we could keep and sent all the women out into the hills. That stinking yetch's men took what we left—"

"Ah, but Nath," spoke up his companion, a lean-faced man with the marks of the cobbler upon him. "We worked it well, did we not? Just enough left in the town to be taken, and not so little that the soldiers became suspicious there was more."

"Aye, Mildo, we fooled the cramph." Three eyes turned in my direction, the fourth inspecting the opposite wall.

I held up a hand, busily chewing an onion, raw and rich and juicy, and spraying among the odor bits and pieces as I spoke. "Now then, doms—I'm just a traveling man." I always enjoyed handing out this one, for it was in its own way perfectly true. "D'you want a ditch dug? A fence repaired—although that's pretty technical—the wood chopped? I ran ten dwaburs without stopping when Telmont's army showed up."

No doubt about it, ragged, not-too-clean, leering, uncouth, I looked my part.

Nath the Peg sniffed and I shuffled out five more copper obs onto the sturm wood table. "You'll join me, doms?"

"Aye, dom, we'll join you."

Their thoughts were transparent. I was probably not a spy for Telmont's quartermasters come to check up on the paucity of supplies from this little town of Homis Creek. But if I were they had me in their clutches and would find me out.

The delicate Och maiden brought the fresh ale with the grace of a being of Creation blessed with six limbs. As she turned to go, I said, "May Ochenshum bless you."

She favored me with a startled look over her shoulder, and fled, and I wondered if it was my words that had surprised her or the bits of onion that sprayed against her shoulders.

Mildo the Last supped and wiped his lips. "We don't take kindly to mercenaries around here and we fooled Telmont. But he'll have this new Emperor Nedfar where he wants him. Aye, that is certain sure."

The cavortings of kings and emperors affected places like Homis Creek only in indirect ways—matters of billeting soldiers and taxes—which were direct enough when they bit.

"How so?" I said, around a fresh onion that crunched beautifully, rich and juicy.

"Why, the emperor's daughter, of course, and her fancy man."

So surprising, these words, that I couldn't stop myself from blurting out along with sprays of onion: "The princess Thefi and Lobur the Dagger?"

"You've heard about them, then? Oh, aye, they're with the army all right. And now he's got them, old Hot and Cold Telmont will make Emperor Nedfar dance to his tune, you mark my words."

Chapter Thirteen

Princess Thefi and Lobur the Dagger

There is a venerable saying on Kregen, attributed to various sources, among whom scholars squabble most fiercely over the competing claims of Nalgre ti Liancesmot, a long-dead playwright, and San Blarnoi, a possibly mythical figure or consortium of wise men of the past, which runs: "When you look too long upon the face of a leem you may grow a leem's tail."

As I stowed the flier in a patch of woods and started out to walk into King Telmont's camp, I recalled this saying, and its meaning. Typically Kregan is that modifier, "May." If you take that ferocious eight-legged hunting beast, the leem, as a symbol for terror and horrific evil, than Kregans do not say if you fight against monsters or devils you will turn into a monster or a devil. You may possibly not grow a leem's tail.

Never think for an instant that I was unaware that because of the deeds I had been called on to perform on Kregen I might grow to be like those against whom I struggled. There are two orders of fighting men, and I believe if you have listened to my words through my story you will understand the kind of fighting man I am, whether or not fate played a part in that. If you do not see that, then I have been spending my breath to no avail.

So, as I walked between the outlying totrix lines with those fractious six-legged saddle animals tugging at the ropes, I pondered how I would react when face-to-face with Vad Garnath and his evil associate, the Kataki Strom.

Bone-headed heroes of many of the stirring tales of Kregen would simply barge in swinging. I'd been like that, once upon a time. I still was, Zair forgive me, but I had learned—not much, a little, enough to make me look first; and that, by Vox,

110

makes the doing of the deed a thousand times harder and more dangerous.

"Hey, dom!" called the bristle-haired Brokelsh Deldar. "You tazll?"

"Aye, dom."

"Then join my pastang, we have a vacancy since that onker Norlgo drank himself into the well. You look handy."

"What happened to Norlgo?"

"Why, he drank himself into the well."

I stopped. The path had been churned up by military boots, some of the ranked tents were decrepit, most were in that middle stage of life when repairs were constant, and only a half-dozen were new. Flags fluttered. Men moved about over the endless fatigues inseparable from an army encampment.

"How so?"

"I told you, dom. Norlgo thought he would drink a score of flagons, and he could only manage sixteen and then he fell down the well and cracked his head open."

"Oh, I see. Let me look around first, Deldar, as to which pastang I join."

"As you wish. It's all the same to me. But you'll find none as open-handed as our Jiktar, who spreads gold every pay day with a lavish hand."

"I thank you for your information." Walking down, casual, not hurrying, it seemed clear to me that recruits were welcomed here. Oh, yes, I was clearly a paktun, well-armed, lithe and limber and wearing the silver pakmort at my throat and with a dangling array of trophy rings in the pakai at my shoulder. Counting tents, counting heads, counting animals—counting damnwell everything and totting it all up in my head—I walked on.

Camps vary considerably from race to race and army to army, but where you have a commander he will usually inhabit a tent larger and more luxurious than the general mob. King Telmont's marquee lofted, striped blue and green, bright with banners, set snugly by the small grove of trees sheltering the well down which, no doubt, sixteen-flagon Norlgo tumbled. I marched up to the guards bold as Krasny work.

"Aye, dom," said the Deldar on duty. He was apim, like me. "We can always take a paktun of the right mettle. You look likely."

"Easy, Deldar. I'm still looking."

He squinted in the radiance of the suns, and showed a snaggle of teeth. "The King's Ironfists offer to take you. You will not do better than that."

This was, given the nature of this army, probably true.

I really had no wish to waste time going through the business of hiring out as a mercenary; but I had to gain entrance into the kingly enclosures. I just wanted this business to be a quick in and out and away clean, with Lobur and, Thefi in tow.

As I have remarked, the problems of retaining a semblance of humanity on a factory production line, of beating the rush hour into the office, or getting to milk the cows, of doing all the humdrum tasks demanded of us here on this Earth are far more pressing than setting off to rescue a princess and her lover from a wicked enemy on a distant world. Paying the bills hits us more shrewdly than swinging a sword at a monster. All the same, I was on Kregen, and on Kregen rescuing princesses and swinging swords are part of normal life.

That is, part of normal life for some folk on Kregen, not all, for folk who take up the adventuring career, who seek their fortunes on that exotic and bizarre world of peril and beauty, for—in short—poor doomed damned souls like me.

"Make up your mind, dom."

"I will—" I said, and then a fancy dandy tricked-out little Hikdar appeared. Now it is possible in some armies of Kregen for a young man with the right connections and qualities to enter on a military career as a Hikdar without going through the tedious business of rising through the ranks as a Deldar. Most Deldars are bluff and rough and bellow—well, to be honest, just about all Deldars bellow.

This Hikdar with the gold bullion and flounders minced over, almost tangled in his own sword, looking agitated.

"Brassud, Deldar!" he called out in a throttled squeak. Brassud is not quite the same as "Attention!" being more of an adjuration to brace up; but it achieved results. "The king is coming!"

That was enough.

Hot and Cold Telmont was on his rounds. To retain some semblance of loyalty among their troops kings have to go out and about from time to time, like politicians kissing babies. Telmont and his retinue trotted into sight.

A gilded bunch, a blaze of gold and jewelry, of plumes and feathers and cloaks. Their zorcas were fine-spirited animals. Among the group riding in attendance on the king came the Princess Thefi and Lobur the Dagger.

Well, now!

This, I had not expected.

If Telmont held Thefi as a threat to her father, as a surety that Nedfar would do as Telmont wanted, then it was to be expected she would be held in durance vile. As it was, here she came, trotting along on a splendid gray zorca, laughing and joking with Lobur, who looked just the rapscallion he was. His smile was brilliant. He leaned across to Thefi and she responded, laughing, and they trotted on in the lights of the suns, and I gaped up at them.

They saw me.

"Jak!"

Well, it was reunion time. I had last seen these two as they escaped in a green-painted Courier voller, eloping and in love. As the swods of the guards stood, stiff as icicles, and the Hikdar aped their pose if not their manner, old Hot and Cold Telmont rode on at the head of his retinue. All I noticed of him was the litter of jewels on his armor and the flowing green cloak, the way he sat lumpily in his saddle, and the face like a half-empty sack of flour rescued from a burning mill.

Thefi and Lobur reined in, and while Lobur sat his saddle, puzzled and half smiling, Thefi impulsively dismounted and then stood, abruptly embarrassed, gripping her zorca's saddle bow.

"Jak!"

"Lahal, princess," I said, and I spoke gravely. "Lahal, Lobur."

Lobur did not answer. He turned an ugly face on the Hikdar. "All right, fambly! Get on about your own business."

Quidang, notor!" babbled the youngster, pink-tinged, and in turn rounding on the Deldar. The Deldar's blunt face expressed no emotion at the kicking order of the world as he bellowed his guard back to duty.

The Dagger looked much as I had last seen him. His dark hair cut long and curled, his nose rather shorter than longer, his casual free air, all reminded me of his past impression— except that I could find no trace of that old forthright candor in his eyes. His dagger swung at his belt. He wore bright clothes, with only a few gems. As for Thefi—well, she looked decidedly the same, beautiful and willful, and also markedly different. She had chosen to elope with Lobur and I had assisted them both. I had thought she might regret her actions when high-flown emotions drove rational thought from her head. In my guise as a gruff old warrior paktun I would not again commit the gaffe of questioning her on so tender a point.

I said, "I am surprised to see you here. I thought you were flying to Pandahem."

Still fixed in that stiff pose by her zorca, Thefi said, "We did, Jak, we did. Then when the Hyr Notor came to Ruathytu—"

"The Hyr Notor!"

She flinched back at my tone, my expression. There was no time to curse myself.

"Why, yes. He received us very kindly in Pandahem. Then in Ruathytu—" She faltered.

Lobur swung an elegant leg over his zorca and jumped down. "You are distressing the princess, Jak. You know what happened in the city? What happened to the Hyr Notor?"

I knew all right. The Hyr Notor was—had been—the Wizard of Loh Phu-Si-Yantong, and even now I did not know if he had been all evil, or if there had been a spot of goodness in him as I hoped. He had been blown away by the Quern of Gramarye fashioned in sorcery by Deb-Lu-Quienyin and Khe-Hi-Bjanching, good comrades both. Quite obviously he had planned to use Thefi in schemes against her father, just as Vad Garnath and King Telmont were now doing.

"I heard," I said.

"We have to resist those devils of Vallia and Hyrklana and drive them back." Lobur's fist fastened onto his dagger handle. His name was Lobur ham Hufadet, from an ancient and honorable family of Trefimlad. But he did not own a fortune. Tyfar had offered the opinion that if Lobur wished to marry his sister then he must do a great deed in the world. Was this the great deed?

As though my thoughts were transparent to her, Thefi said, "And Tyfar? You have seen him? He is well?"

"He is well. Yes, I have seen him. He grieves for you, Thefi, unknowing of your fate."

Then Lobur surprised me, in an area in which I should not have been surprised.

"You call the princess princess, Jak. Have you forgotten?"

I shook my head, a universal gesture among apims. "No. And Prince Nedfar—"

"How is he, Jak?" Thefi let go of the zorca and took a step forward. "We heard such terrible stories—Ruathytu is in flames, and the horrible Vallians have Father chained up and put a crown of mockery upon his head—"

Well, that was to be expected. This belief just made life more difficult for me.

"The prince is well. There is no crown of mockery."

"I do not quite—?"

The zorca hooves clickety-clicking along faded on the warm air, and the shouts of soldiers drifted in, the clink and clatter of weapons training mingling incongruously with the domestic sounds of buckets and plates, knives and forks. One of the important and impressive mealtimes of Kregen was due, and the army drew in deep breaths of appreciative expectation. That warm Kregan air swarmed with mouth-watering scents. It was roast ordel and yellow-juiced shollos and thick gravy and it smelled heavenly.

Trust old Hot and Cold to ride out on rounds when the men were being well fed.

"Why are you here with Telmont, princess?"

She looked startled and then puzzled. The smoothness of her forehead suddenly showed shadowed lines. "But we—"

"We have to fight our enemies, Jak, and that is why you have joined us." Lobur spoke with an edginess that made me think he had his mind on other schemes.

"Fight our enemies, yes. But we have to establish just who our enemies are—"

"Jak!" Thefi burst out. "We know that!"

"I am not so sure. You do not know the half of it."

Lobur's dagger clicked as he loosened it. "You'd better explain what you mean."

"I shall. But I would prefer to talk more privately."

By the suppurating scabies of Makki Grodno! Here I'd expected to have to carve my way through a wall of living flesh and wade through drenchings of blood to free these two, and that would have been the easy part, by Krun. They were here of their own free will, anxious to help King Telmont, and in no need of rescue. It was enough to make a person turn to drink, or temperance, given your previous inclination.

Walking along between them as they led their zorcas quietly

along we skirted past the voller lines. A little wind blew the
serried flags. Telmont was short of vollers, and they were well
guarded. Among them I noticed a courier flier, painted green,
with the big yellow-gold word COURIER blazoned on her
sides. She was number Jay Kay Pe 448 Ve and had been piloted
by cheerful young Bonzo before Lobur and Thefi brought her
away out of Ruathytu. I'd seen to it that Bonzo was all right
and with that little swallowing laugh he'd said he was going
to do what he wanted to do, and I'd told him that the war was
not over yet. He flew Courier vollers for a time yet, did Bonzo.
Any thoughts that I might once again steal that flier away
vanished as I appreciated the strength of the guard details.

"Now then, Jak," said Thefi as we walked on into an open
face where we would not be overheard, "I gather you want to
tell us something we do not know." She shivered. "I feel it
will be evil. . . ."

"Not so, princess. Rather, good news. Splendid news."

After a few sentences in which I tried to explain the new
situation, Thefi burst out furiously. "I don't believe my father
or my brother would believe what the Vallians say! It can't be
true! We have to fight them—"

"No, princess, we do not have to fight them. We have to
fight the Shanks, and I could wish we did not have to do even
that."

"I grant you we must fight the Shanks when they raid," said
Lobur. "But, as for the rest of this fabrication, why, it makes
me think strangely. You have always been a mysterious fellow,
first hailing from Djanduin, then Hamal, and now where?" He
looked at me, his brows drawn down, and his fist on his dagger
handle. "Vallia, perhaps?"

I took a breath—

A party of guards marched briskly along, their spears all
sloped exactly, their helmets shining, for they were of the
King's Ironfists. No difficult calculation told me I could fight
my way through them and probably seize a voller, chained
down or not. I might even manage that with Thefi draped
around my neck and shrieking blue murder that she was being
abducted. Even, perhaps, with Lobur and his damned dagger
to contend with.

Yes, I might have done all those things in the typical bone-
headed way of your barbarian hero—but that would alienate
Thefi. That seemed clear. She would struggle and scream and

in the ensuing excitement some stray arrow or stux might kill her instead of me. That was a chance I would not take.

The truth of her father's position as I saw it was not the truth as she saw it.

I said, "Your father, Prince Nedfar, is now the Emperor of Hamal and in alliance with Vallia, Hyrklana, Djanduin and other forward-looking countries."

Lobur looked disgusted.

Thefi blanched.

"You have been deceived, Jak! You must have been. My father would never join hands with Vallia. Tyfar has told me. He and father would never do it."

"But they have—"

"No! Never! Treat that great devil Dray Prescot as a human being? It is unthinkable."

"But he *is* a human being, princess."

"I wonder!" Her head was up, her chin in the air, and her eyes held a look of haughty imperiousness—and, also, of doubt?

"You know what happened to the Hyr Notor, Jak?" Lobur hauled his zorca along to keep up, for the beast wanted to have a quiet crop at the sparse grass. "Down the Moder we met Ariane nal Amklana, of Hyrklana. She came to the Empress Thyllis for help, we saw her again, and she was with the Hyr Notor when he died."

"I did not know that."

"It was some devilish trick of Dray Prescot's that did that mischief. Now we must resist with all our willpower."

"We must resist the Shanks, the leem-lovers." I spoke firmly, and Lobur jumped, and looked mean.

"You—"

"There is no time left for me to explain it all again. Hamal and Vallia are now in alliance. Did you know, Thefi, that Prince Tyfar and the Princess Majestrix or Vallia are—"

"No!"

Her cry broke forth as an anguished wail. "No, no. That cannot be so!"

In these matters of the convoluted affairs of state and the heart there is no need to spell it all out for a princess. Thefi understood at once, and was horrified, shattered, degraded in her own eyes.

And I'd had enough.

"You misunderstood me, princess. This is no state-arranged marriage. Tyfar and the Princess Majestrix love each other dearly—although they somehow manage to skirt around the subject. It was thought you would help in this."

She put a hand on my arm and looked up into my face.

"Jak, you bring such strange news. And Tyfar. . . . Why, he and this horrible Vallian princess have never met. How could they love each other so soon?" She shook her head, and her hair gleamed. "We must resist the Vallians. King Telmont says so—"

"Old Hot and Cold? Surely you mean Vad Garnath?"

"Maybe." She looked away. "I do not like him. But, Jak— you are strange—and Tyfar and father—it is all—"

"It is all very simple," cut in Lobur. "If we are not to lose everything, we fight the damned Vallians and their allies."

"You, Lobur, were Nedfar's aide-de-camp. Would you obey him if he told you?"

All the forthright candor fled from Lobur's eyes.

"Treachery—?"

As I say, I'd had enough.

"I must leave you to think this over. I repeat, Hamal no longer stands in enmity with Vallia. We have great enemies, greater foes even after the Shanks have been dealt with. Now I must see to my animals and eat and bathe. I shall see you when the suns have gone."

Before they had time to remonstrate, I turned away and marched off. I was fuming. But, then, how else had I expected them to react?

Chapter Fourteen

Chained Like a Leem

The eating and the bathing were accomplished easily enough on payment of a suitable sum; the nonexistent animals no doubt took care of themselves. My voller waited in her clump of trees. I spent the rest of the day moving about and discovering all I could. Telmont had a formidable little army, not over-large but of high quality, and he even had under command a number of regiments of the old Hamalian army, all of whom believed they were acting in the best interests of Hamal. It was those regiments who had allied with Vallia that were the renegades and treacherous werstings.

Try as I might, I could find no other solution to this pretty problem than simply taking Thefi to see her father and letting her see the truth for herself. As for Lobur, he might not wish to face Prince Nedfar, now the Emperor of Hamal. I would not drag the Dagger along by the scruff of the neck, but he ought to be given the chance of making up his own mind about coming with us.

That was it, then.

There were four regiments of swarthmen in whom I took an interest, for the swarth, a dinosaur-like saddle animal of great power and lumbering strength, was often regarded as a mere appendage to the cavalry arm or as the battle-winning strike force, depending on the viewpoint of the riders. These fellows in their harsh scaled armor and blazoned blue and gold looked useful. Also, Telmont had a fine corps of crossbowmen. His churgurs, the solid heavy sword and shield men looked to me to be somewhat thin on the ground. But this army would prove a tough nut to crack.

So I wandered about, spying away in the best cloak and dagger fashion, until the suns set and the first of the night's moons rose. She of the Veils shone refulgently down, all rose and gold, and I took heart. Although claiming to have no favorites among the seven moons of Kregen, I rather fancy I take to She of the Veils just a trifle more than the others. . . .

This was not unimportant, as you shall hear.

By the time the Maiden with the Many Smiles rose over the horizon, I wanted this frustrating business with Lobur and Thefi over and done with.

They had been given a tent of some magnificence by King Telmont, and rather to my surprise I discovered that Lobur was no gilded appendage to the king's retinue, having taken command of a totrix regiment which he strove to improve and turn into the best in the army. With gold and rose moonlight dropping over the lines of tents and animals, I nodded to the sentries at the tent flap and went inside. The information that would have been startling to anyone here, that Jak the Shot was in reality Dray Prescot, had not reached the camp and Nedfar had kept that business on the quiet side. Very few were privy to that item of hot gossip. I wondered, as I watched Thefi approach in the lamplight over the carpets, whether I should tell her.

She looked pale. Her eyes were brilliant.

"Jak! I have been thinking over what you said. It is terrible, terrible—"

"Agreed, princess. Everyone is heartily sick of wars and fighting. But we must brace ourselves. We have to face the Shanks, for they will destroy us if we do not."

"I did not mean that. Everyone knows that. I mean about my brother and that awful princess of Vallia."

I just couldn't help myself. "Oh," I said. "So you've met her then."

"What? No, of course not."

"Then, princess, how do you know she is awful?"

Stupid and petty vindictivenesses like that can be quickly and firmly put down. She stared at me. "She is Vallian, isn't she?" That, of course in her eyes, was explanation enough. I, clever Dray Prescot, was quickly and firmly put down.

"Where's Lobur, princess?"

"Seeing to his regiment. And I have made my mind up. I will not—I cannot—return to Ruathytu. My father would be—would be unkind to Lobur. And I could not bear that."

I studied her. She breathed passion and fire and all the

delightful and worthwhile things of dreams, and I could not
ask her again to think a second time and, perhaps, to betray
her lover. As always, my thoughts of Delia gave me what I
hoped was a better understanding in delicate affairs. How
would Delia react in these circumstances? That is a touchstone
that never fails me.

"Very well—but Telmont bears your father no good will."

"Oh, Jak! Telmont is fighting for Hamal. Once we throw
off the yoke of oppression—"

"Vallia does not—"

She half-turned away and her frown pained me. We still
stood. She had offered no seat, no refreshments.

"We are taking a big swing down into the south and east,
to gather more men. Just north of He of the Commendable
Countenance Telmont has good friends."

The river marking the southern boundary of Hamal, the
River Os, divided before it reached the sea on the east coast
and the two arms enclosed the independent country of Ifilion.
Much of the river and deltas were called the Land of Shining
Mud. You could scrape up thousands of levies there, who
might fight if they were chained and stapled to the ground.
There were other troops to be had. Chido's estates were in that
part of Hamal. And, so Thefi said, some of the realms south
of the river in the northern sections of the Dawn Lands still
would fight for Hamal, since they had been in thrall for so
long. I thought of our abject performances in the Peace Conference. This was one result of shilly-shallying when we should
have been making decisions and implementing them.

Lobur walked in with a swing and a swagger, shouting that
he could only stop for a stoup of ale—no wine for him tonight
on guard duty—before he saw me. He halted, his helmet
swinging by its straps from his fist, and his face congested.
He wore a smartly ornate uniform, but he was a fighting man.

"Lahal, Lobur."

"You are not welcome, Jak. It pains me to say that, after
all you have done for us. But—"

I interrupted and made a last attempt to persuade them to
see that Telmont might protest his honest intentions but that
Vad Garnath pulled the strings. "Between them, and Rosil, the
Kataki Strom, they will try to destroy your father, princess.
It was Rosil who shot Thyllis."

But they would not listen, and Lobur, flinging an impatient

glance at the clepsydra, said he had to be off or those lazy
good-for-nothings would be snoring instead of standing watch.
He left, with a warning look at Thefi which I ignored. He did
not say the remberees.

"Princess—"

"No, Jak. My father is held by the Vallians and we must
fight them to free him. My mind is made up."

Seeing I had failed, I hitched up my sword belt—which is
a useful if redundant preliminary to action—and started to
walk quietly toward Thefi. I picked her up and bundled her
under my arm and walked out of there.

Ha!

The only real bit of luck I had was that Vad Garnath and
Strom Rosil were not in the camp—oh, and that the guards
didn't knock my brains out there and then. They flung iron
nets over me in the evilly efficient way Kataki slavers have,
and iron nets will hold a leem. I fell to the ground, tangled
up, cursing away, struggling to draw a sword and break free.
The nets enfolded me. Katakis with their tails swishing bladed
steel hauled me out. Nasty are Katakis, a race of diffs with
habits that set them apart from the normal run of humanity.
Low-browed, dark, snaggled-toothed, and with those sinuous
whip tails to which they strap six inches of bladed steel, Katakis
are man-managers. Thefi screamed and I cursed and rolled
over, and a Kataki hit me on the head and the night of Notor
Zan enfolded me in darkness.

I woke up, chained and stapled to the ground like some
poor devil of a levy swept up into an army for which he had
no desire whatsoever to fight.

The stars sparkled above, the Maiden with the Many Smiles
performed her serene pink smile, the night breeze rustled the
bushes, and I struggled and was chained like a wild beast.

Two guards stood watch over me.

One said, "You're awake, then?"

His companion said, "When the king sees you, you'll—"

The first one laughed. "You mean Vad Garnath, don't you,
Thafnal? King Telmont is—" He stopped, and looked swiftly
about.

"Aye, Ortyg. Best watch your mouth."

All the notorious Bells of Beng Kishi rang and collided in
my skull. I licked my lips and swallowed. I could move about
half an inch. The chains were thick and strong and of iron.

The fancy dandy little Hikdar trotted up, managing not to trip over his own sword. He put on a big frown, bending his brows down, and I guessed he had caught this guard duty and was not too pleased about it, no doubt having other and more pleasant occupations planned for the night. The two swods looked across as he appeared in the moons light and stood at attention—casually.

"No trouble?" squeaked the little fellow.

"No trouble, Hik."

"Good, good."

I'd given no trouble because I'd been enveloped in the black folds of Notor Zan's cloak. I strained at the chains and could not break them or budge the stakes to which they were stapled. The Hikdar jumped.

"Watch him! There are express orders from Jiktar Nairn. He is to wait judgment from the king himself."

"Very good, Hik."

With a careful flick at his sword to clear it away from his legs, he trotted off.

"Who's he?" I said, in my conversational voice. I didn't give a damn who he was; I wanted to get the conversation flowing easily.

"Hikdar Naghan ham Halahan, and you mind your mouth."

"D'you have a mouth-wet around here?"

The one called Thafnal hoicked forward a bottle. His face was scarred and dark, seamed with seasons of campaigning. "Open your black-fanged winespout, dom, and I'll pour you a draught."

I did as he bid and took in a sloshing mouthful of cheap wine. It was refreshing, tangy though it might be.

"My thanks, dom."

As the stars and moons wheeled across the sky I crouched there, chained like a wild animal, and cogitated. My thoughts were as cloudy as the sky, where dark masses erratically obscured the moons, and then blew free in wispy streamers until the following clouds cast their shadows upon the land.

Just a little of this famous cogitation convinced me that out of a hundred chances, ninety-nine would say that Lobur the Dagger had betrayed me. He was frightened that I would convince Thefi to return, and Lobur would not face her father. This saddened me. It showed how little he understood the depth of her feelings for him.

Also, the unwelcome thought occurred to me that Lobur knew more than he said—certainly not that I was who I was, for in that case my head would be rolling away over the ground—but was probably aware of the true situation in Ruath-ytu through his contact with Garnath. He had not told Thefi. I felt my faith in Lobur slipping away depressingly.

If I hadn't saved him from falling off a rooftop in Jikaida City—and he did not know that Drax, Gray Mask, was me—he wouldn't be alive now and a whole train of incidents that had followed would not have taken place.

In the confusing lights of the moons Hikdar Naghan ham Halahan came mincing back. He looked different, and was trying to strut along with all the pomp his position demanded, and making a strange hash of it. He'd be more dangerous to his own men in a fight, I was thinking, as he wheeled up toward the two guards, Thafnal and Ortyg, who barely took enough notice of him save to come to their sloppy attention. They were so long in the tooth as extended-service swods they could get away with murder among the forest of Hamalian regulations.

"A prowler in the zorca lines," squeaked ham Halahan, his voice higher and yet struggling to sound hoarse. "Get off there at once. I'll stand guard here. *Bratch!*"

That hard word of command made them move. Thafnal said: "He won't get away, Hik—"

Ham Halahan pointed, his helmet casting deep shadows over his face, his cloak wrapped about his uniform. The two swods picked up their spears and marched off, whistling. They knew to a nicety how far to go in baiting jumped-up young officers.

The Hikdar watched them go. He was trembling. They disappeared beyond the corner of the nearest tent toward the zorca lines as clouds threw down shadows.

"Jak! We must be quick!".

In a single heartbeat I stopped my stupid "Wha—?" and instead said, "I thank you, princess. The chains are of iron."

"I have the key. I stole it from Lobur. Here...."

She bent over me and I sensed her perfume. The uniform showed under the cloak, impressive, far too impressive to be that of a Hikdar, however important he thought himself, and it fitted ill. One of Lobur's, of course. The key clinked. The lock made a sound like a wersting savaged by a leem. The chains fell away. I rubbed my wrists, my ankles, but the shackles had not been tight enough to restrict circulation.

"Why?"

She would not look at me. Strands of hair wisped free of the harsh helmet brim.

"You were a good friend to us. I couldn't see you—"

"Is that all?"

Now she looked at me as I stood up, her eyes dark and pained, and I felt for her pain.

"No. Lobur—he was talking to Garnath—"

"That great devil is here?"

"They said—I overheard and I couldn't believe—and yet I still love Lobur—"

"What did they say?" I looked about, and I know my face was as savage as faces may ever become. "We must move away from here." We moved off into the shadows and I held her arm.

"Garnath and my Lobur—what you said is true, Jak. And Lobur knew all the time. He knew! My father *is* the emperor and they plan to destroy him and use me.... Use me to...."

She trembled under my touch.

"It isn't pretty, Thefi. Will you stay with Lobur?"

"I want to.... But how can I? I do not know what to do!"

She wore a sword, a straight cut and thruster used all over Havilfar. The thraxter looked to be a quality blade as I drew it from the scabbard, quickly, before she could move.

"Jak! You will not kill me?"

"Hold still, princess. No—run for the nearest voller if you wish to escape. I will follow."

She turned her head to look where I stared and saw the advancing forms of soldiers, weapons bared.

"Oh, Jak! They will surely kill you—"

"And you too, and still make your father dance to Garnath's tune. Now, run—run for the nearest voller. And, my girl, run fast!"

Then I swung about and switched up the sword, ready to take on the yelling guards who ran in with weapons brandished.

Chapter Fifteen

Hometruths

Thefi had saved me from almost certain death, and now in order to save her I had to face another round with almost certain death. Well, that is life on Kregen. The guards ran on yelling. One or two screeched the chilling Hamalese war cry "Hanitch! Hanitch!" a sound that has risen in triumph over very many battlefields.

My blade slithered across the first guard's sword, turned, thrust, retrieved—all, it seemed, of its own volition. He staggered back, arms upflung, and already the dark blood spouted.

Three more came on, hard, panting, and I foined around and cut and pierced them, and danced away, risking a quick glance over one shoulder. Thefi had reached the voller lines and—by Krun, she was the daughter of her father and sister to her brother!—she pointed imperiously at me and as the guard obediently ran past to join the fray, she took off her helmet and hit him over the head with it. He collapsed in a smother of cloak and his dinted helmet fell off and as Thefi bent with a glitter of steel in her fist I swiveled back to my own fight.

There were a lot of them, and they ran in from different sides, so I backtracked, taking them as they came. Some were what an unfeeling Kapt once called "blade-fodder," some were your ordinary seasoned fighting men more at home in the line with their regiments. Some, three or four, were superior bladesmen. These consumed time. And, of course, I was never unaware that at any disastrous moment I would front up to a man—or woman—who was a better sworder than I was.

If that happened—and it had happened and could occur at any moment—it would be highly inconvenient.

A burly fellow with a tuft of green feathers in his helmet

proved clever, working in combination with his oppo, a slighter man with a wizened face. These two held me up and others were running up, hullabalooing. I just avoided a clever cut at my thigh which changed trajectory with a cunning roll of the wrist and aimed to degut me, blades chingled and rang, I riposted against the little fellow and let my body go with the turn, avoiding the big fellow's degutting stroke. They bored in again and two more started to circle around to my left side.

I yelled.

"By Krun! Behind you, rasts!"

And, with the yell, I leaped.

Cheap, melodramatic trick? Yes. But the big fellow flung a startled look back so that I could ignore him for the instant it took me to engage with wizened-face, circle his blade and punch him through, and then slice down across the throat of the big fellow as he pivoted back. I jumped clear. They fell. The other two hung back. But there were more. I ran. I hared off toward the vollers and saw Thefi at the controls of the green-painted courier voller we had liberated from Ruathytu and in which she and Lobur had traveled to Pandahem and back here.

"Here, Jak! Run!"

Without wasting any more breath I sprinted for the green flier and leaped aboard, tumbling in any old way. As it was, an arrow sprouted from the wooden coaming. I frowned as I untangled myself and then fell against Thefi as she swept the voller into the air. She could not rise at a steep angle, as we would have wished, for the vollers had been staked out in the lee of a gaggle of half-stunted trees. These were small enough, and yet large enough to be an obstacle. We went hurtling along in a wild swinging curve and then straightening to plunge up at the end of the trees.

We never made it.

I was just saying, "Well done, Thefi!"

A mustard-colored voller started up at right angles to our course, coming in from the left-hand side. It hesitated, and then plunged on and Thefi, quite unable to hold the courier flier back or drive her up in time, screamed.

We went slap bang wallop into the side of the maxi-mustard flier and I had a glimpse of Kregen cartwheeling upside down. The courier voller splintered all forrard, turning end over end, slewing away as the maxi-mustardy airboat collapsed sideways.

Thefi and I fell out in a wild tangle onto the grass.

No time to feel winded or take notice of the bruising pain in my left shin or the thwack behind my left ear. Time only to snatch Thefi up, hurl her on stumbling across the muddy grass toward the next flier. She was the penultimate one in the tethered line. Thefi's hair streamed loose, her helmet, its work done, long abandoned. We fled for the voller.

The stupid pilot of the mustardy voller, who had pulled out right in front of Thefi, hung upside down from the coaming, blood streaming from his nostrils. Served the fool right.

"I'll do the chains," I bellowed. "Up with you!"

She did not argue.

The first staple came free with a single heave. The second proved more stubborn, the cunning voller attendants having burred the staple end and cross-pinned it. I ducked out from under the airboat and called up.

"Is there a crowbar, Thefi?"

I looked back. The pursuers, well outdistanced by our brief flight, would soon be up with us, howling like a pack of hunting werstings. The pilot of the voller who had caused the accident, as I now saw, was a woman, not a man. She'd been no heroine trying to halt us, but some incompetent pilot who imagined a voller took up less than half the airspace required. The crowbar appeared over the side and Thefi said, "I'm all ready to go."

"In half a leem's spring."

The crowbar snugged between chain and staple, I leaned back, forces took the strain, balanced, gave. The staple wrenched clear and the chain fell to the mud.

Thefi yelled.

"Guards!"

She did not scream; but the urgency of her tone made me turn sharply enough to crack my head on the voller's keel. I was suffering far too many of these cracks on the head just lately. Half-crouched, I stopped moving. Two boots, black and muddy, showed beneath the keelson. They were positioned in just such a way as would tell the trained eye of a sword fighter that the owner of the boots stood braced and poised, weapon lifted ready to strike down at anyone crawling out from under the flier.

I hefted the crowbar.

The bar of iron cracked against an ankle bone with a most unpleasant sound and the pair of boots hopped madly into the air. In an instant I was out from under the airboat and bringing the crowbar around again in a blow that stretched the guard senseless. His helmet fell off. Others of his comrades were running up, for Telmont had taken the sensible precaution of placing a strong guard on his vollers. The stupid woman who had crashed into us had been attended to and sent off, and the guards must have gone back for a quiet wet until our commotion brought them running back.

Using the crowbar after the fashion of an Aleyexim's trakir, a hefty sliver of iron sharpened at both ends and hurled by the warlike Aleyexim in battle to deadly effect, I managed to knock over the first of the yelling guards. Thefi stared over the coaming, her face apprehensive and yet betraying no real concern.

"Hurry, Jak!"

Without answering—and remarkably heartened by Thefi's obvious confidence—I leaped aboard. She slammed the control levers over to the stops and we shot away.

Looking down as we passed over the last voller, I felt a pungent regret. She was not an enormous skyship, but she was an airboat of good size, of three decks and many fighting tops and walkways, and my regret really did me no credit. Gunpowder had not yet been invented on Kregen—if the Star Lords so willed it might never be invented—and that was most probably a good thing. But right there and then, the idea of toppling a keg of best gunpowder with a short fuse down onto that ship appealed to me with some force.

"Well done, Thefi. Turn a little right and dive below the tree line. I don't think they'll expect us to do that."

She flung me a puzzled glance.

"Wouldn't it be best to make for Ruathytu at once? This is a fast voller."

"If you so order, princess, that we shall do. But I have my own voller parked down there and—"

"Of course!" Her color was up, rosy in the radiance of the moons between clouds. "I see! And you will send me off to Ruathytu in this voller and lead them off on a false scent in yours, no doubt fighting them for the daring of it!"

This was not sarcasm, not irony; it was the hurt of a girl being placed in a situation she detested.

"The thought had crossed my mind—"

"Well, uncross it then, Jak! We fly together."

"Very well. I just hope Garnath or one of his bully boys misses my voller. She was only loaned to me."

Thefi laughed, her head up, her throat exposed.

"My father will buy you a dozen airboats." Then she sobered, quickly—so quickly that I knew she remembered her own troubles with Lobur, black and depressing, and her laughter sounded hateful and mocking in her own ears.

To make any of the superficial and routine comforting remarks would be redundant and clumsy. She had just discovered that Lobur the Dagger was not the man she thought he was. That order of discovery, entailing that degree of hurt, is not survived with the aid of a few kind words.

All the same. . . .

"Your father, and Tyfar, too, may want to condemn Lobur too harshly, for they love you and have been—"

"Worried?"

"More than that, Thefi, more than that."

My voice sounded hard, even in my own head.

"And if they do—they do. . . ."

"But at least we can see Lobur's reasons, why he did what he did. I can understand him, I think. He had no chance with you unless he performed some bold stroke, a jikai—"

"And this is a jikai! Betrayal!"

"When a man loves a woman concepts like that blur and lose their meaning."

She turned her eyes to look at me, over the bridge we had built between us out of our situation. She half-nodded.

"You speak as though—as though you—"

"I know."

Well, my Delia would confirm what I said. No doubt of that at all.

We flew on, and talked desultorily, and soon it was clear that Thefi's thoughts stopped her from speaking altogether. Wondering if I was doing the right thing or making matters worse, I felt I didn't want Thefi to brood too much alone with her thoughts. If this negated my previous feelings on the matter, well, that was my privilege.

"There is a woman," I said. "Whose father—well, she was a girl, then—whose father ordered my head chopped off, at once. I swore at him, I remember, most heatedly. But afterward we fell into a sort of relationship we could both endure. He wasn't such a bad old buffer, and he always wanted to get into

the fighting, although his people prevented him." I was talking
to myself as well, now. This was a point that rankled still.
"When he was killed I had gone—well, never mind that. He
was slain by a damned traitor who makes Lobur a miracle of
upright rectitude by comparison—I think—and I returned too
late. So you see, Thefi, it all works out in the end."

She lifted her head to stare at me, for the weight of her
feelings dragged down her head so that her hair fell forward
over her eyes.

"You are telling me things that pain you. I know. But, if
you can, Jak, tell me. If this woman's father ordered your head
cut off and you are here—the order was not carried out."

"I'm not broken from the ib, Thefi, I'm no ghost. I was
saved by the best comrade a man can have."

"And the woman?"

"You'll meet her. You'll get on, the pair of you."

"Oh, yes? We'll see."

Below us the land fled past and careful scrutiny of the sky
rearward showed no betraying flickers of motion beneath the
stars. The moons shone no reflections from pursuing vollers.

Thefi said, "We keep abreast of all the foreign news, in
Hamal, all the scandals and gossip." Then, right out of the
blue, she said, "We heard the story that the old Emperor of
Vallia ordered that awful Dray Prescot's head cut off, and he
escaped and forced the Princess Majestrix to marry him. It was
a great scandal. That was before Thyllis dragged him around
Ruathytu tied to the tail of a calsany, of course. A pity he
escaped, for then we would not be in such terrible trouble now.
Your story, Jak, reminds me of that scandal." She arched her
brows. "Perhaps you just made that up to make me feel less—"

"No. Did you see Thyllis's coronation?"

"No. But I heard about how Dray Prescot was dragged past.
He was all dirt and hairs, anyway."

"Yes."

The Maiden with the Many Smiles shone forth and iced the
voller in pink. The wind of our passage blew past. I pulled my
lip, ruminating, staring at Thefi. Well, by Zair! And why not
now?"

I said, "I did not make up the story, Thefi. I think of you
as a friend, and you know Tyfar and I are comrades."

"I know. We owe you so much—"

"No, no—or, perhaps, more than you think."

Now that was a damned stupid thing to say...!

"Look, Thefi. We'll work something out with Lobur. I do know about these affairs. I bear him no ill will. Do you believe that?"

She did not reply at once. Then, "Yes, I believe you."

"Good. Then I can tell you that when Thyllis dragged me around Ruathytu tied to the tail of a calsany it was damned uncomfortable. And my daughter Lela, the Princess Majestrix, is deeply in love with Tyfar, as he with her, and it's our job to do all we can to make them—"

She put a hand to her mouth. She let go of the controls. Her face looked like a lily, pale and glimmering above a tomb.

"You—you are joking, Jak? Jak?"

"No joke, princess, except a joke on my fate. And not Jak, although I have grown used to the name. I am Dray Prescot—the awful, horrible, great devil, in person."

She did not faint.

She might well have, seeing that she had been stuffed full of the most terrible stories of the hateful Emperor of Vallia. She swayed. I did not move. Her eyes regarded me over her hand which spread and dug so that her fingers and thumb bit deeply into the sides of her mouth.

So, with intent and not particularly caring for the way I had to say it, I said: "Now you will understand that when I say Hamal and Vallia are friends, and comrades in arms against the Shanks and our other enemies, you will see I speak the truth."

She took her hand away. She breathed in. "I see you believe it."

"I believe it because it is true." Then I brisked it all up and spoke smartly. "Now go and rest in the cabin. I will call you when Ruathytu is in sight."

She did as she was bid.

If I say that as I stood at the controls I did not stand with my back square onto the door of the aft cabin, but rather a little to one side, you may feel contempt. I share that contempt; but, also, I am an old paktun and I would prefer to stay alive rather than be killed through an oversight. Thefi, like most princesses who survived on Kregen, would be quick with a dagger.

She did sleep. A quiet look into the aft cabin proved reassuring, for she lay on the bunkbed, sprawled out and breathing slowly and evenly and not scrunched up into a foetal ball, hard and agonized. Some provisions had been stowed in the flier and a search brought to light smoked vosk rashers and loloo's eggs, with a plentiful supply of the ubiquitous palines. So we could eat when Thefi awoke. She joined me and as we ate she said little, eating enough again to reassure me. She combed her hair and washed her face and dealt with the necessities of life in a way that, princess-like though it might be, revealed she was also a girl in a situation that ought to frighten her into screaming hysteria.

She said, "Why am I not frightened, majister, emperor, Dray Prescot, great devil?"

"Call me Jak."

"Oh?"

"A lot of people do until they are easier in their minds. As to being frightened of me, if you were I would feel insulted."

"I would have killed you and joyed in the doing of it—"

"That's a lot of the trouble, Thefi. Lies make us do things we would not ordinarily dream even of contemplating."

She was not yet over the shock of this—to her—astounding revelation. After all, she was not accustomed to emperors who went off adventuring around the world and whose tastes did not run to gold and flunkies and having people's heads off.

When Ruathytu came into sight she sighed.

"After I have seen Father and Tyfar I am going to wallow through every single one of the rooms in the Baths of the Nine!"

"Every single one?"

She lowered her eyelids. "Well, not in the zanvew."*

Patrols of vollers and saddle flyers whirled up to inspect us and we waved and were escorted down. I recognized some of the flutswods astride their fluttrells, and no doubt my battleship-face was familiar to them also. We touched down on the high landing platform of the Hammabi el Lamma and Thefi was instantly swept away in a bustle of women as Prince Nedfar and Tyfar advanced, beaming, welcoming, all smiles.

"And Lobur?" they asked after the lahals.

I told them.

"There is no sense in pursuing this matter further at the moment." Nedfar looked every inch the emperor he was. "What

---

*Zan: ten. Vew: room.

you say of Telmont's sweep into the southeast concerns us more."

We walked through into private chambers where refreshments were served. Tyfar and his father were concerned about Telmont and his army, yet they ached to hare off—leaving me—to see Thefi. They thanked me, not effusively, but with a quiet sincerity that warmed, as I said, "It was Thefi who saved me."

Jaezila looked ravishing. I refused to worry over the future relationship between her and Thefi. I saw the way she and Tyfar looked at each other, the way they avoided entering too closely into the body-space of the other, the comical and yet frustrating way they circled each other like fighting men seeking an opening. I hoped Thefi, seeing the truth, would help. She might be the catalyst that would precipitate the actions everyone who knew them longed for and despaired of contriving.

Chapter Sixteen

Affray at the Baths of the Nine

Seg said, "Well, my old dom, I'm for the Baths of the Nine. You coming?"

The Peace Conference had died the death. Most of the delegations from the Dawn Lands had gone home to carry on their intrigues and wars among themselves. Ortyg and Kytun had returned to Djanduin and Jaidur and Lildra to Hyrklana. The city prepared for Nedfar's coronation as emperor and we fighting men readied a fresh army to lead against Telmont. There was time to indulge a few burs in the Baths of the Nine.

"You're on, Seg."

"Which establishment? I have taken to patronizing The Sensil Paradise. It is perhaps a little larger than I'd prefer, but the exercise floor is splendid."

"Well, I suppose you can't have it both ways."

There were many establishments in Ruathytu called The Paradise, qualified by gushing descriptives, and the Sensil was, indeed, a fine place, not too far from the Old Walls in the Sacred Quarter. We could take a couple of flyers from the palace and be there in no time at all.

Tyfar breezed into the small room where we spent a deal of time arguing over the maps and eating and drinking and generally trying to keep out of the way. Instantly he declared himself ready to join us in the Sensil.

"After all, when your father is an emperor, there are a devil of a lot of time-consuming nothings to do."

"Yes, Tyfar, and when you're emperor there are a damn sight more, by Krun."

He gave me a hard stare, and I said as though a part of the foregoing: "Not that you'll be emperor—at least of Hamal—for very many seasons yet."

135

Seg laughed and changed the subject. Successions are tricky
problems, as I knew. Drak would return from Vallia for
Nedfar's coronation, and I wanted him to take over being
Emperor of Vallia so that I could have a free hand. I did not
think Nedfar would early relinquish his throne and crown to
Tyfar.

In the end Nedfar joined us with a gaggle of people from
his suite, including Kov Thrangulf. That plain man was most
subdued. After Thefi had eloped with Lobur, Thrangulf had
shriveled into himself. Nedfar's plans for Thrangulf and Thefi
to wed, thrown into disarray, might now never be realized.
Yet I, along with one or two others—not, sadly, including
Tyfar—saw far more in Kov Thrangulf than met the eye.

So quite a crowd of us flew off to The Sensil Paradise.

Taking the Baths of the Nine is more than merely having
a good wash. It is a social occasion. The place was thronged
with people. No one wore any clothes, of course. When you
take a bath you do not customarily wear clothes, although the
folk of Wihtess solemnly wear what they call sponge-garments
when they take a bath, for they have some funny ideas about
the naked human body. The halls were lofty with radiance,
wide with marble floors, heated and kind. The folk filled the
various chambers and rooms with chatter and vivaciousness,
their skins and furs and scales of striking variety. Among the
apims with rosy skins, and brown and black and golden-yellow
skins, the blue and green teguments of Hem-vilar and Olinmurs
added a pleasing color contrast. Very few people paid much
attention to color or texture of the body-covering of the folk
with whom they bathed or swam or played games.

As we walked through into the heated air and the laughter
and horseplay, Seg, very quietly, said to me, "These Hamalese
have got over the war very quickly."

"Aye. I'm pleased."

He caught a ball hurled by one of a group of girls whose
strengths overmastered her skill, and threw it back.

"They caused enough suffering, and, by the Veiled Froyvil,
look at 'em! You'd think they won!"

This comment did not discompose me, for I was well aware
Seg shared my views—in fact he had had a part in shaping
mine—on our coming confrontation with the Shanks and he
was merely feeling the disgruntlement of the fighting man.
Seg, like myself, was no bloodthirsty warmonger. It was just

that his honest sense of wages due for sins committed was outraged by the sight of Hamalese enjoying themselves, like this, now, when perhaps a more studious demeanor would be more appropriate. Then the ball flew through the air toward us again, and we realized that these jolly girls were not unskillful—far from it—but wished us to join in their game.

So we did.

The scented and heated air resounded to the shouts and laughter bouncing off the high walls and roof, and the splashes of divers and swimmers, the click and clack of gamesters in their corners. Everyone worked up a splendid sweat to be washed sweetly off in the pools.

Tall bronze doors with engraved scenes of flower gardens in their panels separated by borders of intertwined flowers gave access to the next chamber. We heard before we saw. The yells of laughter and enjoyment changed to yells of fear and screams of panic. We looked. The high doors opened. Armed and armored men pushed through, slashing with swords to clear a path. Ahead of them, speedily glimpsed through the panicking horde of naked bodies, ran a youth brandishing a sword. He saw us, he saw Nedfar and Tyfar, and he pointed the sword.

He wore a bronze mask, and his helmet bore a tuft of feathers, brown and silver.

The men following him wore over their armor short blue capes adorned with badges. I recognized the badge, for the schturval showed in outline a picture of a sword piercing a heart. This schturval was the badge of the adherents of Spikatur Hunting Sword.

How, I wondered, with a sinking feeling of despair and a scalding feeling of anger, did that fit in with the ominous brown and silver feathers?

Everywhere naked men and women, boys and girls, were screaming and running, stumbling and falling. Like a stone dropped into a pool, the group of hard dark armored men created retreating ripples around them. The youth at their head ran eagerly on, fleeting over the marble toward Nedfar and Tyfar. . . .

"You must get away, Father!" yelled Tyfar. He grabbed the emperor's arm and started to drag him to the side. I knew well enough that Tyfar, himself, would not run. Nedfar struggled.

"I will not deign to flee from miserable assassins . . ."

"His helmet bore a tuft of feathers, brown and silver."

"We are naked and unarmed!"

Seg ignored the emperor and his son. He glanced at me, and I nodded, and so we moved a little ahead. How damned strange it was to be in this situation, one of the classic idiots'—only delights detested and dreaded by Kregans! On Kregen you never go anywhere—if you are a fighting sort of person—without your sword, or bow, spear or axe. But, taking the Baths of the Nine, you expect the proprietors of the establishment to provide guards who check everyone entering for weapons. An assassin must have problems concealing a deadly weapon on his naked body. No doubt the hired guards of The Sensil Paradise were sprawled in their own blood, puddled on the floor of their guardroom.

"Now if Turko were here," said Seg casually, flexing his muscles.

"He is a great Khamorro who can kill an armed warrior with his bare hands. He has taught you a few tricks, Seg, I know. But you'd better let me take the first fellow and his weapon."

The running youth was almost on us now, isolated as we were on the marble floor, the roof high above us, the suns light streaming mingled jade and ruby all about us. Tyfar joined us.

"Ty!" I said very quickly. I usually never called him Ty. "Let me."

"Nedfar is my father—"

The youth with his armor and sword and brown and silver feathers that were the colors of the evil cult of Lem the Silver Leem halted and stared at us. His mask glittered.

"Stand aside, unless you wish to die. The emperor is doomed for destruction."

Tyfar started to shout, "No, cramph. It is you—!"

I leaped.

The young fellow was not expecting a naked and unarmed man to leap on him, clad in armor as he was and wielding a sword. . . . He'd probably never been slave, and when you are slave you become accustomed to nakedness. Mind you, as I took his throat in my grip, I reflected that a bight of slave's chains might have come in handy to throttle him with. I choked him and took his sword away and threw it back. I wondered who would grab it first, Tyfar or Seg.

A single punch laid the young lad low. He was a boy and not a girl; his armor shape would not have accommodated a real girl, only, as Zolta might have said, "Those poor creatures who have not been blessed with the bounty of Zim." As I straightened up, Seg's fruity bellow reached me.

"Stux!"

I dropped lower and the flung spear whistled past above my head. No time to grab it—but as I glared with a malevolent fury toward the assassins the next stux hurtled in. I leaned to the side, took the stux from the air, reversed it, poised ready to hurl it back. Then I changed that plan, satisfying though it was, and tossed the throwing weapon back. With its small cross-quillons beneath the head the pig-sticker would make a handy weapon for a man who otherwise must rely on bare hands.

Seg had grabbed the sword, so Tyfar took the stux.

We did not wait for the other assassins to close in. We went hurtling down into them. And Tyfar screeched, "Hanitch! Hanitch!" I pushed any thoughts of displeasure out of my mind, dodged the sweep of a sword, kicked the fellow in the guts with a tingle all the way from toes to pelvis, grabbed another man's arm, pulled him, stuck two fingers up his nostrils, threw him away, seized the chap at his side who tried to stick me with his rapier. The rapier changed hands. It is a trick.

He staggered back, his hands clasped to his face, and the blood was shared between the rapier blade and his eye.

"Spikatur!" The yells of anger lifted as the rest charged on. "Spikatur Hunting Sword!"

More naked men crowded up to range alongside us and a flung stux punched through the chest of a young Nath Hindolf. He coughed and clutched the ugly shaft transfixing him, and staggered back. I felt the anger.

"Keep out of the way until we have weapons!" I yelled. I felt mad clear through. What a waste!

Kov Thrangulf, his belly thinned over the past months, muscled up, breathing in a snorting rasp.

"I'll take a weapon, aye, and break it over their heads, by Krun!"

I had to flick a spear away with the rapier and then we were at hand strokes with the rest of the assassins of Spikatur.

It was a right old ding-dong, to use a soldier's descriptive.

Seg's sword flashed and glittered, and then fouled with blood. Tyfar might not have been wielding an axe, but his stux went in and out like a trip-hammer, and each time he did not miss his target. Thrangulf snatched up a sword from the limp hand of a dead man and waded in, shouting blood-curdling promises. And, as he did so, so Princess Thefi and a gaggle of naked girls ran yelling from the side room pursued by more armed and armored stikitches. Although, to be fair, we did not call the assassins of Spikatur Hunting Sword stikitches in the same way we dubbed the professional assassins of Kregen as stikitches. The girls ran and we naked men tried to stay close around and so afford some protection.

Jaezila appeared, and she wielded a sword and so I knew she'd dealt with at least one of these ugly customers. As she plunged into the fight at our side, Tyfar went berserk.

"Ty!" shouted Jaezila. She plunged after Tyfar as he tore through the assassins before him.

Just how anyone might expect unarmed and naked men to hold armed and armored stikitches, let alone defeat them, passed understanding. All I had hoped to do was create enough time to enable our friends to escape. And, now, here they were, all yelling and hurling themselves into the fray!

Well, we fought. Some of us were killed. Just how many opponents we had, just how many adherents of Spikatur had broken in, we did not know. We fought them. It was not pretty. Although, in the aftermath, it must have been amusing, not to say ludicrous. As you may imagine.

Tyfar and Jaezila appeared as flashing limbs and flashing blades. Desperate with fear for my daughter, I went headlong into the bunch fronting her and Tyfar, and we sliced and lopped and hacked, occasionally as the opportunity offered time, thrusting.

This was all a desperate chancy business and entirely hateful to me. Jaezila and Tyfar, risking their necks like wild young bloods in a savage challenge of dare and counter-dare! Seg stood with me and we sliced and slashed and took cuts and felt the sting and the blood, and still we battled on.

The people who had fled screaming from the exercise hall flooded back, shrieking and moaning, tearing their hair. We heard their frenzied yells.

"The doors are locked! We cannot get out! We cannot escape!"

The interruption drew a small space about Seg and me, and in the instant I leaped for the glistening form of Jaezila—

glistening with the blood of others—Seg bellowed: "The rasts have worked this sweetly, Erthyr rot 'em!"

"Aye! We have to finish this."

Jaezila insisted on plunging on. Tyfar flung a quick look at me as I hauled on his arm, risking an instinctive blow.

"No, Jak, no! If Jaezila goes on—so do I!"

My rapier flicked up and swept a stux away. I bellowed.

"You young idiot! Get Jaezila to have sense!"

"She is too much like her father!"

By the Black Chunkrah! I pushed Tyfar aside and ran on, and the two black-clad men who tried to cut Jaezila down stared in shocked surprise first at the floor and then at the ceiling as they collapsed. I'd used the hilt, one-two and bang. Now I raced to stand before Jaezila.

Before I could speak, she said, most crossly, "Get out of the way, Father, do!"

"If you get yourself killed—"

We paused in our family conversation then as assassins strove to break past and get at Nedfar. Seg and Tyfar ran up. Tyfar had salvaged an axe. Now his true stature as a fighting man revealed itself in the short economical strokes of the axe, the way he parried and swept on, the trick he had of whirling and then, in a seeming check, sweeping on to slice a neck or a thigh. He was good, was Tyfar, very good with an axe.

The fight swirled about the great hall, and blood swirled in mocking echo in the water of the bathing pool.

Through the armor-clad ranks fronting us, and who would in the end overwhelm us with weight, I glimpsed a thin, a painfully thin, man whose eyesocket glittered with gems. He was urging his men on, although not himself running to the fore.

"Gochert!"

"So that's the fellow," said Seg. "I'll mark him."

His sword blurred and drove into the eye socket of the bulky man whose massive armor failed to save him from Seg's precise thrust. As he fell Seg stepped away and got his blade into a most painful spot through the next man's armor. But blood showed streaked across Seg's arms and chest, and the blood was his own. That blood was precious to me.

The brown and yellow feathers bristled around a Rapa's beak as he hurled his stux at Seg. I leaped, took the spear from midair with my left hand. I reversed it and hurled it back—

but not at the Rapa. He squeaked and ducked away. The stux flew for Gochert. It missed. No time to curse. Time only to cross blades with the next assassin and try to stay alive.

"We're done for, my old dom," Seg panted. "But we've had a good—" Here he parried, riposted, withdrew and the fellow who had tried to stick him—a hairy Brokelsh—dropped with only one good eye, "—time. I've no regrets. Not even Thelda, now."

"We're not done for yet, Seg!" I spoke sharply. Seg, from Erthyrdrin, possessed a fey capacity to seek the future only to fill himself with information no one needs. His wild and yet practical nature was in violent contrast. "We have to hold the rasts. Just hold 'em!"

"Oh, aye. We'll do that."

Then we were pressed back in a confused tangle of blades. Only a few arrows arched, and in that press the assassins would as likely slay their own. Not, from what we knew of Spikatur, that that would deter them. The most obvious explanation for the lack of bows and shafts was the simple difficulty of smuggling them in. As we fought and were forced back and saw good men go down I reflected that I'd smuggled a Lohvian longbow and shafts into places more difficult than The Sensil Paradise. My opinion of the adherents of Spikatur Hunting Sword, which had vacillated up and down, now fell even more. They were going against what I felt to be the best interests of all the people now, and they couldn't even do this job properly.

Tyfar and Jaezila, with Thrangulf and young Hando and the others, pressed back around Nedfar. He was most annoyed. We could all see that even with these assassins' lack of skill, we could not last forever.

The next fellow to tangle with me—he was a Moltingur whose horny shoulder carapace needed to be only lightly armored, and whose faceted eyes and tunnel mouth with its rows of needlelike teeth bore down to devour me—suddenly lifted himself up, tall. His eyes crossed. He looked suddenly perplexed. As he fell I saw the dint in the metal of his helmet flap over his temple. In all that uproar of clanging blades and screams and shouts and the stamp of feet, I heard the rattle of the leaden bullet across the marble.

The man before Tyfar took an arrow through his neck, above the corselet rim.

Then a shower of arrows arched and we saw the rows of men along the balconies shooting down, and slinging bullets. But I knew who had slung and loosed first. Barkindrar the Bullet and Nath the Shaft, for sure.

Jaezila's personal retainer, Kaldu, simply leaped from the balcony rail full into the armored ranks of the assassins of Spikatur.

"Kaldu!"

"Into them!" I bellowed and we all rushed forward, screeching like rampant devils. Which we were.

After that, all the people of Spikatur Hunting Sword wished to do was escape. We chased them to the doors, which now lay unlocked. We did not catch Gochert. He, no doubt, the moment he had seen the plan go wrong, had been the one to unlock the doors and the first to flee.

Panting, blood-splashed, elated, we stood on the steps brandishing our swords, and the good folk of Ruathytu gaped up at this crowd of madmen who paraded naked in the open before the steps of The Sensil Paradise. The air kissed our heated skins. The fellows couldn't stop talking. All I was thankful for was that Jaezila and Seg and Tyfar were safe.

Needlemen were summoned to tend the wounded, and then we went back to wash off all the muck and blood. At least, we were already in the perfect place to do that.

Chapter Seventeen

Delia Commands the Dance

Deb-Lu-Quienyin hurried into the little room we habitually used and, pushing his turban straight, said, "I have to inform you that the empress is coming."

I saw that he teased me, and that he shared my joy. Nedfar had no empress—or empress-to-be—since his wife had died he had not, as he put it, had the heart to marry again. So, since empresses do not flock in great numbers, even on Kregen, I could let a great fatuous smile spread all across my ugly old beakhead.

"Delia!"

"Aye, Jak, the Empress Delia, may all the gods and spirits have her in their keeping."

"When?"

He spread his hands. The mystical powers of Wizards of Loh were very great, very great indeed, and yet I fancy there are gaps and inconsistencies in what they can and cannot do in these fringes of the occult. "She speeds toward Ruathytu. There is wind and freshness and a tumult of sea far below."

"Well, I just hope she's all right—"

"Jak! Majister! I should rebuke you for a Lack of Trust." When Deb-Lu spoke in Capital Letters in these latter days he often did so out of amusement and self-mockery. He was now, in my estimation, just about the most powerful Wizard of Loh there was, certainly in Hamal and most probably in all Havilfar and Vallia combined.

When Seg heard the news he fired up and we started making plans for enjoying ourselves in the short interval between Nedfar's coronation and our departure to deal with King Telmont.

The strong parties of guards who had, perforce, to go everywhere with the notables irked us; but slackness on our part and a relaxation of watchfulness had resulted in the ugly affray at The Sensil Paradise. We could not afford to have Nedfar killed, in a cold political way, and in the warm concerns of friendship.

Coronations, tiresome though they are in reality, are generally regarded as occasions of the utmost importance.

If I say that Nedfar's coronation as Emperor of Hamal proved a splendid affair, filled with pomp and circumstance, impressive and magnificent with its civilized fashions superimposed on but not obliterating the savage Kregan customs underlying all ritual I should have to qualify that judgment. And, too, if I say that in all these grand ceremonies I remember mainly the presence of Delia and the holiday we spent together between the coronation and the battles, I think you will not misunderstand me. My Delia! She grew more beautiful, more lovely, more damned mischievous, every season, so it seemed to me. Her work for the Sisters of the Rose, that mysterious organization of women devoted to good works, the alleviation of suffering, the sword and the whip, kept her apart from me for long periods. Just as, to my sadness, the Star Lords threw me off about Kregen to labor for them. So Delia and I snatched what happiness we could when we could.

Drak came with his mother, leaving affairs in Vallia in capable hands, and we stood for Nedfar at his coronation, and were warmed by the plaudits of the multitude.

"At least the people seem to like their new emperor," said Drak, as we relaxed after the second day of the ceremonies.

"So they should," said Seg. "For a Hamalese he is a fine man, a fine man." He cocked his shrewd blue eye at me. "And I'll admit, just maybe, we may have misjudged the Hamalese in the past." Then he laughed, his reckless mocking laugh. "Crossbows and all!"

"You are incorrigible," said Delia, and we who knew her smiled at the way she thus mocked what the conventionally minded would take as a daring and clever remark. Subtle, is Delia, Empress of Vallia—as I know, by Zair!

During all the junketing we had to discuss the forthcoming campaign against Vad Garnath and King Telmont, and the processions and parades gave us an opportunity to take a look at the forces we might be able to muster. Many of the men had gone home, of course, as that is a sensible course of action when you lose a war. The old regiments were in disarray, many disappeared, many shrunken, many broken up. The Air Service was a parody of its once powerful force. I spent time with Nedfar telling him how we had liberated Vallia.

"And so it is true, Jak, that you employed no mercenaries? We heard the stories at the time, when our armies, commanded by the Hyr Notor, invaded and sought to subdue you, and we could scarcely credit them."

"Don't harp on all that, Nedfar. I know you set your face against Thyllis's crazy ambitions and had no part in the invasion of Vallia. You displease me by referring to what we want forgotten, and the blame you seek to take on yourself."

He smiled.

"We first met when I was a prince and you a slave, I think? And now—well, times change, times change. And the stories about Vallia throwing out the mercenaries are true."

"Yes. But you don't have the same luxury. You will have to employ what forces we of Vallia and Hyrklana have, what Djanduin can bring, and minimize their importance. For Hamal to rise again as a great power of integrity in the world it seems to me you have to do what we in Vallia did. You have to sort out your affairs yourself." I stared at him, willing him to understand. "I could have brought a great army of my Djangs to Vallia, and taken the rebels and misguided ensorcelled wights to pieces. But then, what would Vallians have said?"

"They would not have been overjoyed—"

"No. The same here. You must show the world that it was a Hamalian army that fought and beat the damned rebels of Vad Garnath and his puppet, Telmont."

"I see that. But the Hamalese army—"

"It can and will be done, Nedfar. There will be Vallian support, discreetly as may be, but there. Just in case."

"Now," I said, and I own my voice took a brisker, harsher note I detested, "I must talk about a matter far more important than battles and armies and wars."

"Oh?"

"Aye! Your son Tyfar and my daughter Jaezila—that is, Lela. Cannot you make them see sense?"

He relaxed, reaching out for the wine which stood upon a table whose legs were formed after the fashion of zhantils. A tall blue drape curtained each segment of the windows, the samphron oil lamps were lit, the study was snug and secure; Nedfar liked some of the things I could take pleasure in.

"Sense? I see what everyone sees. But Tyfar is—well, he

is a son to a father. I see your fine son Drak—does he bow
and scrape when you whistle?"

"Too damned right he does not!"

"So how can I—"

A knock on the door—discreet but unmistakably the knock
of the sentry's spear—heralded Delia. She looked radiant,
dressed in sheerest white, her brown hair highlighted by its
own gorgeous auburn tints, devoid of jewelry. She wore those
two small brooches, one beside the other, and a narrow jeweled
belt from which swung a long Vallian dagger. Her smiles filled
the room with more sunshine mustered by Zim and Genodras
together.

Nedfar rose at once.

"Lahal, majestrix."

"Lahal, majister—although, to be sure, you are halfway
between prince and majister this night, I suppose."

"True. And I would not be a half-emperor this night if Jak
here had not—"

Delia looked at me and then at Nedfar. I knew what she
was thinking.

"Nedfar," I said. "My name is Dray."

He nodded, a slow thoughtful nod. "Yes. But I am told that
few people are allowed the intimacy of calling you Dray, at
least, to your face."

"That is true. Although, for some reason, it is not that they
are not allowed as, that—well—they—"

"They shrivel with their effrontery when they look at you,
dear heart!" And Delia curled up, laughing.

Honestly, I really wished Nedfar were not there; and then,
to compound the mischief, other people joined us. The conversation centered on what to do about this silly situation of
lack of communication between Tyfar and Jaezila. I tended to
call Lela Jaezila all the time now, except in formal use. Seg
and Drak had their heads together, drinking and arguing, and
I knew they'd come up with nothing. Thefi was there, flushed
and pretty, and soon the crowd moved to the adjoining chamber, which was larger and had comfortable seats and tables
loaded with bottles. More people came in. This is the Kregan
way, of course. Kregen is a world of joiners, it seems. The
noise rose, and, wherever you listened, everyone was arguing
away about the best methods of lifting the shades from the

eyes of Tyfar and Jaezila and of organizing them and, in general, of seeing to it that their love had a happy ending.

The noise, although loud, formed itself around those two names, so often repeated—Jaezila and Tyfar.

The door opened and Prince Tyfar of Hamal and the Princess Majestrix of Vallia entered.

Silence.

Like fish frozen for centuries in the ice of the polar seas, the good folk who only heartbeats ago had been happily chattering away remained still and silent. The experience was edifying. And yet there was good-heartedness in it, and all the more reason for the flush of guilt to strike the people dumb, for every person there wished only well for these star-crossed lovers.

Delia said to me, "Dray! You will dance?"

As a question it would have brought a regiment of the toughest swods on Kregen to instant obedience.

"I will dance, Delia."

So, solemnly, to the strains of a discreet orchestra—a little band, really of only twenty instruments—we danced and very quickly—thankfully quickly, by Zair!—the room filled with dancers. Tyfar and Jaezila danced. And I wondered if they had any real inkling of that silence when they entered, the silence that Delia's imperious command had filled with the music for the dance.

Anybody might have called for the dance to cover that blank moment of general embarrassment. Oh, yes. But few, damn few if any, by Vox!, could have done it with the charm and skill and downright cunning of my Delia!

These social occasions gave us the opportunity to talk and assess the fighting men and women who would battle for the future of Hamal. And, as I saw it, for Paz, our half of Kregen.

Many of the men who would march out with us you have met in my narrative, and many more who have not been introduced, men I had come to know and respect and assess. Nath Karidge, who commanded Delia's personal bodyguard, the Empress's Devoted Life Guard, the EDLG, was now up-ranked to a zan-Chuktar, a rank of great height. He was a fine Beau-Sabreur, your light cavalryman, from his boots to his plume. Being a zorca man, he did not favor spurs. Deep in conversation with Mileon Ristemer, he became aware of the shadow at his shoulder, and looked up and saw me. Instantly his raffish smile broke out, to be followed by that drawing of himself up to attention.

"Easy, Nath. Your regiment is a credit to you. But I wanted to talk to Mileon here."

"Of course, majister. I will—"

"You will stay and give us the benefit of your advice."

He smiled and looked pleased. In the perfumed air of the chamber where the dancers gyrated and the orchestra scraped and blew away in melodious style, where feathers and fans fluttered and the naked arms of ladies wrapped about their partners' necks or waists as the lines of dancers closed and parted, more than one knot of grim fighting men spoke of the prospects of the morrow.

"Your plan to use the thomplods, Mileon. I have some experience with turiloths who are monstrous great beasts and can knock down a gate as quick as you like."

Mileon Ristemer nodded, absorbed at once. He was a pak-tun, son to old Nomile Ristemer, a banker of Vondium, who had come home to fight for his country. A stout, chunky man, he wore the silver mortilhead at his throat and was now a Jiktar commanding the newly formed fourth regiment of the Emperor's Yellow Jackets, the 4EYJ. He was due for promotion to ob-Chuktar any day now, continuing in command of the regiment. He had ideas, had Mileon Ristemer, on using gigantic beasts crowned with howdahs stuffed with fighting men to act as a species of land-born battleship in the midst of the fray.

"Turiloths?" he said. "The boloth of Turismond. Yes."

"We were besieged in Zandikar and we shot the damned turiloths with varters as they came in."

"Oh, yes, majister, I grant you that. But my thomplods will be in the battle line. It will be difficult to wheel up handy varters or catapults to shoot them there."

"Well, you will have your chance. You have arranged it all with Unmok the Nets?"

Now he laughed and Nath bellowed his enjoyment.

"Aye, majister. He is a little Och I have great respect for. He was talking about going into the wine-making business, but he agreed to contact his sources and supply thomplods. They are not easy to find, being unwieldy brutes at the best of times."

"So why not use boloths, or dermiflons, or—well, Kregen is stuffed with wonderful animals." Here I paused and frowned.

"And the idea of using them in men's battles does not please me."

It was left to Nath Karidge to say, "Agreed, majister. But if we ride zorcas into battle—and there is no animal on all of Kregen to equal a zorca—then anything else must follow."

This argument was fallacious, but it was convincing, for all that. We didn't like it; we liked less the thought of what might happen—what would happen—if we failed to use all our efforts to secure ourselves against our foes.

So, in the ending of that small conversation, one of many of a like nature, it was agreed the thomplods with their armored howdahs, their saxnikcals, or, sometimes, calsaxes, should be started off early toward the southeast. 4EYJ would go along. I forbore to inquire from Mileon, who was filled with enthusiasm, just what the swods of his Guard reigment had to say about acting as nursemaids to a bunch of plodding haystacks. The advantage gained by using thomplods was that they could upset many breeds of saddle animal. Once the thomplods got near enough to the enemy cavalry we trusted they would run off, banished from the battle.

"I have had many barrels of the mixture made up, majister. Our thomplods will have no smell to disturb our cavalry on the march."

Nath said, "And don't forget the water to wash off the mixture, Mileon, just before we start. And—" here he looked fierce "—and if your monsters panic our own cavalry I'll not answer for your fate."

"Well, your zorca regiment will be safe."

"So will Telmont's zorca cavalry."

"So that means," I said, "you have a fine target, Nath."

Because this was Kregen, where customs differ country by country and race by race, it was perfectly proper and natural for the dancing to stop and the singing to begin, which is a civilized occurrence in general favor.

We sang the old songs, and new ones composed in honor of Nedfar and also, I was pleased to note, the alliances that were so new and were to be tested in battle. In the days of Thyllis the Hamalese had tended to the mournful kind of song, at least to the ears of a Vallian. Now we sang songs of greater cheer, and old favorites like "When the Havilthytus Runs Red" were not to be heard. Which was a Good Thing. We sang "When the Fluttrell Flirts His Wing" and "Nine Times She

Chose a Ring." We did not, I may say, in this company sing "Sogandar the Upright and the Sylvie" or "The Maid with the Single Veil."

We Vallians gave them "The Swifter with the Kink," which was perhaps not as politic as might have been desired, since Hamal had no seagoing navy to talk of, and Vallia's galleons were the finest—barring those of the Shanks—afloat, so that we could afford to sing a song poking fun at a swifter, a fast, not very seaworthy Kregan galleass. The evening had grown into an Occasion. We all faced daunting perils in the future and so seized the fleeting opportunity to enjoy ourselves while we could. Delia leaned across to me as we stood by a linen-covered table where the bottles shone and goblets and glasses were filled and refilled. When Delia wishes to show a little style in our self-mocking way, she uses a fan. Now she flicked the fan open to conceal the lower half of her face. Her eyes sparked up explosions in me. Those brown eyes in which I can drown forever. . . . I put down my glass.

Chamberlains appeared and I gave them a look, saying, "We are leaving. No fuss, for the sake of Havil the Green." They retired, bowing, understanding, perhaps; perhaps understanding only that the ways of the high ones of Vallia were vastly different from those they were used to in Hamal.

So Delia and I left the shindig and I had no feelings of being an old fogey traipsing off to bed before the fun had finished. We had battles and campaigns to fight and then would be the time to sing and dance, hoping we would live through the conflicts. Someone started singing "She Kissed the Mortilhead," which tells of a princess who ran away from her palace for love of a paktun. Delia smiled as we left. "That, I think," she said, "will be Seg."

This evening the guard detail on the suite of apartments given over to our use in the Hammabi el Lamma, the Alshyss Tower, was from 1ESW. They had flown in with Drak. Of the juruk I knew every jurukker, every guardsman in the Guard was a comrade. We were jocular, jurukkers and Delia and I. I went in and closed the door. I shut the door and bolted it. Swords in hand, Delia and I went around the rooms. We were on Kregen and in a magnificent palace, and so this was a sensible precaution.

Then we could shut out the whole damned world altogether.

Chapter Eighteen

Mutiny

Mud.

The Land of Shining Mud was—muddy.

Seg picked off splotches of dried mud from his uniform and made a face.

"He's heading for the higher ground away to the west. I've kept the scouts after him. But he still outnumbers us, and—"

"Our fellows will be here in time, Seg."

"Oh, aye." Seg looked around the camp, which appeared to be slipping beneath the mud, and his orderly—Vando the Limp—brought him up a stoup of ale which Seg knocked back in a swallow. "Oh, aye," he said, wiping his mouth. "But if we slip up and Garnath catches us before we're ready—we're for the Ice Floes of Sicce, my old dom."

"We've run rings around him so far."

"H'umph! Well, that's only because you're—" He stopped, blew his nose, made a face and then hauled his longbow forward to look critically at it. "Damn weather."

Nedfar walked across from a campfire, holding a leg of a chicken and gnawing into the meat. "Does the rast still run, kov?"

"Aye, majister. We have him bluffed. He still thinks we outnumber him."

"I wish our forces would arrive." Nedfar swallowed. "We can't go on deceiving Garnath forever. I remember him as a slippery customer, and he has this Havil-forsaken rast the Kataki Strom to advise him, also."

I said, "I wonder what King Telmont is doing in all this?"

"Playing with his women, most likely. He is a cipher."

"He's after your crown," said Seg.

The days passed as what became known as the Campaign of Mud progressed. We had rushed forces into the southeast only to discover that Telmont's recruiting drive had proved phenomenally successful. He had imported thousands of mercenaries. He had drummed up levies—who would probably run away the moment the first shafts rose—and although weak in the air, as were we, now possessed a hardened core to his army and a froth of units of dubious value. The hardened core was large and comfortable.

Deb-Lu had advised me that he felt sure Garnath and Strom Rosil the Kataki had laid their hands on Phu-Si-Yantong's treasure and were using it to hire their clouds of paktuns.

We just had to keep the enemy in play until our army came up.

I heard that Telmont had with him two Air Service Kapts I knew, hard professional warriors who commanded armies, Vad Homath and Kov Naghan. Wounded, they were now recovered. They would prove formidable adversaries, and I could wish they had forgone what they considered their loyalty to their country and given that loyalty and their expertise to Nedfar, who was now their emperor and unacknowledged by both of them.

"He has a great crowd of Katakis with him," said Seg, bending and poking up the fire. "And those damned Jibr-farils have organized themselves into regiments. Not much like Whiptails."

"The Katakis have stepped forward into the world of late," said Nedfar. "As slavers they have—" He looked at me, and said, "Had their uses. But no one likes a Whiptail."

"He has swarth cavalry—"

"Mileon's thomplods should stink them off."

"If Erthyr wills it," said Seg, quite calmly.

Nedfar said, "I do not wish to sound petty or resentful but I find it exceedingly strange that of our few forces here the bulk are Vallians, with Hyrklese and Djangs, and my Hamalese conspicuous by their absence."

"Oh, come on, Nedfar! Your lads are getting here just as fast as they can!"

"Well, the quicker the better."

"We're running rings around Garnath and we'll continue to do so." I made no bones about my views. "I will not throw good men away. We attack when we are sure of beating him. Not before."

So the days passed in the campaign; we marched long hours, camping and marching again, drawing a baffling web about Garnath. There were cavalry confrontations and contests, and occasionally the flyers clashed. The days stretched. The configuration of the country here in the southeast corner of Hamal was of importance to our maneuvers. Everything has a name, of course, but I will not weary you with too detailed a description. The River Os, He of the Commendable Countenance, ran eastward into the sea, dividing into two branches to enclose Ifilion. If there was magic in Ifilion, as was rumored, maybe that was the cause of their independence. To the south of the river, the Dawn Lands stretched and the countries on the line of the river were mostly cowed by memories of the iron legions of Hamal. To the north of Ifilion the land lifted enough so that good grasslands blew under the suns. Every time I thought of that land I thought of Chido, who was the Vad of Eurys there. He knew me only as Hamun ham Farthytu, the Amak of Paline Valley, and he and Rees represented a great deal of comradeship to me in dark days, and formed a void in my present life when I had not seen them again. Well, I would. That I promised myself.

One thing was certain: Vad Garnath would raise no troops in Eurys, for Garnath was a deadly enemy to Rees, Trylon of the Golden Wind, and thence to Chido and to me.

In what I made appear casual conversation I'd discovered that Chido, who had risen to the rank of Chuktar and command out in the west of Hamal, was known to Tyfar, who spoke well of him. "Although Chido ham Thafey retired from the army after—after our defeat. He secluded himself on his estates in Eurys."

"I knew his father, the old vad," said Nedfar. "An upright man. I could hope that the new Vad Chido will join me."

Because we were near Eurys, Chido's name cropping up was a natural occurrence; we all felt he would have to declare his allegiance soon. I could feel for him, as for so many others. The choice was agonizingly difficult.

By maneuvering and marching and counter marching we held off Garnath's two major attempts to launch attacks. We trended more to the east, to draw him away from the higher ground in the west. Tyfar looked concerned as we stood in a mud paddy watching the troops march past.

"If we get our backs to He of the Commendable Countenance and our flank to the sea, Jak—and—"

"Garnath will decide he has us trapped, yes."

"And?"

"Oh, Dray's got it all worked out, Tyfar," said Seg.

"I hope it is worked out. We draw Garnath on, as we have been doing, never allowing him to hit us. Every day our army marches closer. When it is in a position to strike, we stop and Garnath lunges, and—"

"And we catch him between two horns!"

"Well, we hope so. It will take cunning deployment."

"We'll be the anvil, and the army with those thumping great thomplods will be the sledgehammer."

"That is the theory. Had we attempted to draw him further to the west, he would never have followed. He must know an army marches. So we must dazzle him at the end, when we strike."

"Dazzle him! We'll blind the cramph!"

And then I nearly had a mutiny on my hands. A mutiny, moveover, in the crack regiment, the First Regiment of the Emperor's Sword Watch. The lads of 1ESW really threatened to cut up rough. Many of them have been introduced into my narrative and, sadly, many had died. New faces replaced the old. Now there was a spot of bother in Vallia—what that spot of bother was will become apparent later on in my narrative— and Drak had to return. I had told 1ESW that they should serve and guard Drak, as the future emperor. Now they threatened mutiny, saying, in effect, "We are your Juruk and we formed ourselves to guard you, much though we love your son Drak."

I remonstrated with them, drawn up in their ranks outside the tent lines.

They said, "There is a battle coming on. D'you think we will go tamely back and leave you?"

Drak cut that knot by saying he would leave 1ESW. Then he said, "And, father, I shall have to have a bodyguard, I suppose, like Jaidur and most kings and emperors. Yes?"

"Yes. Go and form one and choose good men. I own I shall be glad to have 1ESW back. There is no other unit quite like them."

"I know!"

Then I gave him the same advice I'd given his brother Jaidur when he'd married Lildra and become King of Hyrklana. "Do

not form just one bodyguard. Have at least two and do not
appoint a single Captain of the Guard. You are the personal
commander over all the units of your Juruk."

"I will do as you say."

As we stood to wave the remberees, I said to Drak, sternly,
"And accustom yourself to the idea of being the Emperor of
Vallia."

His protests I would not listen to. He flew off. And his face
was as black as the cloak of Notor Zan.

By Zair! If I was to go off adventuring over Kregen I wanted
the weight of Vallia, at the least, off my mind. I had the shrewd
suspicion that I would not be able thus easily to shuffle off
being the King of Djanduin. Kytun and Ortyg, I felt sure,
would make me see the error of my ways. As for being the
Lord of Strombor—well, I was, and would remain so for as
long as Zair and Opaz willed. Gloag saw to things for me in
Strombor. And—my wild clansmen of Segesthes! Their loyalty could be severed only by death.

Nath Karidge wheeled up, saluting, saying, "Scouts report
that Garnath is following us up with forced marches. Two in
the last three days."

"Ha!" I said as we turned away from watching Drak's voller
vanish into the clouds. "So he's had word from his scouts that
our army approaches his rear! Good! Now we'll play the rast!"

Nath said, "The Kataki Strom has had experience fighting
us. We beat him in Vallia. He will know of the Phalanx."

"He'll know. But will Garnath listen?"

"I'd have thought all Hamalese would know what a Vallian
Phalanx has done to their iron legions."

"Only in the right circumstances. I look forward to seeing
Nath Nazabhan—Nath na Kochwold, of course—and his
brumbytes in the phalanxes."

"They march well. The war ruined the Air Services, more's
the pity—"

"Not so, Nath, not so. For don't forget, Hamal had the most
powerful Air Service of Havilfar. No, we're better off marching
on our own feet."

"Better yet riding a zorca."

"I won't argue that."

They were gathering, gathering here in this corner of Hamal,
the choicest fighting men of Vallia. And the Djangs were here,
as well as not inconsiderable contingents from Hyrklana. Only

token forces marched with us from the Dawn Lands. That wild patchwork quilt of a land demanded great labor for the future. And, in all this, we had to make it seem the Hamalese rid themselves of the mercenaries who fought under the banner of a king who sought to make himself emperor, aided by as miserable a bunch of cutthroat tapos as ever remained unhanged.

Our little force maintained good order and discipline, and we had only two cases which ended with the culprits hanged. There were atrocity stories to be gathered from the huddled villages in the mud, stories of what King Telmont's army had done as they marched through. I thought of Homis Creek, and shook my head, and we did what we could to assist those in trouble.

On the maps the forces drew together as we marched the pins across the colored outlines. Gradually the place where a suitable confrontation might take place became clearer, narrowing down to a relatively mud-free area slightly higher than the rest of the country. It was near the coast, with Eurys to the north, and the river gratifyingly far enough away. Our provisions held out well, and logistics worked wonders. Also, two things operated to assist us here: the army coming down from the north and west carried plentiful supplies, and our flying services brought in fresh food and provender.

There was a well near the place we selected as the site for the battle, known as Plasto's Well. Some of the men began to talk in terms of the great victory we would win at the Battle of Plasto's Well.

Just how decisions reached in conference that should have been secret had circulated among the troops presented a problem I refused to worry about; this little force of picked men were to be trusted to fight and to know when to keep silent. Or so I believed, and by this time any newcomer spy would have stuck out like a neemu among a pack of werstings.

Among the forces arrayed against us was, I discovered, Horgil Hunderd, Trylon of Deep Valley, who, having lost his first three regiments of paktuns had raised three more. We promised ourselves that that unpleasant character would lose the new three.

Toward the end of that month of the Maiden with the Many Smiles we were plagued with thunderstorms. The rain fell down solidly. The very mud itself danced.

In this filthy weather we were reluctant to send the Djang aerial cavalry off on patrol. Our small force of vollers, many of them converted civil craft, performed well. The Suns of Scorpio remained veiled in heavy cloud. And it was wet.

Also, the flying sailing ships, Hamalian famblehoys and Vallian vorlcas alike, were grounded.

For a time we had to pull in our belts. When the weather cleared and the suns shone and the land steamed, the first reports indicated that Garnath had proved a clever and capable commander. During the worst of the weather he had marched his army around us to reach northward, away from the river, and so slip out from between the jaws of our two forces.

"The rast is a cramph and a kleesh," said Seg. "But you have to admire that little maneuver."

"We will still have him, Seg. If you look at the map—here—you will see how Chido's estates extend like a funnel into these low hills. And the sea is there. Garnath will be heavily slowed down if he crosses into Chido's land."

Seg looked at me. He had never met Chido. "You talk as though—as though you know this Vad of Eurys."

I had to ignore the offered opening and so went on to talk of our plans and the way we would turn Garnath's own cunning and expertise to our own advantage. We followed up and a few supplies came in. Feeding an army and bringing up enough provender for the animals are the keys to success in campaigns. The land over which Garnath marched lay stripped and barren, desolate, after he had passed. We found piles of bones, mostly vosk together with the notorious vosk skulls, for the folk hereabouts produced a variety of vosk which provided succulent sweet meat of first-class quality. As the swods said, it was all the damn mud.

Very few people did not like crisp vosk rashers, or a prime side of vosk cooked in the Kregan way. Our own rations were on the frugal side and included vast amounts of mergem, that all-purpose nourishment, and capital though mergem is and invaluable to a quartermaster supplying an army on campaign, mergem is still mergem, and prime vosk is a world apart. We had plentiful supplies of palines, though, so that kept the swods happy.

The promised Battle of Plasto's Well would now not take place.

We maneuvered and marched and, one day when the earth

showed more green growing things than sheets of shining mud,
we gathered for an O group around Nedfar's tent. Our Kapts
and Chuktars attended. Infantry, cavalry, artillery and air, we
stood in all manner of gorgeous uniforms—mostly tattered
now and many faded and bedraggled—and listened as Nedfar
expounded the final plan. For, on the morrow, we had Garnath.
On the morrow, in that finger of Chido's land between the
hills, we would crunch Garnath and his army between our two
forces. It was now inevitable and, I guessed, in the enemy
camp they would see the inevitableness of it, and gird themselves for the fray.

"Tomorrow we shall smash Vad Garnath and his puppet,
King Telmont," said Nedfar. "Through the guidance afforded
us from Havil and Opaz, and also our Vallian and Djang and
Hyrklese allies, Hamal will on the morrow once more lift up
her head in pride. For we shall eradicate the blot upon our
honor."

There was more.

It all boiled down to the simple and gratifying fact; on the
morrow Garnath would get his come-uppance.

On the morrow, then, our army marched out toward battle.
Trapped in the finger of land, Garnath drew his forces up ready
to face us, and drew up more to face to his rear where our
other army, arrived and rested, deployed. This was going to
be a day remembered in the annals of Hamal, and sung and
storied until the Ice Floes of Sicce melted.

In our Earth's Renaissance period when a mercenary army
was trapped like Garnath's army, they often would not bother
to fight. The outcome was certain. The chiefs would gather
and talk terms. It was civilized. Maybe. Maybe nations in arms
and the citizen levy, in changing all that, changed man's out-
look on war for the good, despite the horrors it brought in
train.

Once again the Kapts and the Chuktars gathered around
Nedfar for a few final words before we took up our positions
with our forces. For battle, the uniforms that had been carefully
preserved were brought out and donned, so that the fighting
men blazed with gold, bullion and lace, sparkled with silver,
and the colors patterned the field with fire. Very splendid they
all looked. As for myself, I had elected to wear the brave old
scarlet, with a sensible amount of armor, and I'd hung the

essential armory of a Kregan warrior about me. No man relishes the idea of having his sword snap in the heat of battle—and not another instantly ready to hand. Our forces stood forth arrayed beneath their banners.*

A voller flew in fast and low and she was not one of ours. I was not concerned that any last-minute attempt at assassination could succeed. Long before the voller reached shooting distance she was surrounded by flutduins bearing Djangs of exceeding toughness and escorted to earth. Very shortly thereafter the guards brought the occupants of the airboat in for our inspection.

The sweet scent of blossoms drifted in the air, most refreshing after the eternal stink of mud. The sky smiled with air and suns shine. And we stood in a glittering group of power and magnificence, with our army ranked ready for battle.

The guards marched up in two ranks, spears all slanted, and wheeled out flanking the newcomers. These two stood, staring at us and then at Nedfar, conspicuous in the center. These two stood hardly, firmly, not showing defiance but proudly as men in their own right, and, too, quite clearly men in the devil of a hurry. Some measure of their quality must be gained in that they had persuaded the guard to let them in and to see the emperor in these finals moments before we attacked.

"I recognize you as Prince Nedfar, now the emperor," said Rees, his glorious golden lion-man's face intense with his purpose. "We give you the Lahal. There is a matter of the utmost importance—"

"Gently," said Nedfar. "You presume—"

"There's no time to be gentle," said Chido, dear chinless Chido, now clad as a soldier, looking hardened and mature. But he still could not pronounce his R's and they all came out as W's. "The Twylon Wees and I must tell you—"

"You are the Vad of Eurys," said Tyfar. "You have come to fight at our side? To swear allegiance to the emperor?"

"Listen, you fambly!" bellowed Rees in his old numim roar.

---

*Here Prescot lovingly details all the regiments of the armies, with their commanders and insignie and strengths and equipments. Vollers, saddle-flyers, cavalry and artillery are listed. Many men feature in the muster rolls. They make fascinating reading.

—A.B.A

"The Shanks! There's a whole damn army of the rasts landed on the coast and murdering and pillaging their way inland. This is no raid! They've invaded. And they're here to stay—unless we stop them right now!"

Chapter Nineteen

"We must all wally wound!"

Down in the fingerlike valley the dark masses of Garnath's troops sparkled with light as the suns struck sword and spear, reflected back from helmet and cuirass. In only a few murs the aerial cavalry would clash. Soon the rolling columns of our forces would deploy into line and go rushing down on Garnath and sweep him away to destruction.

Nedfar's face resembled a face carved from marble to stand mute for ever above a silent tomb.

"Shanks!" bellowed Rees. He looked just the same, hot, quick, enormously vital, a man among men, and a good comrade. Maybe his misfortunes had not weighed him down as much as I had feared. The idea that Rees and Chido would not recognize Hamun ham Farthytu was one I could not entertain seriously. Even after all this lapse of time. So I looked like Dray Prescot, with all the foolishness of Hamun's face fled, and my own craggy old beakhead serving me in the office of a face.

Nedfar glanced at me, for I had—with an instinct I had failed to quell—drawn back a fraction. The instinct was not one of flight, I believe, as one of reluctance to jeopardize the character of Hamun. And, also, to let the world see that the Emperor of Hamal and not of Vallia commanded here.

"Dray?"

"There is only one thing we can do." As I spoke I was aware of the eyes of Rees and Chido. Lion-man's eyes, and apim eyes, they sized me up. Yes, the thoughts behind those eyes seemed to be saying, yes, you may be the Emperor of Vallia; but we have spent a large part of our lives fighting your friends. Why should we trust you now?

163

I spoke. I used the didactic, proclaiming style, forceful, rather pompously foolish to me.

"As for Vallia, we will fight Shanks whenever and wherever they may be found."

"Aye!" roared my officers, clustered to the side of the Hamalese.

"And for Djanduin, likewise, I pledge ourselves."

Now the Djangs bellowed.

"And I speak for Hyrklana," shouted Hardur Mortiljid, Trylon of Llanikar. That massive man in full armor and with his arsenal of weapons towered impressively. "We slay Shanks!"

Now the Hyrklese raised their cheer.

Every eye fastened on Nedfar.

Every eye but mine.

I looked at Tyfar.

The choice here was between advantage and honor, between the life and the death of the spirit. The alternatives were clear cut and unambiguous. Tyfar stood poised, as though ready to spring into instant action. I thought I knew him, from the moment down the Moder he had used his intelligence to work out the riddle and his courage to pull the chain that might kill him. I thought Jaezila would not choose amiss.

One of Nedfar's pallans, a man of the utmost honesty, a man who had exhibited extreme loyalty in difficult times, Strom Nevius, leaned forward toward Nedfar. Nevius had a nervous tic about his face, and a bad skin; but he was a man valued in our camp.

"Majister, to do as these people ask is to let King Telmont slip away. Who knows if another chance like this will occur again? And the Shanks can be dealt with later."

Rees heard.

"They are many. They came in a vast fleet. Once they are established you may never dislodge them. And they eat the heart out of Vad Chido's lands!"

Tyfar came to life.

"We must send word to King Telmont. He will direct his army to march with us against our common enemy."

"Garnath will never let him!" shouted someone from the other side of Nedfar.

"We are all Hamalese!" shouted someone else.

"Let us march on our own account!"

"The Shanks will overpower us!"

"Will you take the message?" said Nedfar, and the hulla-baloo died as the emperor spoke. "Trylon Rees, will you take our imperial message to Vad Garnath? Tell him we march to fight the Shanks and invite him to march at our side."

Chido let out a yell.

"That is not possible—"

"Wait, wait, Chido," rumbled Rees. His golden whiskers blazed.

Tyfar said, "What is the problem? We are all committed here to our commands."

"I understand that." Rees stared at us, at our glittering po-pinjay show. His armor was plain and workmanlike. "You are far too committed to leave your commands."

It was perfectly clear that these people here did not know the situation between Garnath and Rees. Garnath had sent assassins and they had slain Rees's eldest son. The two men must have kept apart in the intervening years. The famous laws of Hamal, knowing nothing of Garnath's actions, would un-hesitatingly condemn Rees if he took the law into his own hands. And he was not a man for assassins.

I said, "This fellow Garnath does not know me. I shall go down and tell him where his duty lies. Aye, and old Hot and Cold, too."

Tyfar said, "Jak! He'll have you killed—"

"You cannot go, Dray," said Nedfar. "I forbid it."

Seg laughed.

"Let the Emperor of Vallia go, if he wills!" shouted up Rees. "Let the Vallians do some good in the world for a change."

"We must all wally wound!" That was Chido, spluttering as of old, and yet hard now, bitter with what the years had done to his country and to Rees. Obviously, Chido had taken Rees in and cared for him after the debacle. We three had been comrades. Rather, these two and Hamun had been comrades.

"I'm going, anyway," I said.

With that I broke away from the splendid group around Nedfar and stalked across to my zorca, old Snuffle-nose, a beautiful gray, whom I had not intended to ride in the battle. Generals on white horses, despite the superstitions regarding generals on black horses, tend to get shot at.

Tyfar started, "Jak!" Then, knowing me, he swung on his

father and the assembled Kapts. "Get the army started! We
march for the coast. Vad Chido! You will guide us."

"Right willingly, prince," sang out Chido.

He and Rees stared after me, for I turned back to see if the
folk back there had made up their minds. They had, for messengers sped off to the various banners to carry the new orders.
I swung up on Snuffle-nose and shook the reins.

I felt absolutely no surprise to see Seg riding up. There was
no need for him to say anything. We rode out before the army,
to the edge of the hill, in silence.

Then Seg said, "Your Sword Watch and your Yellow Jackets
will follow. You know that."

"When you are Emperor of Pandahem, Seg, you'll have
your own damn worries about bodyguards. I can't wait for the
day."

"By the Veiled Froyvil, my old dom! I haven't made up
my mind yet."

"I'm not forcing you. I just happen to know it's a job you
can do."

With the accompaniment of the clip-clop of the zorca's
hooves, the creak of leather and jingle of harness, we rode
slowly down the hill, talking about anything save the business
we were engaged in.

"You've really got it in for me, haven't you? Trying to
make me an emperor."

"Ever since the day I took a forkful of dungy straw."

"Ha!"

It would be absolutely superfluous to point out that as we
rode down we were each perfectly prepared to give our lives
for the other. . . .

"They're moving about down there, Dray."

"Like the proverbial ant's nest stirred by a stick."

The masses of infantry looked like blocks of multicolored
glitter. Cavalry rode out along the wings. The artillery, mainly
varters with a few catapults, were lined up ready to swathe in
a sleeting discharge of stones and bolts. As archery and ballistae
do not fire, but loose or shoot, one cannot really speak of
firepower in reference to a Kregan army. The Kregish word
is dustrectium. Their dustrectium down there was formidable.
We rode on. Every now and then Seg turned in the saddle to
glance back. Presently he grunted, and dropped back into the
saddle, looking ahead.

"ESW is moving."

"Then EYJ will be with them."

"Aye. Their rivalry is a bracing experience."

"And just what is that rast Garnath thinking, watching two lone riders come trotting down? We have no flag of truce."

"He's cunning enough to hear what we have to say."

"As to that, Seg, you are right. He knows he is trapped. He'll listen to us."

Seg looked back. "ESW and EYJ are following us, and are picking up speed. I must say they look a frightening bunch."

No need for me to look back. I could imagine what the regiments of my guard looked like, a dark solid mass of zorcamen with a froth of steel, proud with banners, riding knee to knee, or riding knee tucked behind knee in the nik-vove regiments.

Seg said, "Garnath's army will think we're attacking them. For sure."

"You're right, Seg." I patted Snuffle-nose's neck. His spiral single horn cut the air as he nodded. "That could be inconvenient."

"Inconvenient! It could get us both killed."

"You're right, Seg. Well, you'll just have to ride back and stop them. Explain the situation. You carry the weight of authority, and you can quote what I'll do to the lads if they don't obey orders."

Seg's furious bellow made me laugh out loud.

"You cunning, deceiving devil! You planned this! That's why you didn't send word for the Sword Watch and the Yellow Jackets to stand fast!"

"It crossed my mind."

Seg was fuming. "And EDLG are in it, now. You can't expect a fellow like Nath Karidge not to ride after his emperor, can you?"

"Well—my old dom—you ride back and stop 'em."

"Dray, Dray! If we get out of this I'll—"

I nudged Snuffle-nose into a canter. As we went off down the hill I bellowed back at Seg. "I'll see you as soon as Garnath and Telmont move toward the coast. We have Shanks to deal with."

Seg's answer was partially muffled in the stamp of zorca hooves. But words like cunning and devious and ungrateful figured prominently. But he saw that if we didn't stop the

Guard, the enemy would shoot first and not bother to ask questions.

The moment two squadrons of zorcamen rode out from the enemy ranks I knew Seg had stopped the Guard. No doubt the air was a livid blue above the ranks of my lads. The oncoming zorcamen rode with weapons ready. They closed up about me and I shouted: "King Telmont and Vad Garnath! I must speak with them—now!"

A fellow with the insignia of a Jiktar started to bellow his authority, and I cut him to the quick with a few words. I finished: "There is no time to waste, dom. Shanks. D'you understand? *Shanks!*"

The dread name worked like a passport and I was surrounded and we rode rapidly for the slight eminence on the valley floor where Garnath had set up his headquarters.

King Telmont was just as I had seen him last, a figure to be stared at in all its imposing majesty and then forgotten as the *eminence grise*, this Garnath, imposed his will. He was much as I remembered him, and I forced all that old unhappy history out of my head. If the Shanks established a foothold in Havilfar they would spread out and subdue everyone. This was all too clear.

Garnath ham Hestan, Vad of Middle Nalem, ought to have answered for his crimes seasons ago; that he had not I had to attribute to the protection afforded him by Phu-Si-Yantong's sorcerous powers. Well, that particular Wizard of Loh was now dead. It remained to be seen how long Garnath would remain alive.

The odd thing was—difficult though it had been for me to keep silence with Rees and Chido, instead of doing as I longed to do and roar up to them, bellowing greetings, to keep silence before this yetch Garnath was even more difficult. I wanted to let him know who I was, and tell him a few home truths.

That I'd be fighting for my life in the instant thereafter would have been merely a normal occurrence.

Instead, I stared at him with all the powerful look that emperors can bring to bear.

He wore a gilded armor that ill became him. His short military cape was of green and blue; but he wore a sash of brown and silver, the colors of Lem the Silver Leem, that foul cult that many decent men were pledged to exterminate. His thick face shone with sweat trapped in the creases. His dark combed hair glittered with brilliants. His fingers were not as white, perhaps, as once they had been; but now every finger wore a jeweled ring. He looked at once bloated, ridiculous and obscene.

I said, "Shanks. We must march—"

He cut me off. His face congested.

"Yetch! You speak with propriety to me! Who are you?"

"You may call me Jak the Nose."

He might imagine this referred to my own beak of a nose; in fact it was an oblique reference to the Bladesman's duel we had fought, when Garnath had drugged me and I'd managed to summon the Disciplines of the Krozairs of Zy to my aid, and so claim first blood, and force his yetch to grovel on his nose. That, of course, was before I'd encountered Mefto the Kazzur. . . .

"Then, Jak the Nose, you stand in peril of your life."

"As do you of yours. You know you are trapped. Your army is doomed. The Emperor of Hamal offers you the chance of fighting for your country against Shanks—"

"I am the Emperor of Hamal!" said Telmont, starting forward.

"I crave your silence for a moment, king." Garnath spoke without looking at Telmont, his gaze fastened on me. He spoke almost unthinkingly, like one accustomed to rote words that achieve a desired end.

"Yes, but Shanks—"

"Majister!"

Telmont turned away, brilliant of color, smothered in jewels and feathers and fur trimmings, blinding of aspect in the lights of the suns. I quelled an instinctive feeling of pity for him. Time allowed thought for only one aim.

"We must move against the Shanks, all of us, your army, my—the emperor's—army." I stared hard at Garnath, knowing he would never remember Hamun ham Farthytu in connection with this unpleasant Jak the Nose. "You must know what the Shanks will do."

Telmont huffed up to speak again, but Garnath waved a hand, and Telmont subsided.

"Why should I throw away what we have fought for? Your army is quitting the field. Look!"

A single glance back up the hillside showed the blocks of

color thinning and elongating as the regiments formed columns and marched away over the brow of the hill.

"Aye! They march to fight the Leem-Lovers! Will you?"

"Hamal lies in my grasp now. In King Telmont's grasp who is, or will soon be, emperor."

Among the gilded retinue surrounding the chiefs on this slight eminence of the valley floor stood many Katakis. Ranked in the background, waiting, the lines of the King's Ironfists showed the dull gleam of iron and the wink of steel. They would prove first-class opponents. And, looking about, one hand holding Snuffle-nose's reins, I saw no sign of Strom Rosil, the Kataki Strom. No doubt he was with a part of the army, his skills as a soldier being used to the full, for he had been promoted from Chuktar to Kapt, and now was no longer the Chuktar Strom but the Kapt Strom. The damned Kataki Strom, rast of a Whiptail, was the better description.

Despicable of character and unpleasant of personality though Vad Garnath was acknowledged to be, it still seemed to me impossible for a Hamalese not to answer the call to defend his country against the raiding Schtarkins, the Shants or Shanks. Even though Garnath professed in secret the cult of Lem the Silver Leem, still I could not see him refusing to answer his call.

"Will you give the order to march, vad? Now!"

"The Shanks have drawn both your armies off and given me the chance to strike. How can I refuse what the gods proffer?"

"You are a dead man—"

He preened, the sweat thick in the creases on his face.

"I have been reported dead more than once. And the reports have been believed. But here I am, and ready to march—on Ruathytu!"

I said, "I do not think even your Whiptails would obey that order now."

A harsh-faced Chulik, whose yellow-ribboned pigtail was wound around his shaven head ready for him to don his helmet, spoke up. His tusks, which indented the corners of his thin lips, were banded in gold and silver, and studded with gems. He said, "With your permission to speak, Vad Garnath. My men will fight Shanks."

They'd been raided, had these mercenary Chuliks, in their own homelands. Shanks didn't share the usual awe of Chuliks.

There were no Pachaks I could see among those surrounding Garnath and Telmont. A group of Khibil officers, foxy faces alert, indicated their willingness to fight Shanks. A Rapa Chuktar riffled his feathers, and his beaked face betrayed a vulturine appetite for blood as he promised to rip out the tripes of any Shanks that came the way of his regiments.

Garnath's conquested face swung from man to man, and his jaw stuck out in a fashion I saw with wonder was more petulant than grim. The situation was slipping away from him, and he could not grasp that.

A ferret-faced, gimlet-eyed Lliptoh wearing mesh armor and many feathers put one hand to a sword hilt. "As they say in the Risslaca Hork in Balintol, where I come from: 'This is the day of the Seeking After Truth.' I am a hyr-paktun and I wear the pakzhan and I will march against the Shanks, for they are enemies to every man."

This expressed the feelings of the officers gathered here. Looking about, I fancied they might be relieved that they did not have to fight in a battle they were bound to lose; any combat with Shanks was far worse than fighting against fellow men as the Shanks were vindictive slaughters. These fellows were stepping out of the frying pan into the fire, and knew it—and as I saw with joy—welcomed it.

Garnath's fury began to shake him with frightening passion.

He shared the view of the generality of people that all paktuns were merely hirelings, paid to kill, devoid of feelings. That they were not was being revealed to him now.

King Telmont stepped forward again. He wet his lips. He was a man obsessed with rank and position and the baubles and symbols that went with the trappings of power. He was the diametric opposite of an *eminence grise*.

"You say your name is Jak the Nose. Yet you are clearly a person of position, of rank."

Garnath looked about and white showed in his eyes.

"I am skilled in war and I know what is happening. This is a trap! Nedfar's army pretends to march off, to lure us on. It is a trick—"

"You are a fool, Garnath," I said, and I own much of my feelings for this man rasped in my voice. "There would be no need for tricks and traps if Nedfar wished to crush you. As he will, as he will. Your army was doomed. Your men know it, but they have been hired to fight, and so would have fought enough to earn their money, before throwing down their arms. We march to fight the Shanks. There lies a battlefield where men may stand forth to a sterner test."

He frothed and leaped for me.

I backhanded him away.

Telmont looked agitated and the Chuktar of the Ironfists stepped up, flushed, bulky, aggressive and completely at sea now.

"King Telmont. You are a man of honor. Start your army toward the coast. Together we will smash the Shanks back into the sea." My words battered at his indecision.

He wouldn't change in a flash, as they say. He was still old Hot and Cold. But he could see what his assembled officers thought. So, I thought to add a little spice. As I mounted up on Snuffle-nose I looked around the gathered warriors.

"If any paktun wishes to leave his hire in honor, there is a place for him in the emperor's army that marches to fight the Leem-Lovers."

With that, I cantered off.

Mind you, I would not have been surprised had a crossbow bolt buried itself between my shoulder blades.

Chapter Twenty

We Fight for Paz

There was no doubt whatsoever in anyone's mind that this was the most important battle we had ever fought.

There would be other even more important battles in the future if we won this day. If we lost—well, there would be no more of anything quite apart from battles.

From the strength of the Shanks ranged before us the inescapable conclusion had to be drawn that they had at last made the move we had for so long anticipated and dreaded. Their sporadic raiding had turned into a full-scale invasion.

Tyfar pulled his nose as we sat our zorcas, looking out over the host. "Why pick on Hamal? Why now?"

"I would have thought," said Nedfar, "that Hyrklana would be easier for them."

Seg glanced across at me and then said, "It is believed that the Shanks are in communication with—persons—in our lands; where, we do not know. They have been told that Hamal was in turmoil and easy pickings. Hyrklana now has a strong king and is ready once again. The Leem-Lovers would not have known that Hamal now has a strong emperor."

Nedfar's face did not change; but Seg's words came out as he said them, unaffected, making the point, and I saw that Nedfar was pleased.

From the ranks of fighting men a steady hum rose. Everything was going forward quietly and easily. There was time for the imposition of strict silence, although, to be sure, many of Kregen's fighting men do not expect to remain in a disciplined silence during the preliminaries to battle. From a slight eminence where a ruined temple showed splintered walls and fallen columns, the view was breathtaking. Between the sea, a steely bar flecked with light, and the ruins revealed two armies. The Shanks had offered battle and we had accepted, marching up in good order, and now we and the Fish-heads glared at one another across a sandy waste fringed by the sea and gorse-clad slopes.

We were seriously short of cavalry. This is inevitable as wars progress, the toll of saddle animals—whether of the land or flying variety—cannot easily be made up within the normal spans of birth and growth. Animals had been imported, and we had a number of formations of superb quality. Many were the crack cavalry regiments, however, mounted on beasts of indifferent quality, and presenting in many cases spectacles so cruelly ludicrous I will forbear to mention them.

This was one very good reason why Mileon Ristemer's thundering great thomplods were entertained as serious war weapons. We'd armored the huge perambulating haystacks as well as we could against darts and stones. Their castles towered, stuffed with archers, and fleet-footed light infantry ran alongside, ready to guide and assist and to drive off any enemy two-handed swordsmen or axemen who tried to chop the thomplods' twelve legs off.

Vad Garnath, who was here and who had exerted much of his old authority to reassert his position, proved most scathing about our famous thomplods. His relationship with King Telmont had undergone a change. Telmont was no longer so much in the background; but he had the sense to leave the handling of his army to Garnath. No one of his officers mentioned the scene in which Garnath had bowed to the will of his mercenaries; but some surprise was evinced by those hardened professionals, as by his Hamalian regiments, that Jak the Nose was other than he had claimed.

Garnath, swelling up again now that he felt himself back in command, said: "Those stupid beasts will frighten my cavalry with their stink! Keep them away!"

Mileon, quietly, said: "The thomplods are doused down with a mixture that cuts their offensive smell. When we attack, the ointment will be washed off. It will be the damned Shanks' cavalry that will panic."

Well, I said, but to myself, we all devoutly hope so.

Being an emperor, as I have remarked, is often a wearisome burden; there are compensations. One was that I could gallop about freely, with a small troop of 1ESW at my back, to poke my nose into any and everything that went forward. I asked after Lobur the Dagger and Telmont's people informed me that Lobur had disappeared after that fraught night. I thought I knew the Dagger enough to know he would turn up again in his own good time. Rees commanded a brigade of totrix cavalry. He did not know it; but that was my doing, a word in Tyfar's ear had performed the trick. Chido, who was a Chuktar, having no saddle flyers, opted to ride with Rees this day. Because we were on his land he had brought with him a contingent of his own people. These were not soldiers; they were, if such a thing be possible, a willing levy. That they were anxious to kick the Shanks out was an advantage, but not everyone on Kregen is a fighter and I hoped Chido could keep them out of mischief.

Back along our trail lay piles of chains and stakes. I'd told Nedfar, firmly, that I could not fight in any army where poor devils of levies were chained up and stapled to the ground. He'd agreed. If our masses of spear- and shield-armed levies ran off, they would do what everyone expected them to do, and so morale would, instead of being depressed, rise with a fresh resolve. That was the theory.

We outnumbered the Shanks by something like three to two. I would have preferred to have been twice as strong. The Shanks were ferocious fighters and we would be facing the sternest struggle yet.

Nath Karidge listened when I spoke to him. He was kitted out in full fighting fig, and looked magnificent. "I have that to say to you, Nath, that you will—" I saw his face.

He nodded. "I know, majister. And you know I know. But the regiment will fight. We are two short of cavalry for anything else."

"Choose your best squadron. I know I ask a hard task of you, but—" Again I stopped. This time he looked highly devious.

"The Princess Majestrix has told me that she will ride with the empress today."

I came quiveringly alert. "I don't like the sound of that!" I was highly suspicious. "The pair of—Look, Nath, if they start pushing forward and get their necks—well—"

"I know, majister. It will be the best squadron."

"I'd like to chain 'em down for this kind of thing like poor damned levies. Only, being women, they would take exception to that in a quite different fashion. The Sisters of the Rose! Be thankful your Cissy doesn't belong."

He smiled. "Cissy is a member of the Sisters of Opaz Munificent—I think that's the name. Secretive, these ladies."

"Agreed. I wish you well, Nath. May Opaz go with you."

"May the Light of the Invisible Twins shine upon you."

So, feeling that ticklish itch where Delia and danger are concerned, I rode on. I'd speak to her most firmly before the battle, and she would do exactly as she wanted to do afterward.

Another itch bothered me. I could give the greetings and the good wishes to my comrades, and feel free with them before the possibility of death claimed us all. But Rees and Chido? I just could not go into battle without talking to them. So, foolishly, of course, if you consider I was supposed to be an emperor and about to command an army in a crucial battle, I went off to the line of chiefs' tents and told Naghan ti Lodkwara, who happened by rotation to command the duty squadron, to hold fast. Korero the Shield would ride at my back. Cleitar the Smith would carry my standard, and Ortyg the Tresh the flag of Vallia. Volodu the Lungs would be the trumpeter. Targon the Tapster, Uthnior Chavonthjid and many another famed kampeon was there, ready to ride into the worst Herrelldrin Hell at my back.

When I left the tent no one saw me and I exited under a sodsheet at the rear. On my face the foolish smiling features of Hamun ham Farthytu were plastered in that special way I had of screwing them up ready for action. Rees and Chido would know me, for sure.

Borrowing the zorca belonging to Deft-Fingered Minch, the bearded, crusty kampeon who ran my field quarters, I cantered off into the suns shine. Knowing where every unit was stationed was something I had to know—largely because I'd argued like stink in council with the other notables over the placing of the various formations—and so I soon found myself riding up to the knot of officers at the head of Rees's brigade of totrix cavalry. To their side Chido's men stood in raggedy lines.

Well, Rees looked magnificent, and Chido looked—well, this martial figure was dear chinless Chido; but how he had changed!

They saw me.

Now, we had not seen each other for a very long time. I had spotted these two in the Eye of the World, and they had not known I was there. So, now, jaws dropped, eyes bulged, greetings fairly frothed. By Krun! But it was good!

They wanted to know everything. I spun them a yarn and said I was committed to another part of the battle line; but, afterwards! We agreed to a rendezvous at one of our favorite taverns of the Sacred Quarter in Ruathytu. We wished one another well. This moment before impending battle was worth a very great deal to me.

Rees's daughter, the golden lion-maid Saffi, thrived and was still not married but was dogged by a string of suitors a dwabur long. And his son, Roban, was now a powerful paktun, driven overseas through his father's misfortunes.

"But he's coming back, Hamun! He's never forgotten that you once gave him a left-hand dagger."

"That was the day he became a man."

Chido broke in, for that was the day Rees's eldest son, Reesnik, had been murdered.

Chido was married, with two sets of twins, and I was overjoyed for him and we promised great reunions. Then I wished them well, consigning them to the care of Opaz and Krun, and turned away. Despite the risks, despite the dereliction of an emperor's duty, that had been necessary and worthwhile.

And, anyway, I only just got back in time, for Deft-Fingered Minch's personal zorca was being pressed into service with one of our cavalry regiments.

Back again in the brave old scarlet, my weapons slung about me, I stepped out of the front of the tent. If only all the disguises and stratagems I had played on Kregen worked as well!

The name of Garnath had cropped up, to be dismissed. Chido's glance had warned me. But Rees, like a sleeping volcano, had not forgotten. How could any father?

Trumpets pealed. Flags flew. It was necessary for me to ride along the ranks of my men, as the other chiefs displayed themselves before their contingents. Religious ceremonies of many kinds were solemnly performed, and men committed themselves to the protection and mercy of their own deities and spirits.

The time approached.

These spiritual inquiries of the multitude of Kregan deities followed the more material inquiries of the Todalpheme, the wise men who monitored the movements of heavenly bodies and the surge and sweep of the tides. The Tides of Kregen can be fierce and savage beyond understanding—as you know. We had established from the Akhram that we need have no fear of a sudden surprise tide sweeping us away; the water was in balance between the attractions of moons and suns and we could expect a rise of a couple of feet only. Where we intended to fight lay smooth and level and here the tides could sweep in for twenty miles at speeds that would outrun a galloping zorca.

Delia said to me as I patted Snuffle-nose's muzzle, "You will not ride him today, will you, Dray?"

"I thought—"

"Ride Blastyoureyes."

Blastyoureyes was a nik-vove, a shining chestnut, with eight powerful legs and a body to match in weight and speed. He would carry me until he dropped dead. "Very well. And you?"

She laughed. "I ride with Nath Karidge—"

"I see. Then, my heart, mind you keep out of—" I stopped. I breathed in. Then I said, "Take care."

"There is too much in the world to let it go for a foolishness."

She wore armor, mesh and plate cunningly matched, and a scarlet military cape, and she carried weapons. Weapons, I mean of edged and pointed steel. She would ride Yzovult, a splendid chestnut, of the same glorious coloring as Blastyoureyes.

But, in the whole wide world of Kregen and the no less extraordinary world of Earth, there was not a single solitary soul who could match my Delia.

So, simply, we kissed, and she jingled off to ride alongside Chuktar Nath at the head of the elite squadron of the EDLG and I swung my nik-vove and headed off for headquarters. I had words for Nedfar and Tyfar, and for Garnath, too, if he would listen.

As I jumped off Blastyoureyes and handed him over to orderlies of the staff lines I did not know, Seg walked across. His face looked black. "Well, my old dom, and they've gone and done it. Rather, they have gone and not done it."

His fey blue eyes held danger signals. He scowled.

"They have given the vaward to young Tyfar."

Seg Segutorio, in battles in which I commanded, habitually took the vaward. He would take over total command if necessary—had done so, at Kochwald—and he was a man who knew how to sweep a front clean.

"I do not command, Seg, but—and listen!—I am glad."

"Glad for your Tyfar, I suppose."

"If you get maudlin moody you'll be no use! No, glad because it leaves you free to handle all the Vallian forces. Unless you would prefer to handle the Djangs? It is up to you; but I will not command the two together, for the plans call for—"

"I know! Yes, yes! Well, if it is all the same to you, I shall be honored to command the Vallians. By the Veiled Froyvil, my old dom, honor it truly is."

"Good."

"Mind you, the thought of your four-armed Djangs raging into battle tempts a fellow, tempts him direly. . . ."

"You've chosen to command the Vallians, and it's too late. I'll take the Djangs. And we'll see who is first to their Great Standard."

"What, that floating fish thing? Sooner burn the thing."

"It means as much to them as the flag of Vallia to us—"

"Not as much, I'll wager, as your personal standard, Old Superb!"

The scarlet flag, the yellow cross on the scarlet field, my battle flag that fighting men call Old Superb! Well, Cleiter the Standard carried that this day.

That thought made me say, "I'd like to keep the duty squadron of 1ESW if you don't mind."

Now Seg is a fey, wild and reckless fellow; he is also shrewd and practical, not to say cunning. Handing him command of the Vallians meant, since I used the Guard as a division of the army, handing command of that elite unit over, also. So now he said, "Trade me one of your best Djangs for every man you keep out of 1ESW, and you're on."

"Ingrate!"

"Credulous!"

"Quidang, then, Seg. One for one of the best for the best."

Trumpets battered golden notes into the bright sky, for the suns had not stopped still while we maneuvered and mustered under our banners and talked and shouted, swore and prayed, and tried to ignore the fears within us. Flutduin patrols came fleeting back to our part of the line, as mirvols and fluttrells to the Hamalese. The Hyrklese fought with us this day.

"They move! They move!"

So we were off.

A very tame beginning, I was thinking, as Seg wheeled away, not in his usual fashion to the vaward, but to command all the chivalry and pride of Vallia.

My Djangs set up a racket when I cantered up. If sheer noise could win battles, we'd won all-four-hands-each down.

Anticipating this outcome, I wore a flaunting great scarf of orange and gray, the colors of Djanduin, and a Jiktar chosen by lot for the highest honor carried the sacred banner of Djanduin. Looking at the glowing orange and gray and the embroidery and gold bullion, tassels and thread alike glittering, I became aware of Ortyg the Tresh with the Vallian Union flag. I looked away. I couldn't summon the hardness of heart to send him away after Seg—and there were enough Vallian flags waving over the ranks of the army, the files of the Phalanx.

So, in response to the shouts, we, too, moved forward.

The sight uplifted the emotions. Every person of Paz—except for those few misguided traitors we now believed to exist—detested, hated and feared the Shanks. But, these Fish-heads were brave, clever and resourceful men who swarmed up out of their own homelands, locations unknown to us, driven by impulses not too far different from those animating any nomadic clansman, any glory-seeking warrior. Anathema to us, Shanks, Fish-heads, were men still. Pundhri the Serene had preached on this subject, taking as his text the commandments of life developed by a long-dead Pachak. These unwanted thoughts of a rational world where men did not fight and slay other men intruded upon the stern resolve so vital to survival this day.

"We must harden the heart and make strong the sinews," I said, quoting, to N. Strathyn Danmer, an old friend who, as a gerbil-faced two-armed Obdjang, was a cunning, resourceful and immensely devious army commander. He could handle the Djang forces here with as much ease as a drill Deldar flung an audo of swods about the parade ground. Also, he could sense the *point d'appui* and was wise in the way of reserves.

He said, sitting his zorca upright and alert: "You ride again with Djangs now, majister."

I inclined my head. It was a rebuke I deserved. In a good

cause there is no more ferocious or skilled fighter than a Djang, and they go through Katakis by the dozen. Perhaps my Clansmen—but no—idle thoughts. . . .

Garnath's schemes to chain up masses of levies to soak up the first waves of the attack having been rejected, our plans called for these crowds of spear and shield men to draw the Fish-heads into a counterattack that would strike into the confusion. Here the thomplods would have to earn their keep.

"I am going to have an impossible task to hold them back, by Zodjuin of the Silver Stux!" said N. Strathyn Danmer. "Any plan that calls for Djangs to hang back is—"

"The emperor Nedfar commands, Nath, not I. But if we incline gently toward the sea, we will be in a better position."

"Agreed. At least, that will keep them on the move and not sitting fretting."

Danmer cracked out his orders to two of our messengers and they went off lickety-split. From our position on the extreme left of the line we could see the dun masses of the enemy moving forward, crowned with the sparkle of steel. Further along to our right stood the Vallians, with the few contingents from the Dawn Lands, and then the Hyrklese formed a connecting link with the mass of Hamalese who held the right center and flank. Positioned just to the rear of the levies and rising like haystacks over fields of stubble, the thomplods looked impressive and menacing to us. How they would appear to the Shanks remained to be seen.

The air having been cleared, the armies could get down to the main struggle.*

Although this stretch of the coast in Chido's Eurys bore the name of The Level Race, the battle came to be known by another name, which I will tell you anon. It is not my intention to give a full blow-by-blow account. Other currents were at work here to which this great and important battle formed a backdrop. A craggy and bloody backdrop, to be sure; but these

---

*Here Prescot gives the compositions of the armies, muster by muster, roll by roll. It is noticeable that many of the names he lists (many of which I have omitted) are no longer mentioned in his narrative after the battle. They do appear in the casualty lists. Evidently, the battle was far worse than he cares to tell us.

         —A.B.A.

currents of emotion flowing past in the foreground were in their own way no less violent.

Soon the Shanks advanced and the armies clashed and our levies duly ran away.

We could hear above the clangor that shrill and sickening hissing from the Fish-heads as they rushed wildly on. There were all manner of different species or kinds, animated armored figures with fish heads crowned with scales in brilliant colors and designs. As with the feathers of a Rapa, it was difficult to tell if the majority of the scales were natural or decoration.

Now it is quite impossible for a man sitting his saddle to see every part of what occurs on a battlefield and much of what follows was told me by eyewitnesses. The onrushing Shanks, victorious over our poor levies, should have run full tilt into the stink of the thomplods. Their cavalry should have panicked. At that moment, Tyfar with the mass of our vaward, would have nutcracker crunched them in both flanks. Then we Djangs would circle inwards, with the Hamalese right, and with the Vallians as the hinge, close in and destroy utterly....

Something will always go wrong, and you just hope it will not be a big or important thing.

The odd thing was, our plan, simple though it was, would have worked splendidly, for nothing attributable to us went wrong.

The Shanks tipped the balance in the center.

The smell of thomplods is not really detectable by humans; its effect is disastrous upon many animals. Now a fresh smell rose over the mingled odors of leather and sweat and fear and blood. A rich, full-bodied, kitchen kind of smell, a burning and roasting, a crisping sort of smell that brought the saliva to the mouth. Fires were visible through the ranks ahead.

A thomplod in the van which had been forging on like an animated battering ram, his archers loosing again and again and his twelve feet squashing Fish-heads with juicy crunches, stopped. His haystack hide appeared to bristle. He let rip a snorting shriek and backed off, started to turn around, stepping on our own kreutzin, for the light infantry did well with the thomplod protection duty they had been handed. He screamed again, turned around and barged straight back—berserk.

Between the two armies the ground crackled into life and flame. Spots of fire, racing from the Shanks toward us, spots of fire that ran on twinkling legs.

"We could hear that shrill hissing from the fish-heads as they rushed on."

Someone yelled, so I was told: "The cruel bastards!"

The Fish-heads, these Leem-Lovers, had taken a great herd of vosks—those stupid, ungainly, rasher-providing animals—and smeared them with tar and combustibles and set them alight and launched them, squealing, at our thomplods.

Disgusting.

The vosks ran dementedly. Their hides crisped. The hair frizzled. The smell was like an army kitchen the day vosk rashers are on. The squeaks and squeals scratched irritatingly above the expected clangor of spear and shield, the scream of dying men.

The stink of burnt vosk outdid the stink of spilled blood.

By ones and twos, and then fives and sixes as the burning vosks reached them, the thomplods lumbered about and ran.

Our totrix cavalry instantly turned tail and fled.

Many of the regiments we had mounted on other kinds of saddle animals ran.

The zorcas remained unaffected—at least by the smell—and I own to a short but intensely painful moment of apprehension as the Djangs astride their joats from Djanduin held their mounts and reimposed control. The joats quieted. At this moment Tyfar led the vaward forward to what should have been a crunching charge and instead turned into a desperate, scrambling melee.

Lucky it was for Vallia and her allies that we had the benefit of Filbarrka's lancers and archers, for these zorcamen pirouetted and lanced in, mace crunching from the rear ranks, and darted out. The sleeths most of the Shanks rode were no match for zorcas. Green ichor stank on the air, mingling with the raw smell of the red blood of Paz and the stench of the burning vosks.

Thomplods burst back through the lines, and those regiments who were too slow to open ranks and let the beasts through suffered the consequences of slack drill. Seg handled the Vallians magnificently. They opened out and the thomplods careered through and Seg's archers shot the poor devils of vosks to a merciful end. Then the Vallians closed up, and set themselves, and advanced.

Kapt Danmer twisted his Obdjang moustache—the left one, for his right hand held a sword and he, like me, had but the pair of hands. "I cannot hold them any more, majister. We must charge."

"By all means, Natch. And may Djan ride with you."

So, the trumpets pealed and the Djangs let out their joats and those splendid riding animals, the best juts in Havilfar, roared out in a dark and glittering tide.

Perfectly confident that the left wing was now secure and the center about to be closed, I flung a harsh word of command at my squadron of 1ESW. "Hold! You follow me, not the Djangs." And I swung Blastyoureyes and nudged him into his eight-legged flowing motion, heading to the right, heading to where our lines sagged and bulged and where the Leem-Lovers were about to break through in triumph.

For a considerable distance to our rear the sands were covered by fleeing men. Most were the unfortunate levies, but a few bodies held a loose cohesion that told they had once been regiments of fighting men, now huddling together for safety in adversity. We rode on, shouldering aside fugitives. By Krun! The more I looked the more it seemed the whole army was turning tail.

But Nedfar held the center and right. From the eminence crowned by its ruins he could see the course of the battle better than could I, and it was at this time that, observing his left and center were about to be secure, he flung in everything he had on his right. Also, it was at this time, in the small cleared space between Nedfar and the onrushing Shanks, that his massed archers wreaked such horrible confusion upon the enemy. And every Shank that fell was worth two of our men—except for some, of course....

The Hamalese regulars fought like demons. No doubt they smarted with the hurt to their professional pride their defeat at the Battle of Ruathytu caused them. And the paktuns fought as only hard men who fight for a living know how. By the time I reached the knoll and rode up to the ruins, Nedfar—impressive, pointing, dominating his surroundings—had the situation contained. It was not quite under control; but even as I reined in at his side and stared out and down onto the battlefield, my Djangs hit the flank of the forces attempting to halt the Vallians. In a very short time there were no Shanks in that portion of the field—no living Shanks.

"Dray!" said Nedfar. He looked exalted. "I see your people have done all and more than is required. It is all in the hands of us Hamalese now."

"I have no doubts whatsoever."

There were few men left in his retinue. The death toll among messengers and gallopers was high. My squadron of 1ESW waited quietly but inwardly fuming in the hollow behind the rise. As I said to Korero: "If the lads wanted a fight then bodyguarding an emperor in a battle like this is no place to find it."

To which Korero, in his cutting way, had replied nothing.

Over to the right where Vad Garnath struggled to hold a line and prevent the Shanks from overlapping us and striking inwards at the rear of our center—which was exactly what the Djangs were now doing to the Shanks—the Hamalese had a grim conflict on their hands. As we stared a shout of joy broke from the group around Nedfar. Up from the rear, kicking sand, racing with their six-legged ungainly gait, came the totrix cavalry, rallied and raging to rejoin the fight.

Rees and Chido would be at the head of that headlong onward rally, furious they had been cut out of the battle and determined to show us all their true mettle. Nedfar gave fresh urgent orders and more of his aides galloped off. Now it did seem as though we people of Paz could successfully resist the Shanks. And, through it all, I was aware of the detachment, of the way in which I rode about so grandly directing operations and had not even drawn a sword from its scabbard. This was a far cry from the sweat and muck and blood of the heat of battle.

The passions that burned in the forefront of the battle backdrop, also, passed me by and left me with just the same manner of detachment. In the event, in the two events, I own I was glad I was passed by. In this wise. . . .

"I shall ride to join Garnath's wing," I shouted at Nedfar, and in no time at all Blastyoureyes was carrying me thundering off to the right with my little group of 1ESW hard on my heels. We hit at the same time as the returning totrix cavalry, smashing into a screeching horde of Shanks who thought they had won. A single squadron, superb though they were, could make little difference and the bulk of the work was done by the totrix cavalry, with those elements who, having recoiled, reformed to press on again. The swarth cavalry lumbered up afterward at their slower gait and they tipped the scales. For a few moments we were in a real battle, with men yelling and animals rearing, with the lethal sweep of steel and the sudden spurt of blood. Then the Shanks were no longer facing us, and the totrixmen let out bright yells of triumph. I saw Rees. His golden lion face lowered down upon a pile of corpses, tumbled any old how in a welter of red and green.

I felt my heart kick. Chido...!

I cantered over, with the nik-vove avoiding the heaps of slain. Rees looked up. Still his face bore no readable expression.

"You are all right, Chuktar?" My voice was rough-edged.

"Perfectly, thank you."

"You looked as though you have lost someone dear to you."

I know I felt what I could not express, a great proud emperor sitting a magnificent charger among the slaughter, talking to Rees like a stranger. Chido, I wanted to scream out, Chido....

"Yes, majister, I have lost someone. Someone, I own, I now see to have been dear to me. But not, I fancy, in the way you may imagine." He looked down and touched a headless corpse with his boot. The corpse rolled away, slithering.

There, a trident's tines through both eyes and the third smashing the bridge of his nose, lay Vad Garnath.

Rees looked up. "This—person—was known to me."

"Well, he is dead now. You can forget him."

A trumpet pealed, high and carrying brilliant overtones, a series of notes piercing the sky. I looked away. I had work to do. I would see Rees and Chido in the Sacred Quarter.

I rode away. Only when I was returning to the headquarters was the realization borne in on me that I had spoken deucedly oddly to Rees. Any normal reaction would have been one of sorrow for a friend lost. Who would know, here, of the deadly enmity between Rees and Garnath? Well, that would be explained away, for emperors often do not operate under normal rules—and that is not always a good thing, either.

Figures fought beneath the old ruined temple on the rise.

Thinking that, I was glad Rees had not had to slay Garnath in the end, and that that evil man had met his death from a Shank trident—how appropriate! a worshipper of Lem the Silver Leem slaughtered by the Leem-Lovers!—I saw the scene ahead more clearly.

Nedfar fought for his life, surrounded by swordsmen.

I dug my heels into Blastyoureyes and sent him galloping madly ahead. We thundered up the rise, his eight legs pumping in wonderful unison, and I flung myself off, blade in hand, to roar into the fight. My lads followed and in only moments the swordsmen were dispatched. Nedfar held his arm from which the blood flowed. He, like Rees, looked down on a pile of corpses.

"Nedfar! You are unharmed?"

"Just a scratch, Dray. I'd have been dead—Spikatur, they are from Spikatur Hunting Sword."

"So I see."

"I'd have been killed for sure—but for him."

Nedfar pointed to Lobur the Dagger who sprawled across two dead men. The sword in his fist was snapped off. I advanced, beginning to kneel down, when Lobur sat up, dazed, looking past me up to Nedfar.

"Prince—I mean emperor—I wronged you, I know. But—"

"Keep quiet, Lobur, you great fambly," I said. "You have a hole in your chest we could drive a damned thomplod through."

"Jak?" He frowned, dizzied by his wound. "What are you doing here?" He gazed about. "I betrayed you to Garnath, and—"

"Garnath is dead. And you have been an idiot, a get onker; but you must rest now." I heard the voices, light, excited, tumultuous with events, and I said, "And here is Thefi to see you."

As I turned she paused on the slope of the rise, staring at her father, and then at Lobur. She screamed and rushed forward to fling herself on him.

"Easy, Thefi, easy. He's only punctured. Let him breathe."

Thefi bent over Lobur and her hair fell loose and shrouded her face as she kissed him. "Oh, Lobur!"

The other ladies walked forward, content to let Thefi have her moment. In the background Nath Karidge and the EDLG stood in their ranks—and they were bloodied and the bright uniforms were slashed and torn, and their ranks were thinned. I looked at Delia as she walked forward with a swing at the side of Jaezila, and I own I felt the faintness of relief.

"Dray!"

I pulled myself together. Time enough for the stories afterward. I could not allow detachment. Delia was safe! That mattered.

"You promised you wouldn't get into the fight—"

Jaezila said, "When Ty went in—well, I wasn't going to sit around doing nothing. And mother came too."

"Between us all it looks as though we've won," I said. "All of us, all peoples of Paz. We've come a long way together this day. This fight, the Battle of the Flaming Vosks, will be remembered as a beginning. And as an end."

After that there ensued a great deal of talking and excitement and rushing about clearing up and seeing to the wounded and burying the dead. The fish smell would persist for days. The reaction made us all tremble. Seg was safe, thank all the gods of Kregen. And Tyfar trotted in, his equipment just about ripped to shreds, wearing an enormous smile and waving a Shank trident.

Delia took my arm.

"A great deal has happened, dearest, and I know you will say there is a great deal more left to do."

"As there is. You are leading up to something. So?"

"You want to lay down the burden of empire and let Drak take over. I agree. Oh, and, Dray Prescot, if you think I shall allow anyone to call me the Dowager Empress—!"

I laughed. "Of course not. We're young!"

"We are young. Also, can you guess what old Hot and Cold has in his baggage train?"

"Apart from scantily clad young ladies, you mean?"

"We-ell, they could figure. . . . And I shall be less than scantily clad, believe me."

So I guessed. But I let Delia tell me.

"King Telmont has a full outfit, all in tents and marquees, with huge boilers and furnaces and pipes and things. He has the whole works, a complete mobile Baths of the Nine."

"Lead on," I said. "What are we waiting for?"

Attention:

DAW COLLECTORS

Many readers of DAW Books have written requesting information on early titles and book numbers to assist in the collection of DAW editions since the first of our titles appeared in April 1972.

We have prepared a several-pages-long list of all DAW titles, giving their sequence numbers, original and current order numbers, and ISBN numbers. And of course the authors and book titles, as well as reissues.

If you think that this list will be of help, you may have a copy by writing to the address below and enclosing one dollar to cover the handling and postage costs.

DAW BOOKS, INC. Dept. C
1633 Broadway
New York, N.Y. 10019

LIN CARTER

Grand Master of Fantastic Adventure

Now Brings You...

The Adventures of Eric Carstairs in Zanthodon!

- ☐ JOURNEY TO THE UNDERGROUND WORLD (#UE1499—$1.75)
- ☐ ZANTHODON (#UE1543—$1.75)
- ☐ HUROK OF THE STONE AGE (#UE1597—$1.75)
- ☐ DARYA OF THE BRONZE AGE (#UJ1655—$1.95)
- ERIC OF ZANTHODON (Forthcoming in 1982)

and

- ☐ THE WIZARD OF ZAO (#UE1383—$1.75)
- ☐ LOST WORLDS (#UJ1556—$1.95)
- ☐ THE PIRATE OF WORLD'S END (#UE1410—$1.75)

—Illustrated—